Love and the
Game 3

Love and the Game 3

Johnni Sherri

www.urbanbooks.net

Urban Books, LLC
300 Farmingdale Road, NY-Route 109
Farmingdale, NY 11735

Love and the Game 3

ISBN 13: 978-1-64556-203-0
ISBN 10: 1-64556-203-4

First Trade Paperback Printing May 2021
Printed in the United States of America

10 9 8 7 6 5 4 3 2 1

Distributed by Kensington Publishing Corp.
Submit Orders to:
Customer Service
400 Hahn Road
Westminster, MD 21157-4627
Phone: 1-800-733-3000
Fax: 1-800-659-2436

Love and the Game 3

by

Johnni Sherri

Where we left off . . .

Plus

It had been over a month since that tragic night of the fire, and although today was my birthday, I could barely stand to form a smile. Aria was still in the hospital, where she was preparing for major skin-graft surgery. The procedure would cover the right side of her body, including a small area on the right side of her face. Since her burns were so severe, she was in constant pain and was currently trying to wean herself off the morphine they had prescribed. Even though I was thankful she had survived, her condition was still depressing.

Not only was I messed up in the head over that, but my mother and I were still beefing too. I just couldn't get over the fact that she would actually shed tears over a sorry-ass nigga like Ronnie. And then there was my friendship with Perri, which at this point was practically nonexistent. Despite the fact that she had moved back home and broken it off with Derrick, my pride just wouldn't let me look at her the same. I had even moved back into an apartment-style dorm with Jorell on a permanent basis just so I wouldn't have to see her as much.

Although I wasn't rocking with Perri like that anymore, I had to admit that she continued to impress me. Somehow she had been able to reenroll at Georgetown for the spring semester and had also got a part-time job. But even with us attending the same school, we moved like two ships passing in the night. While my classes were during the day, hers were mostly scheduled in the evenings. Not to mention with all my basketball games and the practices I had to attend. Perri, on the other hand, had been unable to regain her spot on the womens' basketball team.

I didn't feel up to doing anything for my birthday other than maybe having a few people come through, but Tez insisted on throwing a small party for me at the house. He was like my big brother, so I always found it hard to turn down his generosity. He went all out when ordering the food and liquor. He even sent my mother and the kids over to Mr. Phillip's for the night, so I knew the least I could do was appear to be enjoying myself.

It was around ten o'clock that night when I found myself down in the basement, taking shots of Henny with Jorell at the bar. Lil Wayne's "Lollipop" blared through the surround-sound speakers, and the faint scent of kush could already be smelled drifting through the air. Several of my teammates were already there playing pool, and even a few girls that I was cool with were in attendance. Everything was all good until Perri and Nika came downstairs.

Perri was dressed in a simple pair of black skinny jeans and a red long-sleeved crop top that revealed a sliver of her flat belly. On her feet were a pair of red-and-black Js, and her long hair was slicked back into a high ponytail. Although her attire was casual, she looked good enough to eat. I hated the fact that I was still attracted to her.

"Hey, Plus. Happy birthday," Nika said, giving me a hug. "I see you got that bush cut off yo' head," she said jokingly, rubbing her hand over my fresh new haircut.

"Had to," I said. I hugged her again and saw Perri standing not far behind her.

When our eyes met, Perri gave a small smile and a coy little wave before saying, "Happy birthday, Plus."

I raised my chin to her and kept my conversation short. "Thanks."

Nika then went over to Jorell and gave him a hug as well. "Hey, big head. What y'all over here drinking on? We wanna take a shot too," she said.

"Nah, lightweight, you don't know how to hold ya liquor. I don' already seen you in action, remember?"

"Oh my God, it was one time, Jorell. Will you just let that go?" she whined.

While those two fell out laughing at their own inside joke, Perri and I just stood there awkwardly, looking at one another. She twiddled her thumbs and rocked back on her heels, while I did my best to get through the uneasy moment. I scratched a spot behind my ear that didn't even itch and looked her over once more. I was just about to tell her that she looked nice when Brianna walked up and put her arms around my waist.

"What's up, birthday boy?" she said, giving me a tight squeeze.

"What up, Bri Bri?" I offered, leaning down to hug her back.

When I looked up, I saw a glower appear on Perri's face that was undeniably intended for Brianna. Inwardly, I chuckled, because Brianna was just a friend. Even though she sometimes flirted, I never took it there with her, because I didn't see her that way. However, now that the opportunity had presented itself, I couldn't help but be a little petty.

I threw my arm around Brianna's shoulders and looked at Perri. "I guess I'll catch you later, then," I said before walking off with Brianna.

Perri's eyes followed Brianna and me as we trekked across to the other side of the basement. When we plopped down on one of the leather couches and started playing drinking games with a few people from school, I could feel Perri's eyes burning a hole through me. Just to be spiteful, because I knew she was watching, I leaned over and whispered in Brianna's ear.

"So did you have trouble finding the house?" I asked over the music.

Brianna shook her head and was all smiles, probably because I was finally paying her some attention. Either that or she was beginning to feel the effects of that green monster concoction in her cup.

Before I knew it, Perri got down from the barstool that she'd taken a seat on and rushed past me, with Nika in tow. Judging by her expression and the way she cut her eyes over at me before she climbed the stairs, I knew she was pissed.

I released a deep sigh of frustration and ran my hand over my low-cut waves. "I'll be back, yo," I told Brianna before getting up from my seat.

Seeing Perri hurt didn't bring me as much pleasure as I had thought it would, and I knew I needed to go make things right. I had been avoiding her by seeing Camille only in the evenings, when Perri was away at class, or on the weekends, during those hours when Perri was at work. The shit had to stop. I was twenty-two years old and needed to start acting like a grown man rather than a childish little boy. Whether I liked it or not, we would be bonded forever, and I needed to remember that.

After going upstairs, I immediately looked for Perri in her bedroom, but she wasn't in there. As I came back out into the hall, I heard crying. I leaned my head up against the bathroom door and heard Perri and Nika talking inside.

"He's found someone else," Perri cried.

"Well, have y'all talked?" Nika asked. Perri must have shaken her head no, because Nika then said, "Well, just go tell him how you feel."

All of a sudden, I heard the sound of someone gagging and vomiting in the toilet.

"See, girl? This shit with him is making you sick," Nika said.

The next thing I knew, there was a long moment of silence on the other side of the door, followed by Nika's dramatic gasping.

"No, Perri!" she breathed. "Please tell me you're not pregnant."

My mouth damn near fell to the floor, and my heart instantly began to race. But before I could even get my emotions in check and wrap my head around what I had just heard, I heard Jamal calling out my name. I walked to the edge of the hall and stood just before the first step of the staircase and peered down into the foyer. Standing there were Jamal and Shivon, with their coats still on, as though they'd just arrived. I opened my mouth to speak, but something behind them caught me completely off guard. A familiar set of bright blue eyes.

The fuck? I thought.

Chapter 1

Plus

"Nigga, the fuck is you doing here!" I snapped, rushing full speed down the stairs.

I watched TK's bright blue eyes widen in horror at the mere sight of me. I hadn't seen his bitch ass in well over a year, yet here he was in the flesh, standing in Tez's crib like everything was cool. To say that I was furious would be an understatement. After all that shit he had pulled, fucking Tasha behind my back and getting her pregnant, he knew damn well his ass wasn't welcome anywhere near me.

As I pushed Jamal out of the way, TK flinched and immediately held his hands up, trying to guard his face in defense. I was so full of anger that I didn't even care if he was trying to come at me on some peaceful shit. All I saw was red, and before I knew it, I hauled off and punched him. I heard the sound of his facial bones crack in the process.

"Oh, shit!" abruptly chorused the crowd that had quickly formed around us, but my eyes remained solely on TK. I hadn't got a clean shot, but his nose was definitely starting to bleed. Not wasting any time, I jumped on that nigga and brought him down to the floor.

And as I hammered away, delivering blow after blow to his face, I heard Jamal panicking behind me. "He didn't come here for all that shit, man. Damn!"

All of a sudden, I could feel several hands grab my back and lift me away from TK's body. I tried my best to fight my way out of their hold, but whoever it was had a good grip on me. The entire time I was being lifted to my feet, I just glared down at him. This nigga just lay on the floor, curled up in a fetal position, covering up his face like a fucking coward. He wasn't even trying to fight me back, which only infuriated me more. I literally could feel the blood pumping through my veins like rushing water flowing into an open stream.

"Get the fuck out!" I yelled. Finally, I stood on my own two feet, and I realized that Jorell and Tez were actually the ones who had taken hold of me.

My nostrils were flared, and my chest heaved up and down. I was like a bull in the ring, filled with so much rage that I could barely control my own breathing. The only thing I knew for certain that would calm me down was pounding on TK's bitch ass some more. So again, I tried my best to get at him. I attempted to push through Tez and Jorell as they struggled to hold me back.

"Calm your ass the fuck down, yo! We not doing all that rah-rah shit up in my crib, man," Tez snapped.

He turned back and faced TK, who was now being helped up off the floor by Jamal. TK's pale face was now a bright shade of red and was half covered in blood and bruises. He slowly stood up and rubbed his jaw before wiping the blood from his mouth with the back of his hand.

"Look, man, I'm not trying to fight you! We already did that shit," he said, shaking his head.

"Obviously, I didn't beat that ass good enough the first time, nigga, since you still think shit is sweet. Fuck you come here for!" I yelled, spit flying from my mouth, as Tez tightened his grasp around my arm.

The crowd was still gathered around us, watching the entire scene unfold.

TK threw his hands up in the air. "Look, man, I'm sorry, all right? I messed up big-time by fucking around with Tasha. I carry that shit with me every day, bruh, knowing I fucked up our brotherhood." He let out a light snort, then shook his head. "And the crazy thing is, the shit wasn't even worth it, yo. I can't stand that bitch."

Tez stepped in front of me and walked up real close on TK. Instantly, that nigga's eyes doubled in size, and I could see the look of pure fear on his face. While they both stood over six feet tall, TK was slender, whereas Tez was all muscle. Not only that, just like me, TK had grown up in the Millwood housing projects and knew exactly what type of nigga Tez was. Of course, now that Tez had a legal business, with a fiancée and a son at home, he had toned a lot of that down, but there was no mistaking what he was capable of.

With a quick pound of his fist, which crashed into his other hand, Tez chucked up his chin. "Look, I don't give a fuck about none of that bullshit you talking. What the fuck you doing in my house, nigga?"

TK held his hand up. "My mama, man. She's in the hospital, dying of cancer."

Shit! Ms. Rita had been a like a second mother to me while I was growing up.

TK went on. "Ms. Tonya was at the hospital, visiting, the other day and told me that I should swing through here. She figured enough time had passed where we could bury the hatchet, ya feel me?"

"Wrong. We ain't burying shit!" I spat, feeling Jorell tighten his grip on my shoulder.

Tez turned around and cut his eyes at me. "Yo, chill out."

I let out a deep sigh and ran my hand down my face. "Look, I'm sorry about Ms. Rita and all. I truly am. But you and me, we ain't got shit else to say to one another," I told him.

Defeated, TK shook his head and shrugged his shoulders. "A'ight."

As he, Jamal, and Shivon all walked out of the house together, I turned around to see Perri and Nika standing on the stairs. Perri and I locked eyes before she gave me a half smile. My mind was still fucked up, first from hearing she might actually be pregnant and then from dealing with TK's dumb ass, but somehow, I managed to send a small smile back her way. Just as I was about to head over and tell her we needed to talk, Brianna walked up and looped her arm through mine.

"Hey, you all right?" she asked.

I looked down at her and nodded my head. "Yeah, I'm good, shorty."

"You sure. Wanna talk about it?"

Shaking my head, I let out a light chuckle. "Nah, not really. But you go back down and enjoy yourself. I'll get up with you in a minute."

Just as Brianna turned to walk away with the rest of the dispersing crowd, I looked over to see Perri heading back up the steps. However, Nika stayed put, ensuring that she would get my full attention with her obvious frown and a hard roll of her eyes. Instantly, I knew it was because of Brianna. Perri probably thought that Brianna was someone I was dealing with and that I was trying to flaunt her in her face. But it honestly wasn't like that. I only tutored Brianna, and the only reason she had got an invite tonight was that I was being childish, trying to make Perri jealous.

I walked up to Nika, who still had that scowl on her face as she held a red cup in her hand. "What you got your face all frowned up and ugly for?" I asked.

She sucked her teeth. "Shut up, Plus. You need to stop chasing after all these hoes and—"

"Ain't nobody chasing after no hoes, Nika," I said, cutting her off.

As soon as I stepped up to walk past her, she put her hand on my chest to stop me. "Don't hurt my girl, Plus. She really loves you."

I gave a slight nod, fully understanding. "I know. And I love her ass too."

After walking up the stairs, I went right to Perri's room, where I saw she had her door closed. I knocked twice, but I didn't wait for her to answer before I walked in. She was lying back on the bed, tossing her basketball in the air, with headphones covering her ears. She'd already kicked off her shoes, which were sitting next to her on the floor. Her amber-colored eyes widened at the sight of me as she quickly sat up straight in the bed. As she put her headphones down around her neck and pulled her knees up to her chest, I trudged over. Dragging my hand down my face, I sat on the edge of the bed. She just tucked her lips inward and stared at me.

"Why you up here by yourself?" I asked.

She shrugged her shoulders. "I just don't feel like partying anymore, I guess."

I gave a little nod, allowing the silence to creep back in between us. You know, one of those awkward moments where there's so much to say, but no one says a word. As we stared at one another, all I could hear was the faint sound of music playing down in the basement.

"Look, I need to ask you something," I finally said, breaking the silence.

Slightly tilting her head to the side, she lifted her chin. "Okay."

"Are you pregnant?"

She gasped, her eyes ballooned, and her head shot up from her knees. "I'm gonna kill Nik—"

"Nah, it wasn't her. I heard you throwing up in the bathroom earlier," I said, cutting her off.

Her bright eyes dimmed and glossed over as she softly shook her head. "Plus, I honestly don't know if I am or not," she told me, then gave a heavy sigh before lowering her legs down on the bed.

"'Cause, you know, on Christmas—"

"I know, Plus, and I already know what you're gonna ask. If I'm pregnant, I don't know by who," she said, looking me in the eyes. I guessed she could see the disappointment on my face, because then she added, "I'll take a home test tomorrow, and if it's positive, will you go with me to the doctor?"

Nodding my head, I gave her a small smile. "You already know I got you, P."

I took a deep breath and swallowed, feeling a bit uneasy, as I slid my hands in my pockets. So much was racing through my mind, like her actually being pregnant by another nigga this time around. I know it might sound crazy, but I really didn't care if the baby was someone else's. I still wanted her. I *loved* her.

I glanced over at Perri and realized that there was so much I wanted to say to her. Things that I definitely couldn't hold in any longer and needed to get off my chest. But just when I was about to open my mouth to speak, she blurted out, "I'm sorry, Plus."

"No, I'm sorry, P," I said not even a second later. I slipped my hands out of my pockets, reached out, and gently pulled her to me. "I feel like every time things start to go right between us, some bullshit happens to pull us right back apart. I love you, and I don't want us to waste any more time not being together."

As she nodded her head, I could see her golden-brown eyes immediately soften and fill with tears.

"I wanna marry you," I let out.

Perri's face immediately lit up, and the corners of her mouth turned up in a pretty smile. "You do?" she asked lowly, with her eyebrows dipped in.

"Hell, yeah, I do." I released a soft snort of laughter at her reaction. "Perri, you and I were made for each other. No matter how bad shit gets with us. No matter who else we've been with in the past, I swear," I said, putting my hand up to my chest. "You are, and will always be, the only girl for me." Gently, I stroked her cheek with the back of my hand. "Please forgive me for all the fucked-up sh—"

Before I could even say anything else, Perri leaned in and crashed her soft lips against mine. Easing into a gentle kiss, she wrapped her arms around me and pulled me down onto the bed. When she straddled my lap and pressed her breasts against me, I could hear the eager sounds of our breathing picking up speed. And I felt the pounding of her beating heart right up against my chest.

"Damn," I muttered into her mouth, feeling myself rise beneath her. "I love you so fucking much, P."

"I love you too," she whispered.

Sliding my lips down to her neck, I picked her up and gently laid her back on the bed. I removed her shirt and tossed it across the room before kissing my way down her body. My mouth landed on top of her bra, and I kissed each breast separately, inhaling her sweet scent. Hearing her soft, subtle moans in anticipation, I snaked my tongue down a trail that led to her stomach. After unzipping her jeans, I tried my best to tug them down, but they were too tight, so Perri had to lift her hips to help.

As soon as I got her pants completely off and dropped them down on the floor, I slid in between her legs. After diving face-first between her fleshy thighs, I allowed the warmth of my mouth to hover over her panties. "Damn, I missed you, P. Can I taste you?" I whispered against her, knowing that shit was going to drive her wild.

"*Please*," she breathed, damn near begging through a moan.

With the tip of my tongue, I teased her clit through her panties and eventually peeled them off with my teeth. Seeing just how smooth and hairless she was down there made me think back to our very first time. Perri had definitely grown up over the years, and it was funny how time and maturity had made all the difference for me. "You're so fucking beautiful, baby," I muttered.

When I looked up at her and saw her chest heaving up and down with urgency, I knew that she wanted me just as badly as I wanted her. Plus, she was wet as fuck. Slowly, I slid my tongue up and down the length of her lips. After gently parting them, I dipped in and out of her center. Her hands immediately came to the sides of my head as her back arched up from the mattress, her thighs squeezing around my face.

Ahhh," she moaned.

I continued to kiss, pull, and suck until she was at her peak. As she shivered against me, I cupped her cheeks in my hands. Then I lowered my pants and wedged myself between her thighs. I didn't waste any time before pushing myself deep inside her. A loud moan came from her lungs as she reached around for the covers. But I grabbed both of her hands above her head and interlaced her fingers with mine. Stroking even deeper, I watched her pretty face contort from a pleasurable pain.

"Gahdamn, P," I groaned.

"Plus," she breathed, her body tensing as she squeezed her eyes tight.

"Open up for me."

When she opened up her legs a little wider for me, I rolled my hips in a circular motion. Then I slowed it down just a bit so that I could take my time, bear witness to the sheer ecstasy on her face, and take in the sounds of our wet bodies moving as one. I wanted to feel every push, pull, and squeeze of her body as I dove deeper inside her. Then suddenly I could feel her fingers digging deep into my shoulders. Her eyes were still sealed tight as her body began to seize.

"Plus!" she cried out.

I leaned down and kissed her lips, steadily working my hips against her. It wasn't until she opened up those pretty-ass eyes of hers and locked them with mine that I felt myself cumming. "I can't . . . Fuck!" I growled. Feeling my entire body tremble on top of hers, I came inside her. We lay like that for what seemed like forever, with my face resting against hers, our weak limbs entangled. The sound of our heavy breathing eventually slowed, in sync.

Even though it was my birthday, I never did make it back down to my party. I just stayed up in the room with Perri the rest of the night. And whenever I felt her body begin to shift, like she was trying to get away, I made sure to pull her back close and hold on tight to her. I didn't know what the future held, nor did I care at this point, as long as she was in it. Never, ever would I let her go again.

Chapter 2

Jorell

It was just before two in the morning when Nika and I were out on the back deck. We were smoking the last of my blunt, just talking and laughing. Above us was a pitch-black sky, and other than a few scattered stars, the only source of light was the small bulb by the back door. The party was over now, and besides Tez and Myesha cleaning up inside, things had settled down quite a bit. It was February and cold as fuck outside, so after zipping up my jacket, I threw my arm over Nika's shoulders and pulled her into me.

She looked up at me, shivering, her nose red and her curly hair blowing slightly beneath a purple hat her grandmother had probably knitted for her. "How's Jornelle?" she asked.

I took another pull before letting the smoke escape from my lips. "She's straight," I said.

Simply nodding her head, Nika looked out into the yard, beyond the covered pool.

"Maybe you can meet her one day. The right way," I proposed.

She let out a little snort before snatching the blunt from my mouth. "I'm sure that'll go over real well with Meechie," she said, then took a quick puff on the roach before tossing it to the ground.

I wasn't even going to set myself up by carrying on with that conversation, so I said, "How's Grandma doin'?"

"She's doing good. Still asks about you sometimes."

"Oh yeah?" I smiled.

"You should come up and see her sometime."

Tilting my head to the side, I narrowed my eyes. "Shawty, you trying to set me up. Grandma ain't cussing my black ass out," I said, making her laugh.

"Oh, I forgot. I gotta tell you something," I said, quickly switching subjects.

"What?"

I could feel myself getting excited before the words even flew out of my mouth. "I entered the draft. Just got my letter yesterday," I revealed.

A wide smile spread across her face, which caused me to smile as well. "Oh my God! I'm so proud of you, Jorell." She turned and wrapped her arms around my neck to give me a tight hug.

Being that close gave me the opportunity to take in her scent, to smell that sweet perfume in her hair. When she pulled back, swiping the curls back from her face, I looked down into her pretty brown eyes. Mane, Nika was a classic beauty: soft brown skin, delicate feminine features, and wild spiral, cinnamon-colored hair. My la' baby was beautiful as fuck, and I'd be lying if I said I didn't miss her ass something serious.

"You pretty as hell, shawty. You know that?" I told her, flicking her chin with my finger.

I could see her cheeks instantly growing flushed as she turned quickly to look away. "Whatever," she muttered dismissively.

"Why you say dat?"

She shook her head and stared out into the yard.

Then suddenly a thought occurred to me. "Oh, I see," I said, tossing my head back with snap of my fingers. She turned back to face me with a peculiar look on her face, so I stepped in a bit closer and wrapped my arms around her waist. "You just scared of giving me that pussy again, huh?"

She sucked her teeth and rolled her eyes. "You're not getting none, Jorell."

I couldn't do shit but laugh. "Ain't nobody said I was trying to. Shit wasn't even on my mind, to be honest," I lied. Hell, every single time I was around Nika, I couldn't help but remember the way her body felt, the way her lips tasted, and the way she always made a nigga feel.

Narrowing her eyes knowingly, she pursed her lips to the side. "Uh-huh. I'm sure," she said, slipping her hands into the pockets of her coat.

"I'm serious. I 'on' look at you like that no mo'."

Her eyes widened a bit before a quick look of embarrassment flashed across her face. "Oh," she let out softly, lips still quivering from the cold.

I knew she was still feeling me just as much as I was feeling her, but was too damn stubborn to admit it. With my index finger, I lifted her chin. "Nah, you know you'll always be sexy to me, shawty. Always."

When she licked her lips, I took that as an invitation to kiss her. Leaning down, with my eyes still locked with hers, I pulled her in close. But just before our lips were about to meet, my cell phone started buzzing on the rail of the deck. We both glanced over and saw the name Brenda flash brightly across the screen.

"Oh, I forgot, it's three in the morning and big-booty Brenda's probably looking for you," she said, her voice filled with sarcasm, as she rolled her eyes again.

I let out a deep sigh. "Mane, that's just some random ho I'm talking to. Ain't even that serious, shawty."

"Yeah, whatever," she said, pulling away from me.

After grabbing her by the arm, I pulled her body back into mine and whispered in her ear, "If you want a nigga, all you gotta do is say the word. You already know this."

After a moment of silence and contemplation on her part, she shook her head. "I'm going back in the house. It's too cold out here for me," she said.

Just as she was going back in, Plus was coming out, with a gray hoodie pulled up over his head. "What you still doing out here, yo?" he asked when Nika had disappeared inside.

"Smoking. Was just talking to Nika and shit." I shook my head.

"Ah, you trying to get back in with her?" he asked knowingly with a smirk.

I shrugged my shoulders. "I don't know, breh. I mean, I want to, but then again, I don't. I don't know what's going to happen now that I've entered the draft. Plus, shit is still confusing with Meechie."

"Y'all still fucking?"

I just nodded before sending a shot of spit out into the yard. Whenever I went back home to Prichard, or when Meechie would come up to visit me with Jornelle, she and I always kicked it. I always made it clear that we weren't back together, but she was still my baby's mama, so we had a natural connection. Now, to be clear, shit with her could no way compete with what I had once had with Nika, but Meechie definitely still had a hold on me.

"Well, don't force nothing with Nika if you ain't ready. She's a good girl."

I just nodded in agreement before another thought hit me. "And where the fuck was you all night? Here it is your birthday, and I ain't seen yo' ass since that goofy nigga TK left."

Plus gave a slight grin. "I've been upstairs, chilling with Perri. We're back together now," he revealed.

Feeling my eyebrows bunch together, I turned to look at him. "Damn. Fa real?"

Nigga started cheesing from ear to ear. "Yeah, man. I told her I wanna marry her."

"Yeah . ." I said, letting my voice trail off, as I nodded my head. "I can see that."

"What you mean?" he asked.

"I mean she's been the one for you since you were knee high. You don't do shit without thinking about shawty first. So like I said, I can definitely see that."

I barely noticed it, but a slight look of frustration crossed his face before he rubbed his hand down his jaw. "She might be pregnant again, though."

My eyes stretched a bit. "By Derrick?" I asked.

He shrugged. "Or me. Remember when we went down there for Christmas?"

"Oh, shit." I let out a light chuckle. "Breh, you was fucking his girl?"

He let out a light snort and shook his head. "Nah, he was fucking *my* girl."

"Damn," I muttered. "So how you feel?"

"I mean, I hope it's mine, but if it's not, it's not like I'm gonna turn my back on her."

I nodded. "Yeah, I feel you. That's baby mama right there."

After a small chuckle, he quickly glanced over his shoulder. "Yo, you better not let her hear you say that shit."

"Breh, ain't nobody scared of Perri's manly ass," I said jokingly.

Plus balled up his fist and tagged me in the shoulder. "Yo, don't make me fuck you up out here, nigga."

I waved him off before slapping hands with him and bringing him in for a brotherly hug. "A'ight, mane, I'm 'bout to get up out of here."

After both of us headed back inside, I glanced over to see Nika drinking a glass of juice in the kitchen. "Shawty, it's late. You need a ride home?" I said to her.

She shook her head. "No, I'm spending the night."

I gave her a slight nod before walking out the front door. As soon as I slid into my cherry-red Impala, I cranked up the engine and called Brenda. She was a local chick that I had met out in DC one night, at the club. I already knew what was up as soon as I saw her name come through my phone. She and I had been fucking around for the past month, mostly around the midnight hour.

After telling her I was on my way, I sped across town and made it to her house in no time. She stayed in some run-down apartment off Ames Street with her mother. The parking lot was littered with trash, and all the street-lights were broken except for this one that constantly flickered on and off. After pulling up my sagging pants, I jogged up the steps before knocking at her door. When she opened it up, she looked up at me and put her finger up to her heart-shaped lips.

"Shh. My muva asleep, so you got to be quiet," she whispered.

Brenda was a pretty dark-skinned girl, with brown Chinky eyes and full, pouty lips. Her hair was always styled in long micro braids that fell right to the top of her fat ass. But even with all of that, shawty wasn't the type I would ever wife. She was twenty-four years old and didn't do shit but lie around the house all fucking day. I was simply a nigga at the end of the day, twenty-two years old, looking to get fucked and sucked like the rest of them.

As she led me back to her bedroom, I pinched her ass cheek that was spilling out the bottom of her boy shorts. Suppressing a giggle, she turned around and swatted my hand away. Once we got into her bedroom, she closed the door softly and locked it behind her. I barely got my coat off before she skipped over and started tugging at my sweatpants. Once they were down around my ankles, she sank to her knees and pulled my dick out of my boxers. I sat on the edge of her bed, in my hoodie, my bare legs cocked, with my boots still on my feet. Without warning, she quickly popped it in her warm mouth.

I bit down on my bottom lip and closed my eyes. "Shit," I hissed.

"Mmm," she moaned as she guided me to the back of her throat.

Mane, Brenda was sucking me off so good that she had my toes curling in record time. Just as I was about to nut, I pulled her up off her knees and ripped open a condom. After she shimmied out of her shorts, she straddled my lap and eased down on my length.

"Ooh, baby," she whined softly, tossing her head back in pleasure.

She tightened her grip on my shoulders and started rocking her hips back and forth. Shawty could definitely ride that dick, that's *fo' sho'*. I held on to her plump ass for dear life until every muscle in my body locked up. And after just five minutes of her gyrating and her sensual moans, I could no longer hold on. I trembled and jerked inside her until the last of my seeds had erupted into the condom.

"Damn, baby. You didn't let me get mine," she whined, panting. She was still straddling my lap as her head rested on my shoulder.

I shook my head sympathetically before lifting her body up and moving her to the side. "Damn, shawty. You ain't get yours? That's fucked up. I got mine, though."

I stood up and walked over to a small wastebasket in her room. After removing the condom and throwing it away, I quickly wiped off and pulled my sweatpants back up around my waist. When I walked over to her bedroom door to leave, she grabbed me by the arm.

"You leaving already?" she asked, with a frown on her face.

"Yeah. I'll call you tomorrow," I lied.

After she walked me to the front door, she reached up and tried to kiss me on the mouth. I quickly turned my head, making her lips collide with the side of my face. The last woman I had kissed—*like, really kissed*—was Nika, and I wanted to keep it that way for a while. I ain't never in my life been into kissing random bitches, anyway, but I also wasn't a heartless nigga, either. I leaned down and gave Brenda a tight hug before giving her booty a gentle squeeze.

"I'll check you later, shawty," I whispered in her ear.

"Okay. Don't forget to call me."

Chapter 3

Perri

"Well, the test did come back positive, Ms. Daniels," the doctor said, holding my patient chart in her hand.

I instantly closed my eyes and swallowed back the lump in my throat as Plus gently squeezed my hand. It had been a little over a week since his birthday party at the house, and as promised, he was right there at the doctor's office, by my side. Although I had already taken two home tests, both of which were positive, I had still held on to an inkling of hope that perhaps I wasn't pregnant. But hearing the doctor actually confirm it in that moment made me anxious. I knew without a doubt that Daddy, Tez, and Ms. Tonya would be disappointed in me *again*. And the mere thought of having to tell them brought instant tears to my eyes.

"P, you know everything's gonna be all right, right?" Plus said lowly, smoothing back my hair. "I promise."

I nodded my head, not because I knew everything was going to be okay, but because it was just the natural thing to do.

"Okay, Ms. Daniels," the nurse said, putting on her latex gloves. "We're going to do an internal ultrasound to hear the heartbeat and see just how far along you are."

My heart began to pick up speed. Knowing that I was only minutes away from possibly hearing that this was Derrick's baby made me nauseated. I hadn't seen or heard from him since the New Year, so I didn't even know what I was going to do if this baby was his. Slowly, I nodded my head. I felt numb all of a sudden, as if this were just some sort of dream. *Or nightmare.*

Once I got undressed from the waist down, I lay back on the table and allowed her to put the instrument inside me. I was extremely tense and uneasy, but Plus was right there every second of the way, holding my hand. As soon as she cut the ultrasound machine on, a rapid heartbeat reverberated throughout the entire room. And as the screen next to me lit up in black and white, I could see a tiny flicker of sorts. It was blinking with speed.

"Right there," the doctor said, pointing to the screen. "She's got a strong heartbeat."

"She?" Plus asked, with his eyebrows raised.

"Or he." The doctor smiled. "It looks like you're right around nine weeks, Ms. Daniels."

A lone tear trickled from the corner of my eye as I glanced over at Plus, feeling somewhat relieved. "Christmas," I whispered.

From the way his eyes widened, then immediately softened, I could see that he was too choked up for words. He simply nodded his head in response before leaning down to kiss me on the lips. With Derrick being on the road so much, he and I hadn't been together sexually since before Thanksgiving, so I knew without a shadow of doubt that this was Plus's baby. After printing out a picture of our little bean, the doctor left us alone in the room. I got dressed and headed back up front, where I made sure to schedule all my prenatal appointments.

Once Plus and I were back in his car, driving toward Tez's place, I silently stared out the window. There was so much racing throughout my mind that I kept quiet. I kept wondering what our families would think—what this all meant for us now. Plus must've sensed my anxiety, because he didn't even try to initiate conversation. He just drove silently, listening to the soft music playing on the radio. But every so often during the drive he would make sure to lean over and comfort me, affectionately touching my thigh. Although it was only a small gesture, it somehow put my mind at ease. It seemed that no matter what Plus and I had been through over the years, we'd still proven to be the best of friends.

When there was only ten minutes left in our drive, Plus cut the music down. Still staring out the window, I could see him glancing over at me through my peripheral.

"So how do you feel?" he asked.

I shrugged. "Scared as shit," I admitted, leaning my head against the cool glass.

"What you scared for?"

Shaking my head, I sucked in a deep breath. "That I'm gonna disappoint my father. That I won't ever finish college. Won't ever be able to play ball again . . . shit, everything." I sighed.

"Well, in a few months I hope to get picked up during the draft, and wherever I go, you're going with me."

I shook my head fervently and turned to look at him. "No, I don't want to be a burden and mess up your pla—"

"Perri!" He raised his voice so loud that I was a bit taken back. "I'm not that same selfish-ass eighteen-year-old! I love the fuck outta you," he said. When he tucked his lips inward, I could tell he was attempting to calm himself. "And I would be honored to have you and my children by my side. Wherever I go. Y'all ain't no fucking burden, so don't even say that shit," he said as he took my hand in his.

Just from his hardened glare and the conviction in his voice, I could tell that he meant every word he said. I simply nodded my head, and just as my head collapsed back onto the headrest, the waterworks started to flow. Plus reached over and grabbed my hand.

"Everything's going to be fine, P. You gon' finish school, and we're gonna get married. Wherever the NBA takes me, you, Camille, and my son will be right there with me."

"Son?" I asked, cutting my eyes over at him.

He cracked a boyish smile and shrugged his shoulders. "Don't kill a nigga's dreams, P. Damn," he said, making me laugh.

"Well, one thing's for sure, I know I can't even mention getting an abortion around Ms. Tonya. She would kill me."

Plus sucked his teeth and removed his hand from mine. I knew that he and Ms. Tonya weren't exactly talking these days, but I didn't think it ran that deep.

"You know you need to fix things with your mother, right? Especially now that we're having another baby," I said.

The way Plus kept his eyes fixed on the road ahead, you would have thought he hadn't even heard me. But seeing his lips all pursed and twisted to the side let me know that he had.

"Please talk to her. For me," I urged.

After a few seconds of silence passed between us, he gave a slight nod. "Fine. I'll go talk to her tomorrow. When are we going to tell everybody about the baby?"

"We have time."

Plus just nodded his head again and reached out to cut the radio up, but I put my hand on top of his to stop him.

"Can I ask you something?" I said.

He looked over at me with crinkled brows. "What's up?"

"What's your relationship with that girl? The one from the hospital and the party?"

Just as we came to a red light, he pressed down on the brakes and looked me in the eye. "I'm tutoring her. She's just a friend. That's it."

"Are you sure?"

Plus shook his head, with an exhausted look in his eyes. "Shorty, I don't want nobody else but you. Ain't been thinking about nobody but you for the past year. That's my word. Now let's get home so you and my baby can get some rest," he said, then leaned over to peck me on the lips.

I could tell that things would definitely be different this time around. We would actually be together during this pregnancy, and Plus was going to be the overprotective father to be. An instant tinge of excitement washed over me as I thought of it all, and slowly but surely, my nerves over this unexpected pregnancy started to subside.

Once we made it to the house, I quickly hopped out of the car. The smell of Myesha's pepper steak and rice smacked me in the face as soon as I walked through the door.

"Mommy, Mommy!" Camille squealed, running straight toward me. I scooped her up in my arms and kissed her cheek as I made my way in the kitchen. Myesha was standing by the stove, while Tez and MJ sat around the table.

"Oh, that's all you see?" Plus asked Camille. He pretended to be hurt as he fake cried. "That's how you do Daddy?"

"Hi, Daddy," she said with a giggle, reaching out to give him a hug.

He took her out of my arms, then leaned over and kissed me on my lips. I didn't care that Myesha and Tez were right there in front of us. I closed my eyes and kissed him back deeply. "Go get cleaned up for dinner, P. I got Camille," he said as he pulled back.

"The fuck! Y'all together now?" Of course Tez was the first one to speak up. Although Plus had been staying over every night since his birthday party, this was actually our first time displaying this type of affection toward one another around the family.

"Yeah," Plus said, his cheeks suddenly hiking into a smile.

Tez nodded his head, then came over and dapped Plus up before pulling him in for a brotherly hug. "That's what's up. 'Bout time, nigga," he said.

We all chuckled at that before Myesha came over and gave me a hug, as well, and congratulated both of us on finally getting it together.

While everyone else stayed downstairs, I went up to take a quick shower. After I got out, I sat on the edge of my bed, with my towel still wrapped around me. I glanced down at my cell phone screen and saw that I had two missed calls and a text message from Nika. She knew that I was going to the doctor today, and was probably trying to find out the outcome. I decided to shoot her a quick text.

Me: It's official. I'm pregnant.

Nika: Duh! By who?

I rolled my eyes. Did she have to make me sound like such a ho? I thought.

Me: I'm nine weeks pregnant. Happened during Christmas.

Nika: Aw. See? I knew you and Plus were made for each other. Congratulations, best friend!

Me: Thank you. And don't let Plus hear you calling me your best friend.

Nika: Whatever! I'm not scared of Plus. Call me later.

Me: Okay.

As soon as I put the phone down on the nightstand, Plus entered the room and shut the door behind him. "What's taking you so long in here?" he asked, walking toward me.

"Just texting Nika. Why? Is the food ready?"

With lust in his eyes, he licked his full brown lips. "I 'on' know, but a nigga's definitely ready to eat."

Before I could even respond, Plus came in close and slowly unwrapped the towel from around my body. He pushed me back on the bed and kneeled down on the floor, pulling my thighs to the edge. Without hesitation, he dove face-first between my legs and allowed the tip of his tongue to travel up and down the length of my folds. A loud moan came from the back of my throat upon contact, and my pulse quickened beneath my skin.

"Oh, Plus." I squirmed, clenching the sheets, as Plus licked, sucked, and penetrated every inch of my core.

His hands savagely gripped my thighs as his muted words, expressing just how much he loved me, floated around the room. His mouth on me was pure perfection, and within a matter of minutes, I found myself climaxing hard. My body trembling and panting, I came down from the most euphoric high.

Later that night, as we all gathered around the table, I had to admit that it felt good to finally eat as one big, happy family: Camille, Plus, and I, along with my brother and his family. I could only pray that everyone would take the news of my pregnancy well. I honestly didn't want another baby right now, but knowing that Plus was fully in my corner this time around somehow lessened the emotional burden.

We loved each other, and this time I truly believed that we were going to get it right.

Chapter 4

Nika

It had been a few weeks since Plus's birthday party when I found myself sitting in my grandmother's living room with Clarence from the church. It was a rainy Sunday afternoon, and my grandmother had invited both Ms. Bernadine and her grandson over for dinner after service. I had given my grandmother the silent treatment the entire ride home after church for doing that shit, but did she care? *Hell no.* At sixty-seven years old, Grandma Pearl did what she wanted and could care less whether or not it hurt your feelings. She had been promising Ms. Bernadine a Sunday dinner, and today she'd finally hold up her end of the bargain.

"So how much longer do you have before you graduate?" Clarence asked, pushing his glasses up farther on his nose.

He had on those "old men" polyester pants, belted around his bulging stomach. As he rocked back and forth in Grandma's recliner, the old afghan swinging off the back, I could see at least six inches of his socks.

"I graduate this May," I answered, hearing the light chatter of Grandma and Ms. Bernadine coming from the kitchen.

"That's awesome. Pharmacy tech?"

"Radiology tech," I corrected.

"Well, I have one more year before I get my bachelor's in accounting. Going for my master's and my CPA license right after that." He cheesed, exposing the gap between his two front teeth.

At this point I started to completely tune Clarence out. Don't get me wrong. He was a very nice guy, but my mind was on Jorell. Although I hadn't spoken to him since the party, all I could think about was the almost kiss we'd shared. I would never admit this to him, but I truly missed him. I knew that at any given time, I could call him and we'd be back together, but I didn't want to go back to all his lying and cheating ways. We were better off as friends.

"So I said to Professor Woods, do you really think that's necessary?" Clarence chuckled at what I guessed was supposed to be a joke. Belly jiggling, he slapped his hand down hard on his right thigh.

I had gotten so wrapped up in my thoughts about Jorell that I had hardly even heard a word he'd said. Looking over at him, I gave a little smile in hopes that he would see I was somewhat engaged. Then suddenly my cell phone vibrated in my lap. Tucking my curly hair behind my ears, I looked down at the screen to see that it was Jorell. *What a coincidence.*

As Clarence continued on with his story, I slid my finger across the screen and opened up the message.

Jorell: What you doing, la' baby?

I rolled my eyes at the fact that he was always trying to charm me. *La' baby, tuh!* Fighting to stop the corners of my lips from turning up into a smile, I quickly responded.

Me: Out on a date.

That'll teach his ass a lesson, I thought.

Jorell: Nigga must be lame as fuck if you texting me back.

I did my best to suppress a laugh.

"I know, that's so funny, right?" Clarence asked, then gave a piglike snort. "So yeah, there we were, sitting in the library, when Dr. Cuszig comes waltzing by and . . ."

Once again, I had tuned him out and sent Jorell another text.

Me: He is not lame! He is so fine. Clean cut, tall, light skin, with wavy hair. Muscles galore.

Glancing over at Clarence, I bit back my laughter. He was everything but fine. *Poor guy.*

Jorell: See, now I know that shit won't last.

Me: Huh?

Jorell: Nigga ain't even yo' type.

Me: Well, then, what's my type?

Jorell: Tall, dark, and handsome. A nigga with locs and gold fronts.

I rolled my eyes but couldn't help but smile.

Me: Ugh! Yuck!

When I laughed out loud this time, Clarence's gaze shifted down to the cell phone in my hands. "Oh, I was wondering what you were laughing at."

"Sorry. I was just shooting a quick text to a friend. You were saying?"

Jorell: Yeah, right. You know you still want this dick, shawty.

Scrunching up my nose at his distasteful choice of words, I let out a hard sigh. Jorell was so damn full of himself. Just as I tossed my cell phone over to the next cushion, Grandma called out and said it was finally time for dinner. I got up and headed toward the kitchen, Clarence following behind me. I didn't even bother to bring my cell phone.

***

"You still haven't told them?" I asked, looking over at Perri.

It was several days after dinner with Clarence and Ms. Bernadine, and I was at the coliseum, sitting in the stands with Perri. This would be Plus and Jorell's last time playing Villanova, so of course, she had wanted to come out and show her support. Over her long-sleeved white shirt was Plus's jersey, which she wore with pride. She rocked it with a pair of light blue jeans, Timberland boots, and gold hoop earrings in her ears. Her brown hair was pulled back into a high ponytail, which she had reluctantly let me braid into a fishtail down her back. Since this would be my first time seeing Jorell in a few weeks, I had decided on a pair of fitted dark blue jeans and an olive-colored body shirt. I wore low brown heel booties and a brown blazer to match. And I had on light gold jewelry, with just a bit of soft makeup on my face. My hair was clipped back on one side, and my natural curls were hanging down on the other.

Perri shook her head. "Nah, it's still not the right time. Plus hasn't made things right with his mother yet, and I want him to do that first before we tell everyone that I'm pregnant," she said, keeping her eyes fixed on the court.

The next thing I knew, she hopped up from her seat and whistled loudly through her fingers. "Defense, Taylor! Defense! Shit!"

I looked down at the court just in time to see a player from the other team making a three-point shot on Plus. With a frown on her face, Perri plopped back down in her seat.

"Girl, you are so intense when it comes to these damn games," I told her.

"Gotta be, yo. I love the game, and I love Plus," she quipped. Then she shrugged her shoulders, like it was no big deal. I just smiled, admiring the conviction in her voice. After all the back-and-forth between the two of them throughout the years, I was so glad that they were finally together.

After the game was over, with Georgetown winning by only two points, we fought through the crowd at a snail's pace. On our way down to meet Plus, we saw the girl that he was with at the party. She was walking beside another girl, and low and behold, she had on the same jersey as Perri: navy blue, with the number twenty-three displayed on the back, and the word *Taylor* just below the collar. I wasn't going to be the one to say anything about it, but luckily, I didn't have to.

"Yo, you see this shit," Perri said, turning back to me and pointing at the girl, who was only a few feet away.

Not wanting to be one of those girlfriends who hyped their friends up over every little thing concerning their man, I simply nodded my head. Perri had been on cloud nine since she and Plus had gotten together, and I'd be damned if I was going to be the one to ruin that.

"I swear, if this nigga is on some bullshit, yo . . . ," she said, letting her voice trail off as she shook her head. "I'm gonna kill his ass," she muttered.

After weaving our way through the herd of fans, we found ourselves at the usual waiting spot just outside the locker room. We were both posted up against the wall, with a few other people we didn't know, when the girl and her friend strolled by. I didn't say a peep, but judging by the look on Perri's face, I knew she was about to go off. The girls finally stopped and stood on the opposite side of the hallway, just a bit down from where we were.

Placing a comforting hand on Perri's hiked shoulder, I looked over at the girl. Overall, she was fairly attractive. She was petite, with skin two shades darker than a paper bag, and shoulder-length black hair, which she wore with a simple part on the side. She was just an average-looking girl. No flawless dark skin like Tasha's, no bright, amber-colored eyes like Perri's. She was just regular, not that looks were the only thing that mattered. I just knew that Plus would end up looking like a fool to risk everything for this one particular girl.

After waiting another fifteen minutes or so, the guys all started to file out of the locker room, each picking up waiting friends and family along the way. Then, finally, Plus came through the door. He was wearing a gray Russell Athletic sweat suit with a hood, and a navy blue book bag hung over just one shoulder. His hair-covered chin was raised, and his dark eyes scanned the small crowd, to the point where it was obvious he was searching for someone. That was when I looked over to see a poorly hidden smile on Perri's face. With a kick of her foot, she pushed herself off the wall. It was then that she and Plus locked eyes, and a wide smile spread across his lips, placing his perfect white teeth fully on display and everything. They were so damn cute.

As Plus started shuffling through the crowd, in a hurry just to get to her, he made an abrupt stop mid-stride and looked back. Perri must have noticed it, too, because she began making her way toward him, with me quick on her heels. But before we even got close, I noticed that he was looking down to talk to ole girl. Then he nodded his head, as if he was starting to engage in a conversation. Closing my eyes, I said a silent prayer that Perri wouldn't have to dig in anyone's ass today.

"Ahmad?" Perri called out to him over the clamor.

He turned around and smiled at the sight of us standing there in front of him. And before even saying hello, he leaned down and gave Perri a sloppy kiss on the lips. In the meantime, I kept my eyes on ole girl and her friend, who was right beside her. I noticed the quick roll of her eyes as her weight shifted from one hip to the other. And the single rigid line her lips made as they compressed tightly together.

With his arm now draped around Perri's shoulders, Plus looked back behind him. "Oh shit . . . um, yeah," he stammered. "Brianna, this is my girlfriend, Perri. Perri, this is a friend of mine from school, Brianna," he said, making the introduction.

"Sup?" Perri mumbled, raising her chin and looking down at ole girl like a nigga.

"And this is my homegirl Nika," he added.

Barely parting my lips, I gave a snarky "Hey."

"Well, I guess I'll catch you later," Plus said to Brianna.

"Tutoring on Monday, right?" she asked, her eyes lighting up all hopeful like.

I let out a quiet groan.

"Yeah." Plus nodded his head.

As the three of us began walking away, I felt an arm slink around my neck, and the fresh smell of Irish Spring whizzed past my nose. I looked up to see Jorell trekking next to me, his gold teeth shining amid the tight dark skin of his handsome face and those locks hanging loosely beneath his red fitted cap.

"What y'all doing after this?" he asked.

With Perri still by his side, Plus said, "We gotta get home to Camille. I don't want Myesha to think we using her as our permanent babysitter and shit."

Jorell nodded his head before looking down at me. "What about you, shawty? You gon' hang out with me for a bit?"

"I rode with Perri."

"I'll take you home," Jorell said.

I shrugged my shoulders before looking over at Perri. "I guess I'll text you when I get in, then," I told her.

"A'ight. Don't forget," she said.

"Aye, baby, did you see me out there tonight? That three I put up on Sutton's ass?" Plus asked, making an imaginary basketball shot with his hands.

"Yeah, I saw you." Perri twisted her lips the side. "And the twelve points he got off on you too."

"Ahh!" Jorell cracked. His fist balled up at his mouth, he laughed. "Perri's manly ass is mean, bruh. Don't give a fuck about yo' ego at all!"

After getting out of the building, we went our separate ways. Jorell and I walked up the block toward his Impala. As soon as we got in, he reached over me and opened the glove compartment. He pulled out a clear plastic bag full of weed and a few papers, then tossed them carelessly on my lap.

"You gon' roll?"

"Nigga, I swear, that's all you do is get high. I don't even see how you're an athlete," I told him. After opening up the bag, I pulled out a single piece of rolling paper. The strong scent of fresh marijuana immediately smacked me in the face.

"So where we going at? To the crib?" he asked, then licked his dark brown lips. His eyes traveled down my body as his hand rested between us on the gearshift.

I shook my head. "No, because then you gon' think you getting some. You ain't slick."

He cracked a knowing smile, partially exposing the gold teeth in his mouth.

"Let's go do something," I suggested.

"Like what? Ain't shit to do."

"I don't know . . . Let's go get a drink. Feed me."

Tossing his head back a bit, he let out a chuckle. "Ah! Shawty, you trying to get a date outta me. What? It ain't working out with ole boy?"

Rolling my eyes, I felt my cheeks growing warm. "Shut up, Jorell. Friends can go out to eat."

"Nah, you trying to be my la' baby again, but, hey, it's all good, shawty. Don't get embarrassed now."

After Jorell cranked up the engine, we decided on the bowling alley. Pinstripes was right by campus, but I didn't want to run into any of his little groupies, so I told him to go to Lucky's instead. The parking lot was jam-packed when we pulled up, and I could hear the bass of the music playing inside the place. Naturally, I began dancing in my seat, getting hyped like it was a club. I hit the joint one last time, and when I passed the last bit back to Jorell, he cocked his head to the side.

"Shawty, how you gon' be talking about me smoking all the time when you stay smoking up all my shit?"

"Boy, just come on here," I told him before opening up the car door. I immediately felt the cool air on my face as I stepped out into the night.

Once we got inside, Jorell paid for our lane and got our shoes. He even went over to order us a pepperoni pizza and a pitcher of beer while I picked out a ball. The atmosphere in there was crazy. Hip-hop music was bumping, and there was complete darkness, with the exception of the bright neon lights flashing throughout the place. Once we got to our lane, I sat down, changed into my bowling shoes, and put our names up on the screen. I typed in *Nika* for me and *Big Head* for him.

He looked up. "Nah, take all that Nika shit down. Put la' baby up dere," he said, his Southern accent strong. Then he leaned down to finish tying his shoes.

I sucked my teeth but ended up changing my name, anyway. Once everything was programmed and ready, I stood up from my seat and peeled off my brown blazer, exposing the olive-green bodysuit hidden underneath. I tossed the blazer onto a chair. Being that I was first, I stepped up to the platform and bent down to grab the bright pink ball.

"Damn, la' baby. Fuck has Grandma been feeding you, shawty?" I heard Jorell say from behind me.

Still bent down, I craned my neck around to see Jorell's eyes practically glued to my ass. His locks, now pulled back off his face, revealed that all too familiar lust in his gaze. Although I had gained a few pounds, I didn't want to add any fuel to his fire by acknowledging his comment. I simply shook my head, picked up the ball, and got into position. I could still feel a slight buzz from the weed. Without bending my knees, I took a single step and hurled the ball down the lane. As I watched it roll down a continuous path, only to curve and end up in the left gutter, I heard Jorell erupt in laughter behind me.

"Breh, how you gonna ask me to go bowling when yo' ass don't even know how to bowl?" he called.

He stood up from his seat, then tucked his gold chain inside the collar of his sweatshirt before waltzing over. With a cocky-like grin on his face, which showed that metallic shine on his teeth, he stepped up to me and gave a little wink. "Watch and learn, la' baby . . . Watch and learn," he said.

After taking a seat, I folded my arms across my chest and rolled my eyes. Once he got his ball, he stepped up and did some little hop before tossing the ball hard down the lane. The ball crashed loudly at the other end, making all ten pins fall upon impact. Immediately, he raised both hands in the air like he'd just won an Olympic gold medal.

"Now, that's how the fuck you 'posed to bowl," he boasted, turning around to face me.

I waved him off, my lips pursed, before getting up to take my turn. As I got into position this time, I felt his warmth coming up behind me. His body was suddenly pressing up against mine, his chin settling on my shoulder. Then his strong, lanky arms reached around to help me hold up the ball. I took a deep swallow, in hopes that it would help the unexpected change in my breathing pattern.

"Move your legs a little farther apart," he said lowly, separating my legs with his knee.

Between the natural scent of his locks, that Irish Spring soap, and his voice tickling my ear, I had to struggle just to keep my eyes open. I widened my stance, as he had instructed, then allowed him to guide my hand back slowly with the ball.

"Shawty, don't throw it too soft. Put a little sum'n' on it," he whispered, his cheek still pressed up against mine.

I tried my best to focus on the lane ahead.

"And you see that middle arrow right there?" he asked. I nodded.

"That's where I want you to roll it."

When he finally moved away from me, I did exactly like he'd told me to. After sucking in a huge breath of air, I took a small step, with my legs slightly spread apart. Then I pulled my arm back and hurled the ball down the arrowed path. It rolled straight toward the center pin. As soon as I heard that initial clatter, which was followed by the sound of each single pin dropping one by one, I just jumped for joy, my arms and legs out wide like I was some sort of high school cheerleader cheering a winning touchdown.

"Oh my God!" I shrieked. "I did it!"

I turned around and ran right up to Jorell, then leaped into his arms. "I did it! I did it!"

He just laughed, allowing me to wrap my legs around his waist. "Get down, gul. You embarrassing me," he finally said, with a smile. Those were only his words, because he held me close, with his arms firmly around my waist.

When he finally put me down, I had my arms still wrapped around his neck. I didn't know if it was the strike or that damn weed. Or the mere fact that we were finally spending time together. I was smiling so hard, my face hurt.

"Now gon' 'head and say thank you," he said.

I playfully rolled my eyes before saying, "Thank you, Jorell."

"And don't forget my kiss, shawty." He childishly puckered up his dark brown lips, closing his eyes. Hands splayed across the small of my back, he pulled me near.

I didn't know why I hesitated, because I wanted that kiss just as bad as he did, if not more. On the tips of my toes, I leaned in close and met his lips for the first time in months. Nothing over the top, no tongue. Just his two lips pressed against mine, with our eyes closed.

Two games, several glasses of beer, and a pepperoni pizza later, Jorell drove me back home. A waning moon and only a few stars lit up the darkened sky as I stared out the window. When we pulled up in front of Grandma's house, Jorell put the car in park. The clock on the dashboard read 1:45 a.m., but we just sat there, taking in the quiet. All the lights were off in the house, and only the one on the porch illuminated us in the driveway.

"Thanks, Jorell. I really had a good time tonight," I said as I looked over at him.

Jorell did a quick lift of his shoulders before swiping his palm over his tired face. Then he cut his eyes and licked his lips. "Anything for my la' baby."

Leaning over the console, I placed a soft peck on his cheek, then opened the car door and planted a foot on the driveway. With one last thought, I glanced over my shoulder. "Drive safe and text me when you get home."

"Fo' sho'." He winked.

Chapter 5

Plus

It had been two weeks since we confirmed Perri's pregnancy. I hadn't seen or even talked to my mother in that time, so I was feeling tense as I turned into the Millwood projects. It was about five in the evening, and although the streetlights were already on, darkness had yet to take over the sky. Young hoppers were hanging out on the corners, while kids were still riding their bikes up and down the streets.

As I pulled up to Mr. Phillip's place, I glanced down the way at my childhood home. It was still charred from the night Ronnie had set it on fire and destroyed it, only now it had wooden boards covering up the windows. I took a deep sigh and ran my hand over my head before stepping out of the car. A heavy resistance washed over my body as I walked up to the door. I wasn't ready to talk with my mother. I didn't want to hear any bullshit-ass excuse she would give for crying about a nigga that had beat my ass for years. A cracked-out nigga, he had repeatedly stolen from her and had treated her like shit. This was the same nigga who had damn near burned her home to the ground with my sister still inside. *Nah!* There wasn't shit she could say to me regarding Ronnie. But even with all that said, I knew we needed to move forward; she was my mother, after all. And I had made a promise to Perri.

I knocked on the door, feeling that tightness in my jaw as I chucked up my chin. Mentally preparing myself for the bullshit. Seconds later I heard the bolts and the chain unlock. Mr. Phillip opened up the door and stood back to let me in.

"Your mother's in the kitchen," he said, placing a supportive hand on my shoulder, as if he knew exactly why I was there.

While I headed into the kitchen, Mr. Phillip plopped back down in his recliner in the living room. I released a shaky breath at the sight of my mother, in a floral-print housecoat, standing by the stove. She had pink curlers in her hair and dingy powder-blue slippers on her feet. The all too familiar smell of sloppy joes, one of my childhood favorites, filled the air. She must have sensed me behind her, because she turned around with a spoon in her hand.

"Finally made your way over here to see me, I see," she said. Her voice and her body language revealed that she was unmoved by my presence. She turned back around and stirred the meat in the pan.

I sat down in a chair by the old kitchen table. Legs out wide and elbows resting above my knees, I tried to figure out just where to start. How to break the ice with my own mother. But it turned out I didn't have to. Moments later, she came over and sat two sloppy joe sandwiches in front of me, along with a cup of red Kool-Aid. She took a seat directly across from me at the table, and her eyelashes fluttering and her lips pressed together, she looked as if she was trying to find the right words to say.

"You gon' 'head and eat. And just listen."

Nodding my head, I lifted one of my sandwiches to take the first bite.

"I never told you the story of how me and Ronnie met."

The mere mention of this nigga's name had me clenching my jaw. My mother must have noticed the irritation in my expression, because she said, "Just eat and listen."

I took a bite of my sandwich.

"Ronnie was my high school sweetheart. Started dating when were just fourteen years old." She smiled at the thought, while I rolled my eyes. "He was smart and the starting quarterback for Frederick Douglass, even in his freshman year. He was that good . . . better than good. So good, in fact, that by the time he was a senior in our high school, he had offers for a full ride at more than six major universities." She let out a little chuckle. Staring across the kitchen, she recalled that time in their lives.

She went on. "While Ronnie had his heart set on going to Florida A&M University, I didn't know what I was going to do after graduation. I was just a fast-tail cheerleader. Popular, at best, but no real plans for my future. The summer after we graduated high school, I found out I was pregnant with you."

My eyes ballooned across the table, and she noticed my face right away and shook her head.

"I know what you're thinking. Ronnie isn't your father. I cheated on him with Armand Taylor." She smiled and bit down on her lip. "He was all wrong for me. Nothing but a thug, out there selling dope in the streets, but . . . I loved him." She sucked in a huge breath and closed her eyes, indicating that there was more to the story. "I—I . . ."

After laying my sandwich down on the plate, I looked up at her, needing more. "You what?" I asked.

"I didn't want to hurt Ronnie. He was a smart boy, a good boy. A lot like you."

I groaned at the comparison before taking another bite of my sandwich.

"So I allowed Ronnie to believe it was his baby. To the point where he turned down all his scholarships just to stay here and help me raise you." Her eyes shifted down with regret, and she pressed the tips of her fingers against her mouth. "I had two men claiming you without even knowing the other existed."

"Damn," I muttered in disbelief, my chest suddenly tightening.

"Eventually, I came up with a plan, though, or so I thought. By the time I was six months pregnant, I had made up my mind to just tell Ronnie the truth." She shrugged her shoulders and shook her head. "I was in love with Armand, and I thought, 'Hey, maybe Ronnie can even get his scholarship back,' yah know? But before I got a chance to tell Ronnie you weren't his, Armand found out and confronted the both of us. Whipped Ronnie's ass so bad . . ." She swallowed and shook her head. Squeezed her eyes tight at the memory. "He almost killed him," she added with a shaky breath.

"I had to beg and plead just for him not to. It was . . . a crazy time, Ahmad," she continued. "Both your father and Ronnie refused to talk to me . . . for months. It was only after I gave birth to you that your father even started coming back around. Eventually, he forgave me, and we later married." She smiled.

"Mmm," I muttered with disappointment. "So how did you end back up with Ronnie?"

"After your father went to prison for drug trafficking and someone killed him in there, I began to drink. A lot. That's where I ran back into Ronnie. Down at the bar off Old Branch."

I didn't know why my mother was telling me all this. All it did was make me realize how much I didn't even know her. Never in a million years would I think my mother would do half the shit she was telling me, and even after learning about all of it, I still didn't believe it was a good enough reason for her to let Ronnie treat me the way he had. Nigga used to punch and hit me all the time over the littlest shit. Although he had stayed in our house, I had never looked up to him as a father figure, because he'd been consistently drunk. Eventually, I had attached myself to Mr. Phillip and Tez, had looked to them to learn how and what a real man should be.

I let out a little snort and shook my head. "So why you telling me all this shit?"

"Because I want you to know why I cried in that hospital the night Ronnie died. I brought him to this place. I might as well have given him every bottle of whiskey and every needle he put in his arm. I did it! I killed him!"

I sucked my teeth.

"No, it's true, Ahmad! Every time Ronnie laid his hands on you, or even me, for that matter, I kicked his ass out. I even called the cops on him a few times, but each time he would come back, promising to do better. Convinced me that he would be there for you and Aria both." She shook her head. "Hell, I already had one child without a father. I didn't want two, and besides, deep down, I knew that I was the real reason for him being the way he was. The resentment he had toward you and the alcohol abuse . . ."

All of a sudden, my mother reached across the table and grabbed my hand. "I'm sorry, Ahmad. I'm sorry for letting him hurt you. Sorry for not being a better mother and your protector." Tears trickled from her eyes, and her shoulders began to shake. "Please forgive me," she croaked.

I hated seeing any woman cry, especially my mother. Instantly, I got up from my chair and went over to hug her neck.

"Please forgive me, Ahmad . . . please," she begged again through a whisper.

Feeling choked up myself, I didn't say anything. Just nodded my head in response. At the end of the day she was my mother. There wasn't anything or anyone that could destroy the love I felt for her in my heart.

After we both calmed down, I went back over to finish my sandwiches. But before I could even take a bite, my cell phone started to ring. I looked down and saw that an unknown number had appeared on the screen.

"Yo," I answered.

"Yes, I'm trying to reach a Mr. Ahmad Taylor."

"This is him."

"Hi. I'm Nurse Brown, calling from UM Prince George's Hospital. We have a Perri Daniels here, and she told us to call you."

My mother overheard that. "Perri! Is she okay? The baby?" My mother's neck jerked back, and her eyes narrowed in panic.

"What happened?" I said into the phone.

"Sir, I'm not at liberty to say over the phone, but we need you to come up to the hospital now."

"Fuck!" I quickly hung up the phone and shot up from my seat so fast, the chair literally fell back on the floor.

"What's wrong, Ahmad? What's wrong?" my mother asked, her voice clearly filled with fear and alarm, as she looked at me.

"It's Perri. She's at the hospital," I replied, frantically looking around for my keys, as pure panic began to settle into me.

"At the hospital! Phillip!" my mother yelled. "Phillip, get in here!"

Perri's father walked into the kitchen, with a confused look etched on his face. "What's going on here? What's wrong?"

"It's Perri. She's in the hospital," my mother told him.

"Hospital! For what? Was she in an accident?"

"I don't know, but we gotta go. Now!" I said.

As soon as we entered the hospital room, I saw Perri curled up on the bed. Wearing a hospital gown, with a band around her wrist, she lay trembling in a fetal position. No nurses or doctors were present. I saw that her face was red and swollen, giving away the fact that she'd been crying.

With my mother and Mr. Phillip following behind me, I walked up to her bedside. When she peered up at me, I easily read her amber-colored eyes. No words were even needed in that moment, because everything was written all over her face. I just softly nodded my head, only to see her break down and cry.

"Talk to me, baby," I said lowly, leaning down to press my face against hers. I gently rubbed her hair, feeling my heart shatter into a million pieces while I pretended to be strong.

"The baby's gone," she whispered.

"Who's gone? What happened?" Mr. Phillip asked. He was now on the other side of her bed, rubbing her back.

An instant lump formed in my throat as soon as I tried to explain. "Perri and I—"

Suddenly, the doctor walked into the room, with a clipboard in his hand. "Are you family of Ms. Daniels?" he asked.

"Yes, I'm her fiancé, and this is her father, Phillip Daniels," I said.

My mother cut her eyes over at me. "Fiancé?" she whispered.

"Good. I'm glad you're finally here," the doctor said. "Ms. Daniels came in earlier with complaints of bleeding and severe cramping. Unfortunately, Ms. Daniels was in midst of a miscarriage, and because she was just shy of twelve weeks, we had to do a D&C procedure to remove the remaining tissue from her uterus."

"My God," her father gasped.

The sound of Perri weeping in the background damn near broke a nigga's heart. "Why didn't you call me?" I asked her.

"It wasn't a lot of blood at first, and I did text you," she said with a sniff.

"Ms. Daniels will be just fine. We would like to keep her overnight for observation, and we'll discharge her probably sometime tomorrow afternoon."

"Do you know what caused it, Doc?" I asked.

"Sometimes these things just happen. All her lab work came back normal, and from what we've been able to tell, Ms. Daniels is a very healthy woman." He placed a comforting hand on Perri's shoulder and said, "I'm very sorry for your loss."

As soon as the doctor walked out, Tez came charging through the door. "What's wrong! What happened!" he asked all in one breath. The nigga's chest was heaving up and down, so I knew he had to have been running.

"Perri, did Derrick even know you were pregnant?" Mr. Phillip asked.

Perri slowly looked from him to me. Bright eyes still glossy and red, she silently pleaded for help.

I cleared my throat before looking Mr. Phillip in the eye. "Actually . . . ," I started, then took a deep swallow. "She was pregnant with my baby," I admitted.

"Da fuck!" Tez spat, throwing his arms up in the air. "Y'all some confused-ass niggas, I swear, yo," he muttered.

"Oh my God," my mother gasped, shaking her head.

"So when were y'all going to tell us? As far as we knew, you two were keeping your distance from each other. When did this even happen?" Mr. Phillip asked.

"When Plus came down for Christmas," Perri explained lowly as her head dropped down in shame.

"Christmas!" My mother shook her head, probably realizing that Perri and Derrick were still together during that time. "And what's all this fiancé stuff you were talking about?" she asked, looking over at me.

"It's not official yet, but I already told Perri that I plan on marrying her."

"Marrying her?" Mr. Phillip repeated, his eyebrows raised.

"Yeah, if I get drafted, I want her and Camille to go with me."

Perri reached up and touched my arm. "We don't have to get married, Plus—"

I looked down at her and gently pinched her chin between my fingers. "Look, I hate that we lost our baby, P. I really do. But if I'm being completely honest, none of that shit changes how I feel about you. I would've married you before even knowing you were pregnant. The baby was just one more thing tying us together forever. And I want to be with you forever, 'cause . . . I . . . I love you," I confessed. I heard my mother release a dramatic gasp as I stared intently into Perri's eyes.

Perri gave a half smile and sniffed back her tears. "I love you too, Plus."

An awkward silence fell upon the room, while Perri and I remained in our own little world. As we gazed into each other's eyes, we finally did not give a damn who knew that we were together. I think both of our parents were at a complete loss for words, but after a few seconds, Tez cleared his throat and approached Perri's bedside.

"Well, how you feeling? You gon' be a'ight?" he asked, brushing his hand over her frizzy hair.

"Yeah." She nodded, looking over at me. "I think I'll be just fine."

Chapter 6

Jorell

It was late on a Thursday night when I found myself back at Brenda's place. We had just finished another round of meaningless fucking, and here I was, lying back against the headboard, smoking a blunt. Usually, I would be in and out, but since her mama wasn't home, I had decided to chill for a bit. Brenda was curled up, quiet and content, beside me. She was sucking on her thumb as she watched *For the Love of Ray J* on the television screen.

I hadn't seen Nika in months. Occasionally, we would talk over the phone or by text, but it seemed that, for whatever reason, I was slowly pushing shawty away. Not that I didn't think about her all the time, because I did. *Hell,* she and that damn kiss at the bowling alley ran through my mind on a daily. It was one of the many things that let me know I needed to just let her be. I loved her little ass way too much to even let her deal with a nigga like me. Twenty-two years old and just wild as fuck. A nigga that liked to smoke, drink, and fuck different bitches throughout the week. *Nah!* Nika was too good for that shit. Then there were Meechie and Jornelle, who I knew would always be a priority. Not to mention, the NBA draft coming up next week. Once I got drafted, who knew where I'd even be at this time next year? There were just too many fucking factors that made me believe we were better off as friends.

Suddenly my cell phone vibrated on the nightstand. Right away, I noticed that it was Meechie calling. No matter what time of day or night it was, I always made sure to answer her calls because of Jornelle.

"Yuh," I answered, then felt Brenda's hand come to rest on my chest. She was already getting too clingy, making subtle moves like we were an official couple. I slid her hand out of the way and sat up on the edge of the bed.

"Hey, whatchu doing?" Meechie asked.

My eyebrows gathered from both my confusion and frustration before I glanced over at the clock. Seeing that it was almost three in the fucking morning, I ran my hand over my face.

"What you need, Meechie?" I asked, then gave a deep groan.

"Um . . . I was just calling to make sure you got our tickets for the draft. And to let you know we'll be coming up there this Thursday."

More knots formed in my forehead when she said that. "Shawty, I thought you said y'all was coming with my mama on Saturday for graduation?"

"No. I changed my mind. Thought we could spend some time together with Jornelle before then."

With the phone tucked between my ear and shoulder, I let out another low groan and reached down to grab my sweatpants off the floor.

"A'ight. Let me just hit you tomorrow," I said.

It was not that I didn't want to see my daughter, it's just that Meechie liked to pretend we were one big happy family whenever the three of us spent time together. I considered her my family, based on the sole fact that we had a child together, but that was as far as the shit went. That was the only reason why she had even been invited to my graduation and draft night in the first place. I didn't have feelings for Meechie anymore. Hell, a nigga had even promised himself that I wouldn't hit this time when she came up.

"Um, you must be busy if you can't talk."

I sucked my teeth. "Mane, you ain't saying shit! Just sitting on the phone, breathing in my gahdamn ear. Is Jornelle good?"

"Yes."

"A'ight then! Like I said, shawty, I'll hit you tomorrow," I spat. Shaking my head, I hung up the phone.

When I stood up from the bed and pulled my sweatpants up around my waist, I felt Brenda's long nails graze my back. I quickly glanced at her over my shoulder. "What you doing?" I asked, only to turn back to pick my gold chains up off her nightstand.

"I just thought you would stay for a while. You know my mama ain't gon' be home till tomorrow sometime," she said.

I leaned down and grabbed my T-shirt from the floor before turning around to face her fully. She had those long micro braids hanging down, covering both of her perky breasts. "Nah, I gotta get back," I told her.

As soon as I lifted my arms to slide my T-shirt on, she reached up and planted a kiss on my chest. She made sure to slide the tip of her tongue down the center of my abs while she stared into my eyes. *Damn!* My dick instantly sprang to life.

"See? Why you playing? You play too much, shawty," I told her, trying to gently push her away, but she held firm. Then she closed her eyes as she French-kissed my skin.

"You know you don't want to leave. Look," she mumbled. Lips still in place, she reached down to grab my length through the sweatpants I was wearing.

"Damn, shawty. You doing too much," I muttered weakly. Finally, I closed my eyes and allowed my T-shirt to drop carelessly on the floor. Before I knew it, Brenda was shoving my pants back down to my knees, and I was right back where she wanted me.

One would think that I'd be used to the bright lights and blaring crowd of McDonough Arena, but today I just wasn't ready. I wasn't wearing a Hoyas jersey, nor was I carrying a ball down the court. Today I was actually graduating from college. The arena was packed, and with all the excitement around me, I could barely hear the president announce the graduating class of 2010. Not even a second after I moved my tassel to the other side of my cap, I shot up from my seat and looked up in the crowd. While everyone was on their feet, cheering, I watched my mother pump her hands in the air to "raise the roof." Even from that far away, I could literally feel how proud she was of me.

As all the graduates began filing out, I found Plus among the crowd. Like me, he was dressed in a navy blue cap and gown. The only difference was that he had several gold cords and stoles draped around his neck. This nerdy nigga actually graduated summa cum laude, with a degree in biophysics. He dapped me up before pulling me in for a brotherly hug.

"Come on, mane. Let's get out of here," I told him.

Once we were out in the lobby, we began looking for our families. I immediately spotted my mama, who was on her tippy toes. Her narrow eyes were scanning the crowd; she was undoubtedly looking for me. I had started rushing toward her when Plus tapped me on the arm.

"Aye, I see my fam over there, yo," he said, pointing just a few feet away from where my mother stood.

My eyes followed him as he walked off, and that was when I spotted Nika. My la' baby was so fucking pretty as she stood there in a coral-colored sundress and heels. Her soft brown hair was in its usual coils, and her full pink lips held a natural smile. She was standing next to Perri and Myesha. I was so caught up in staring at her that when my mother came over and threw her arms around my neck, I flinched.

"I'm so proud of you, baby," my mother said. Hugging me tightly, she rocked us both from side to side. After my mother let go, I glanced behind her and saw Meechie walking up, with our daughter down by her side. I instantly reached down and scooped Jornelle up in my arms.

"Congratulations, Daddy!" she squealed.

"Thank you, baby," I said before kissing her cheek.

After I put her back down, Meechie leaned over and hugged me around the waist. Before I even realized what she was doing, she lifted herself up on the balls of her feet, her lips pushed out and her eyes closed, in a hopeful attempt to kiss me. I didn't want to embarrass my baby's mama like that, so I just turned my head, forcing her lips to meet the side of my face. When she opened her eyes, I could tell that she was a bit surprised, but she didn't say anything.

"Ms. Annette," I heard Nika say.

I looked over to see Nika giving my mother a hug.

"How you doing, baby?" my mother asked.

Somehow over the past year those two had built a relationship just by talking over the phone.

"I'm doing good. Just came to support these two knuckleheads." Nika pointed to Plus, then over at me. Then I watched as she winked slyly at my daughter, wiggling her fingers in a wave.

When she and I finally locked eyes, the corners of her lips turned up into an even bigger smile. "Congratulations, Jorell. I'm so proud of you," she said, leaning over to give me a hug. I know I probably took that shit overboard, but I squeezed her little body so tight that I lifted her up off the floor. I took the time to inhale her sweet scent as my face lightly grazed the soft skin of her cheek. But before I could even set her back down to the floor, I heard Meechie clearing her throat behind me.

I let go of Nika and craned my neck around. "What? You need some water or sum'n'?"

"Don't be disrespectful, Jorell. You are completely ignoring your family, after we came all this way to see you," Meechie said, glaring at me, with those big lips of hers all pushed out.

"Mane . . . Meechie gon' 'head with that bullshit na," I said, waving her off. Then I turned back around and focused my attention on Nika, who looked like she was on the verge of an attitude as well.

Women.

The next thing I knew, Meechie came up and grabbed me by the arm. She twisted me around a little so that she could wedge herself in between me and Nika and get in Nika's face. "Look, don't you see this man is with his family? You don' said your little congrats. Now gon' 'head about your business," she snapped. She shooed Nika away with her hand, as if Nika were a peasant or a child.

It was only for a split second, but I saw Nika's eyes widen with fury before she regrouped. Somehow she quickly managed to soften the expression on her face. Her lips turned up into a phony smile, and she began batting her eyes in a condescending manner. "Jorell and I are just friends, Meechie. I'm not trying to keep him from his *family*. Trust. I just came over here to speak to Ms. Annette and congratulate him." Nika then looked up at me and placed her hand on my shoulder. "Again, congratulations, Jorell. I truly am proud of you." And with that, she walked away.

"Lord, y'all kids got too much drama going on for me," my mother muttered, shaking her head.

I didn't open my mouth to say shit, but Meechie knew exactly how pissed off I was just from the way I glared down at her. All she could do was lower her head, with a dumbass look on her face. I took my daughter by the hand. "Come on, Ma. I want you to meet Plus's mama."

Over my past four years at Georgetown, my mother had come to see me play only one time. We didn't have a lot of money for her to be catching flights back and forth, so she had mostly watched me on TV. I understood, so I had never griped about it, but that was also the reason she had never met any of Plus's people before.

When we walked over, Plus was standing there with Camille in his arms. His mother, along with Perri, Mr. Phillip, Tez, Myesha and even Nika, were all gathered around.

"Hey, Ms. Tonya, I wanted you to meet my mama, Annette," I said.

Ms. Tonya came up and embraced my mother. "Good to finally meet you, Annette. These boys of ours have truly made me proud today," she said.

My mother patted me on the back. "Yes. Finally, a college graduate in the family."

"And who is this beautiful little girl?" Ms. Tonya said, looking down at Jornelle, who was hiding behind my leg.

I gently pulled her in front of me. "This is my princess, Jornelle," I said.

Ms. Tonya, along with Perri and Myesha, all cooed while my daughter stood there timidly, twisting from side to side.

Tez stepped closer. "I'm taking everybody out to dinner at Joe's Seafood. Y'all wanna join us? My treat," he said. He was holding MJ, who somehow managed to sleep peacefully amid the clatter.

I looked over and saw my mother shrug her shoulder. "That's fine with me," she said.

After we all made our way outside, I realized that Nika was walking away from the rest of us.

"Hey, where you going, yo?" Perri asked, following behind her.

"I'm going to let y'all go out and enjoy this *family* time. I just came to the graduation," she said. I knew right then that she was leaving only because of Meechie.

"Nika, what the hell are you talking about? You *are* family," Perri said, sounding confused.

Nika glanced over at me before she shook her head. "Nah. I'll catch up with y'all later." She paused. "And, Plus?" she called out, getting his attention. "Congrats again."

Feeling frustrated, I watched Nika run off toward her grandmother's car. By the time we separated from Plus and his family and piled into my car, I was so damn pissed. I hated to argue with Meechie in front of my mother, because she always seemed to take Meechie's side, but I swear I could barely hold my tongue.

After cranking up the engine, I turned around and glared at Meechie in the backseat. "Stay in yo' fucking place, Meechie! Last time I'm gon' tell you that shit," I spat.

"Stay in my place! Nigga, what the fuck are you talking about?" she replied, snaking her neck around.

"You know what I'm talking about. All that shit back there with Nika was uncalled for. I'm not even with that girl no mo', and here you are, out here showing yo' ass like I owe you something!"

"Oh, so, just because we're not together now means you get to disrespect me . . . in my face?"

"Disrespect you! How?"

"You was all hugged up on that girl, Jorell. And then you wanna sleep with me whenever it's convenient for you. I don't fucking think so."

"All right now! That's enough!" my mother shouted. "Y'all not about to sit here and argue like this in front of Nelle."

I could only clench my jaw to keep myself quiet at that point, because my mother was right. We didn't need to be fighting around Jornelle any more than we already did. And that was some sad shit to admit, given the fact that we didn't even live in the same state anymore. Meechie and I were always arguing on the phone, and we butted heads even more when I came back home to visit. Mostly because she still wanted to be in a relationship with me, but I didn't feel the same.

Once I saw Tez's car drive off behind Plus's, I pulled out and followed them. It took us twenty minutes on the highway to get to the restaurant. As soon as I parked the car, I asked my mother if she could take Jornelle inside while I talked to Meechie in private. With a reluctant look on her face, she agreed. After they got out, I noticed that Meechie stayed in the backseat rather than sliding up front. I glanced at her through the rearview mirror and noticed her childish, nonchalant attitude as she looked down at her nails.

Sighing deeply, I leaned back in the seat. "Look, shawty, you been real good to me over the years. And even more importantly, you been a damn good mother to Jornelle. There's no way in hell I could have walked across that stage today if it wasn't for you staying back at home, taking care of her. You sacrificed big-time, and I know that," I looked back at her in the mirror and saw tears slowly pooling in her eyes.

I went on. "And because of that, I'm gon' always love you. I'm gon' always make sure you straight, ya feel me?" I watched as she sniffed and slowly nodded her head. "But, if I'm being completely honest, I just want to co-parent with you. I don't want no relationship right na'."

"You don't want a relationship, or you don't want one with me?" she asked, looking up to meet my eyes for the first time since the conversation began.

"I—I . . ." *Fuck.* I really didn't want to hurt her. "I'm not trying to be with you, Meechie. I don't know." I shrugged. "I mean, at least right now I'm not. But in all fairness, I'm not trying to be wit' nobody. I'm just praying like hell that I get drafted next week. That's all I'm focused on right now." I watched as the tears finally spilled down her cheeks.

"Fine," she muttered. She scooted over in the seat and aggressively opened the door.

"Aye! Meechie—" I yelled out.

I was cut off by the hard slam of my car door.

Chapter 7

Plus

With my hands and forehead pressed up against the warm glass, I stared out the hotel window. As I looked down at the busy streets of New York City, I suddenly felt Perri's soft hands slide around my waist. She reached up to palm my bare chest and pressed her face against my back.

"You ready to get dressed?" she asked in a whisper.

After checking into the Renaissance Hotel last night, we'd spent the past sixteen hours cooped up in our room, fucking. During our rest breaks in between, we'd ordered room service and just watched the highlights run on ESPN. I swear, I loved that Perri and I shared the same interests: sex, food, and basketball. Every day that we spent not fighting what we felt for each other and just actually enjoyed being together was a testament to the fact that we had been created for one another.

Perri had taken it hard the first few weeks after her miscarriage; she had felt sad, had slept a lot, and had and just not eaten like she should. But now Perri was finally back to her normal self, and it felt so good to have her by my side. Especially, since tonight was the NBA draft.

"Yeah. I just can't believe that today is finally here. Shit just seems so surreal," I told her.

"You deserve it, Ahmad. I'm so proud of you."

"But you don't even know—"

"Shh," she whispered, making sure to cut off any doubtful words. Slowly, she slid her hand down my abs and into my basketball shorts before stroking my dick.

I smiled. "You nasty, P, you know that?" I could feel her nodding her head and smiling against my back as my muscle hardened in her hand.

"Come on. Let's make it quick," she said.

I turned around and lightly squeezed her chin with my hand, bringing her face in close to mine for a kiss. "Ain't nothing quick about my shit," I said against her lips.

She pulled back and rolled her eyes. "Nigga, quit bragging and just give me the d—"

Hurriedly, I picked her up and tossed her over my shoulder. Listening to her sound almost girlish as she squealed, I carried her over and flung her down on the bed. She was wearing one of my T-shirts, with nothing on underneath, and was just looking sexy as fuck, with her bushy hair all wild and those bright amber-colored eyes peering back at me. I bit down on my bottom lip at the sight of her resting back on her elbows before I decided to slide down my basketball shorts. She licked her lips in a concentrated stare as she watched me stroke my length. I lowered my face between her thighs and slithered my tongue between her folds.

"You want me to make it quick?" I asked teasingly. Then I went back and, with the tip of my tongue, stroked her once more.

"No," she breathed, bringing her hands to my head as her back arched up from the mattress.

Just when her moans began to echo through the room, the phone on the nightstand rang. "Fuck!" she groaned, slamming her fist on the bed.

The whole family had checked into the hotel earlier today, so we knew we couldn't ignore the call. I got up from the bed and reached over to grab the phone.

"Hello," I answered with a sigh.

"What time does Perri want me to come up and do her hair?" Nika asked.

I looked down at Perri, who was still sprawled out on the bed. "Yo, what time you want Nika to come up here?"

Perri quickly sat up and glanced at the clock. "Oh shit! My hair!" she said, grabbing the shaggy brown mass on her head. "Tell her to give me, like, thirty minutes, and I'll just come down to her room."

Before I could even relay the message, Perri hopped up from the bed and went into the bathroom. When I heard the shower running, I contemplated whether or not I wanted to join her. It was almost four o'clock in the afternoon, and I knew that the car would be pulling up shortly after six, so I quickly decided against joining her. Whenever Perri and I made love these days, I liked to take my time. I'd spent too many years not appreciating those small things about her, and now that I had her, I wanted to pamper her. Make her feel beautiful and study her body so that every sexual desire she had would be fulfilled.

Once she came out of the bathroom, I headed in and took my shower. By the time I got out, Perri had left. I got dressed in a simple navy blue suit with a royal-blue silk tie. The outfit was something that Perri and Myesha had helped me pick out. Once I was ready, I called down to my mother's room to make sure she and Camille were dressed.

"Hey, Ma. Y'all ready?" I asked.

"Yes, we're sitting here waiting on you."

"Okay. I'm on my way down."

I hung up the phone, headed out of my room, and ran into Tez in the hallway.

"A'ight, li'l nigga. I see you," he said jokingly, brushing the lapel of my jacket.

He had on a simple white T-shirt and his black basketball shorts. His locks were pulled back behind his neck, and he had some Nike slides on his feet. His eyes were red as fuck, and I could smell the weed on him, so I knew he was high. That was fine, though, because he, Myesha, and Nika weren't going to the draft. They were just going to go to the after-party. I had only three tickets to the draft, and they were reserved for my mother, Perri, and Camille.

"Where's Myesha and MJ at?" I asked.

"They in the room," he said, pointing down the hall. "I just came from outside."

I let out a little snort of laughter. "Yeah, I can smell you."

He shook his head. "Copped this good shit from my mans, yo. But I'll hook you up later on tonight, when we celebrating and shit."

After dapping him up, I headed down to my mother's room. When she opened the door, Camille, who was now almost three and half years old, ran up to me with a Barbie doll in her hand. My baby girl looked so beautiful with her curly hair pulled tight at the top of her head. Baby hairs framed her caramel-colored face, and those bright eyes flickered back at me. She was dressed in a frilly pink and gold dress, with gold shoes. Just by looking at the tiny gold bracelet around her wrist and the small diamond earrings in her ears, I knew that Tez had had a hand in her appearance. He was always buying Camille things like that, and I appreciated him for it. If God blessed me again tonight with an NBA contract from a team, I would make sure to pay Tez back tenfold for everything he'd done for me.

"Daddy's baby looks so beautiful," I said, picking her up in my arms. I kissed her cheek, then asked, "You ready?"

"Yes, Daddy. But it's taking a really *long* time," she said dramatically, rolling eyes. Camille was a little drama queen already, and I didn't know where she had gotten it from, because Perri was so chill.

"Come on, let's go find your mama." I looked over at my mother, who was all dressed up as well, sporting a simple formfitting black dress with pearls. "You ready, Ma?"

"Yes. Let me just grab my purse. Perri said she's gonna meet us down in the lobby," she said.

Once my mother had grabbed her things, the three of us headed down to the hotel lobby. Perri was not there. We sat and waited for a few, but when the clock hit a quarter past six and Perri was still a no-show, I knew I had to locate her. The car would be pulling up at any moment now, and I didn't want to be late. I lifted Camille from my knee, stood up, and walked over to the house phone so I could call up to Nika's room. It just so happened that at the exact same time, I heard the elevator doors chime to my left. I looked over and saw Perri stepping off the elevator, with Nika following close behind.

Stunned into complete silence, I felt my jaw instantly dropped. In a strapless sequined black dress, Perri looked more breathtaking than ever before. Her long brown hair was now straight and pushed back from her neck, showcasing the delicate curves of her collarbone and shoulders. The makeup on her face was soft and pink, with the exception of her smoky eye shadow, which intensified the bright color of her eyes. And on her feet were a pair of black high-heeled sandals, which I knew she could barely walk in.

"Damn, bae," I muttered lowly, my eyes still roaming her curvy figure in that body-hugging dress.

She blushed, then let out a little laugh.

"What?" I asked, trying to figure out what was so funny.

"That is your first time calling me that . . . bae. Is that the corny shit you're gonna start doing now that we're together?" She laughed again.

I took both of her hands in mine and pulled her to me. Looking down at her pink-painted lips, I licked my own. "Yeah, bae." I nodded, with a smirk.

She leaned in and placed her lips on mine for a quick kiss. "Well, you look good too . . . *honey darling*," she said mockingly. I laughed as she thumbed her lipstick off my lips.

Then I heard Nika say, "Y'all are getting on my damn nerves."

I looked over Perri and saw Nika standing there, with her hands on her hips. "Stop hating, shorty." Then I glanced over to where my mother was still sitting, and pointed. "Y'all see Camille over there? Can't tell my baby that she ain't no real princess today." I smiled, shaking my head.

Before we could all make it over there, Camille jumped down from my mother's lap and ran toward us. Her long pigtails swung as her tiny dress shoes clacked against the marble floor.

"Hey, pretty girl," Perri said, leaning down to pick her up.

Nika pulled out her phone and took a few pictures of us before my mother told us that it was time to go, as she could already see our car pulling up.

I grabbed Perri by the hand, then looked over at Nika. "Make sure you, Tez, and Myesha are all dressed and down here by eleven," I said.

She nodded her head. "All right. We'll be ready. Good luck."

"Thanks."

***

As soon as we entered Madison Square Garden, I caught sight of Jorell, who was seated with his mother and daughter. We all went and spoke to them first before making our way over to our own seats just a few tables away. Surprisingly, it didn't take long for them to announce me in the first round. I was LA's number one pick of the night. There had been a lot of rumors that it was going to be a toss-up between me and some white kid named Luke from Nevada. But as luck would have it, I was chosen to rock that purple and gold.

I was all smiles as I walked up on that stage to shake hands with the commissioners and accept my jersey. With cameras flashing brightly in my face, I stood proudly next to Mr. Phil Jackson himself. On the podium I made sure to thank my entire family, including Perri. As I looked down into the crowd, I could see that Perri was beaming. My baby girl was bouncing and clapping in her lap, while my mother sat next to her and cried.

After I made my way off the stage and took my seat again next to Perri, I reached over and gently squeezed her hand. "You okay with moving to LA?" I whispered in her ear.

When she turned to face me and look me in my eyes, I could see a staggered expression on her face. "You know I'd follow you anywhere, Ahmad."

She was right. We'd had this conversation over a hundred times in the past two months, and each time we had vowed never to separate again. I nodded, then kissed her lips.

Several picks and a few hours later, Coach Phil Jackson took the stage once again. Only this time, he was going to announce the Lakers' final pick of the night. I swear, it could've only been fate that he called out my boy's name. Jorell sprang from his seat, kissed his two fingers, then raised them high up in the air. Perri and I were up on our feet too, whistling and shouting so loudly that I could feel people starting to stare at us. We didn't care, though. We just kept right on cheering as he took that stage.

Once that was over, everyone exited the building. We kept running into anxious reporters, and cameras flickered in every direction. I told Jorell that after we dropped my mother and Camille off, we would meet him at the after-party. It was being held on the rooftop of the Peninsula Hotel this year. Due to the bumper-to-bumper traffic, it took us just shy of an hour to get back to the hotel. By the time we pulled up, Camille was asleep, long limbs dangling from Perri's arms

As we entered the hotel lobby, Perri passed Camille over to my mother. "I see Tez and them right there," she said, pointing across the room.

Tez and Nika were standing there without Myesha. I could only assume that she was up in the room with MJ. While my mother headed toward the elevators, we walked over in Tez and Nika's direction. Tez was dressed down in a gold and navy Versace shirt and dark blue jeans. His locks were pulled back, showcasing the large diamonds in his ears. And each of his wrists sparkled under the lighting of the chandeliers.

"Congrats, homie," Tez greeted, dapping me up. "We watched it down here at the bar. LA it is, huh?"

"Looks like it," I replied.

"Well, that's a damn good look. I'm proud of you," he said, touching my shoulder.

Then Nika walked up and gave me a hug. "Congrats, Plus," she said. She, too, was dressed up in a short red dress and gold heels. Soft, curly hair framed her face like a lion's mane, with a gold dangling earring on each side. Like Perri's, her makeup was soft and natural. Although this meeting had not been planned, I knew my boy Jorell would be happy to see her.

"We gotta wait for My', y'all. Shorty gon' have a gah-damn fit if we leave her," Tez said, shaking his head. "Ain't neither one of us been out since we had MJ."

A few minutes later, Myesha walked out of one of the elevators. She strutted over in a silver minidress and high silver heels. Ever since she'd had MJ, Myesha's body had appeared even curvier and more appealing than before. Her booty had doubled in size, and with the way her dress draped down in the front, you could see most of her cleavage. I stretched my eyes wide before pretending to look somewhere else, because I knew Tez was going to spaz the fuck out.

"Hey, y'all," Myesha greeted, with a little wave.

"My', what the fu—" Tez began, but he cut off his own words when he sighed, then clenched his jaw. I watched his eyes slowly roam her thick frame. "I thought you said you was wearing the other dress?" he asked, his forehead scrunched from anger and confusion.

Myesha nonchalantly shook her head. "No. I changed my mind. Y'all ready?" she said, quickly changing the subject as she looked toward Perri and Nika.

They both stepped up and looped their arms through hers. "Yeah, come on. Let's go," Nika said.

While Tez and I just stood there, the three of them swished toward the front door. Even Perri managed a seductive sway of her hips, despite walking in those high-heeled shoes. My eyes were completely glued to her round ass, until Tez smacked me on the arm.

"I can already see it's gon' be some bullshit tonight, yo," he said. "But come on. Let's bounce."

Chapter 8

Perri

I swear, it felt just like déjà vu when Plus and I stepped out onto the rooftop of the Peninsula. The music was blaring, and people were dancing and mingling right under the night's stars. The waiters were dressed the same in black ties and vests, and they walked through the crowd, holding trays of champagne and caviar. I even spotted some of the same NBA players from last year, when I attended the draft with Derrick. Of course, they each had a pretty, exotic-looking chick hanging on their arm, like an ornament dangling from a tree. As Plus held on to my hand, we made our way over to the bar, with Nika, Tez, and Myesha following close behind.

"I'd like a Long Island iced tea. What you want, bae?" Plus looked over at me with a devilish wink. *Bae*.

"Um . . ." I hesitated, because I wasn't much of a drinker. I would much rather smoke weed instead.

Myesha leaned over the bar and spoke for me. "She'll have a Fuzzy Nipple. As a matter of fact, make that three of them," she said.

My gaze shifted toward my brother, who was directly behind her, tugging down the back of her dress. Knowing Tez, he was probably still pissed that she'd even chosen to wear that little shit, but for the sake of not ruining

Plus's big night, he bit his tongue. Myesha knew that too, which was why she had changed clothes at the very last minute, not giving him time to protest.

After the bartender made our drinks and passed Tez a beer, we walked around until we found Jorell. Like Plus, he was still dressed in his suit from earlier. He was talking to a few players that I didn't recognize. As soon as his eyes landed on Nika, he licked his dark brown lips.

"Dere go my la' baby," he said. He summoned her by raising his chin as his lustful gaze traveled her body.

She rolled her eyes just to keep from smiling. "Congratulations, Jorell," she said, going over to give him a hug. As he placed his hands around her tiny waist, he leaned down to whisper something in her ear. I could only imagine what he said that caused her to smack his arm playfully.

Tez and Myesha then walked over and congratulated him as well. And while the four of them engaged in conversation, Plus was pulled away by one of the owners. As he'd been doing recently, Plus introduced me as his fiancée. Feeling conflicted, I cut my eyes over at him, but he didn't look back at me. Despite the fact that I loved the sound of him calling me his fiancée, he hadn't officially proposed or even given me a ring.

Once we wrapped up the conversation with Mr. Chevy, Plus was pulled away by someone else that wanted to meet him. When I was here with Derrick, he wandered around without me, but now I stayed by Plus's side. In fact, our palms grew sweaty from never letting go of each other's hand. This simple act alone made me feel claimed and cherished, like he was proud to show me off.

When Plus realized that my glass was empty, he leaned down and whispered in my ear, "You want me to go get you another one?"

I nodded. "Sure," I said.

He let go of my hand for the first time that night, then headed over to the bar. Feeling awkward as I stood there by myself, I naturally watched the scene around me. Then suddenly, in the corner of my eye, something caught my attention. It was Mia. She was standing there by her lonesome in a purple cocktail dress. Her round, pregnant belly was obvious underneath. She was so big that it looked like she could give birth any day now. A short spell of nausea instantly washed over me as I thought about the child I had just lost.

I shook my head and swallowed that back as I quickly added up the months in my head. Suddenly I realized that Mia had to have gotten pregnant while Derrick and I were still together. My eyes nervously scanned the crowd until they landed on him. I had to admit that Derrick looked handsome as he stood there in his dark gray suit, talking among the crowd and smiling and laughing every so often to showcase those deep dimples of his. Freckled face and all, he looked nothing short of money, with his fancy watch and expensive shoes. For some reason, my stomach started to twist into knots. This was the first time I'd seen him in over six months, and I guess I just didn't know how to react.

As if he could feel me watching him, Derrick unexpectedly looked up and locked his eyes with mine. He raised his chin up to acknowledge me, then licked his lips. I gave a small closed-lip smile before peeling my eyes away from him. Rocking back on my heels, I noticed Plus trekking in my direction with two drinks in his hand.

When he finally walked up to me, he tried to pass me my glass. "I have to use the bathroom real quick," I told him.

"Oh. It's right over there." He nodded in the direction of the restrooms, which were only a short distance away.

After lifting myself up onto the balls of my feet, I softly kissed his lips. "I'll be right back."

I didn't really have to use the bathroom. As soon as I entered the ladies' restroom, I leaned over the sink to catch my breath. "I will not let these people ruin my night," I mumbled to myself. After splashing a small bit of water on my face, I stared at my reflection in the mirror. Given that Plus was going into the NBA, I'd known that there was a small possibility I'd run into Derrick again, but seeing him here tonight had caught me completely off guard. In my heart, I knew that I didn't want Derrick. I was completely and madly in love with my best friend, Plus. But I'd be lying if I said that seeing Derrick here after all this time, with Mia nonetheless, didn't make me feel some type of way.

"Ooh," I heard someone moan abruptly.

I looked over my shoulder at the bathroom stalls but saw nothing out of the ordinary. I reached over, grabbed a paper towel, and gently dabbed my face with it before looking down at my clothes. As I was adjusting the strapless dress around my breasts, the bathroom door swung open. In wobbled Mia, holding her lower back with her hand.

Pulling my eyes away from her to look back in the mirror, I could hear her heels clicking across the tile floor. Instead of going a few sinks down, she took it upon herself to stand right next me. As she pulled her lipstick out of her purse, a large sparkly diamond glistened, and I couldn't help but notice the engagement ring on her finger.

"You know," she said, rolling up her tube of red lipstick, "it was never going to be you."

I'd been in such a happy space lately—with school, Plus, and just life all around—that I quickly decided not to give Mia any of my energy. Instead, I just stepped back and smoothed my hand down over my dress, acting as if I hadn't even heard her.

"You were ghetto trash, just trying to use him for a come up. I'm glad you've latched onto another baller, because Derrick is so over you," she said evenly. Circling the red lipstick around her lips, she looked at herself in the mirror.

I just shook my head and let out a light snort of laughter before heading toward the door.

"Glad you found a father for that little bastard child of yours *too*," she snidely added. "Derrick was never really into playing the whole stepdaddy role, ya know?"

Hearing her speak about Camille in that way instantly caused the "nigga" in me to rise up from the dead. I could literally feel the muscles in my body lock up at once as my left eyebrow rose from dismay. "The fuck you say?" I asked lowly, with my back still toward her.

"Oh, I think you heard me, Perri. Loud and clear. Because I don't speak ghetto, Mami. Just plain old English." Even with the ass whupping I'd put on her back in Miami, she still hadn't learned not to fuck with me.

Without even thinking, I spun around on my heels and rushed toward her. Before she even had a chance to blink, I raised my hand and slapped her hard across the face.

Whap!

"You bitch!" she screamed, holding the side of her face.

With both of our chests heaving up and down, we stared at one another briefly. And then, out of nowhere, Mia screamed, "Argh!" She charged toward me like a madwoman and pushed me back against the wall.

Now, I didn't believe in fighting pregnant women, but at this point, I considered it self-defense. She was clawing at my face and pulling at my hair like a damn maniac. I did the only thing I could do in that moment, which was to use all my strength and push her off me. Without warning, Mia flew back and landed flat on her ass on the floor.

Plus must've heard all the commotion as he stood outside the bathroom door, because he barged in, with an alarmed look on his face. "The fuck is y'all doing in here!" he spat, first looking at me behind the door, shaking with anger and adrenaline, then down at Mia, who was still sitting on the floor, in disbelief.

The next thing I knew, Derrick came up behind him. "Mia? You all right in here, Ma?" he asked, brushing past Plus to make his way farther inside.

"This bitch pushed me to the floor, Derrick! I told you she still wanted you," Mia cried, pointing up at me.

I scoffed, then rolled my eyes before noticing that both Derrick and Plus were glaring at me. "What?" I asked, shrugging my shoulders.

"Come on. Let's get out of here," Plus said, taking me by the hand.

Just as we were heading out the door, I could hear someone moaning softly. "Ahh." I looked over my shoulder one final time and saw Derrick helping Mia up from the floor.

When we got back out to the party, Plus let go of my hand. "What the fuck was that back there, yo?" he said sternly.

"She started with me first," I said, then started chewing on the corner of my lip.

He cocked his head to the side and narrowed his eyes with skepticism. "So you still out here fighting pregnant women, I see."

My head immediately jerked back at his words. I couldn't believe he had the nerve to bring up Tasha's birdbrained ass, especially at a time like this.

"Don't get fucked up out here, Ahmad! I already told you she started with me first. She started talking shit about Camille, so I slapped her ass. The fuck did you want me to do?"

"I want you to act like a fucking lady! Act like you don't give a fuck about her or that *nigga* in there!" he barked, pointing toward the bathroom door.

Taking in a deep breath to calm myself, I suddenly realized the reason Plus was going off. He actually thought that I'd been in there fighting over Derrick. He assumed I still had feelings for him, which in all actuality couldn't be further from the truth. As expected, seeing Derrick for the first time since our breakup caused me to feel uneasy. I mean, let's be honest. Both of us were now rubbing elbows with the ones we had cheated with, and Mia appeared to be a thousand months pregnant. But no, I didn't want Derrick back. Don't get me wrong. He was definitely a keeper for someone, just not for me. My heart belonged to Plus and would be his forever.

"It's not what you're thinking, Ahmad, I swear," I told him, grabbing the side of his arm. "She kept saying little slick shit to me in the bathroom, and I tried my best just to ignore her. I'd even started to walk out, but when she called Camille a little bastard child and some other shit, I just . . . I fucking lost it," I said, flinging my hands out like wings. "Pregnant or not, you already know I wasn't about to take that shit lying down. So I . . . I slapped the piss out of her," I explained.

The next thing we heard was abrupt screaming and shouting from somewhere in the crowd. Alarmed, we looked across the rooftop and saw Tez cracking a beer bottle over some dude's head.

"Oh shit! We gotta get the fuck up outta here," Plus said, pulling me toward the exit.

Along the way he grabbed Tez, who at this point was totally enraged. After I took ahold of Myesha's hand, the four of us ran to the door in a frenzy and funneled into the stairwell.

Galloping down the steps, two at a time, I looked back at Myesha. "Where's Nika?" I asked, still in motion.

"She's with Jorell," she answered. We were moving so fast that all you could hear were the loud echoes of our labored breathing and the pounding of our shoes.

When we reached the bottom floor and exited the building, Plus looked over at Tez. He was bent down, holding his knees, in an attempt to catch his breath. "Yo, what the fuck just happened back there?" Plus asked, borderline pissed.

"Niggas was trying to grab all on her and shit, yo. I told her dumb ass not to wear that little shit!" Tez spat, shooting an angry glare in Myesha's direction.

"What I chose to wear is not an open invitation for niggas to touch me, Montez. I've already told you this," she argued back.

Plus shook his head and ran his hand over the freshly cut waves of his hair. "I ain't even got a foot in the damn door and y'all niggas already trying to get me kicked out," Plus mumbled in annoyance.

However, Tez didn't pay him any mind. Instead, he snatched Myesha by the hand and rushed her down the sidewalk toward our car. "You somebody's muva now. You can't be coming out of the house dressed like no gahdamn ho, Myesha," I heard him say in the distance.

As I cautiously looked up at Plus, realizing how we'd all just ruined his big night, I sighed and placed an affectionate hand on his shoulder. "So . . . ," I said, letting my voice trail off from amusement.

He looked down at me, with a frown still etched on his face.

"You ready to go, *honey darling*?" I asked lightheartedly. Truth be told, "honey" was the pet name my mother had for my father.

Fighting against the corners of his mouth, which so desperately wanted to turn up into a smile, he looked at me and let out a little snort. "Yeah, bae. Let's go."

Chapter 9

Nika

One hour earlier . . .

After planting himself directly behind me, Jorell slipped his large hands around my waist. "Damn, shawty, you look good enough to eat," he whispered against my ear.

I did my best to hide my blushing and my smile as I pushed the blowing curls back from my face. Then I craned my neck and peered up at him. "Thanks," I said before quickly turning back around. Rather than taking a sip from my straw, I managed a huge gulp of the pink Fuzzy Nipple concoction in my glass, hoping to ease my nerves. I didn't know why, but I was feeling tense.

Jorell was already a flashy kind of guy, but tonight he looked especially handsome in his black suit and cranberry-colored tie. Somehow he looked taller than normal, broader, and even more mature. His locks were freshly twisted and pulled back from his smooth, angular face. His ears were lit up from the diamonds in them, and his hand sparkled, thanks to a simple golden pinkie ring. Tonight was probably the first time I'd actually seen him without his gold fronts, and I found myself loving the look. His natural teeth were surprisingly white and perfectly aligned.

As the music continued to pour from the speakers, I watched people dance and intermingle across the floor. Eventually, Plus and Perri went their own separate ways through the crowd and began speaking with execs and other players on the team. Myesha and Tez decided to do their own thing too, it seemed, as they headed back over toward the bar. Considering that Jorell and I hadn't come to the party together, I felt extremely uncomfortable standing there with just him. This was made worse by the fact that we were surrounded by a few other players and their dates.

"Yeah, I have to tell Lisa that shit all the time, bro," said a tall brown-skinned guy with a Mohawk. "I tell her to slow up on spending that bread, 'cause, hell, I don't even know when I might come to the end of my contract."

Since no formal introductions had been made, I could only assume that he was another basketball player and that the lady on his arm was Lisa. Although heavily made up, she was a beautiful woman and looked to be of Hispanic descent. Her long, silky brown hair and warm vanilla complexion were indicative of that.

"Yeah, you definitely gotta be conservative with your money," another player said, chiming in. This guy was extremely tall—damn near seven feet—with skin the color of clay. The lady on his arm was a shade darker than Lisa, but I could tell that she, too, wasn't quite black.

Biracial perhaps?

As the conversation continued, I could feel Jorell's hardened manhood pressing into me from behind. Every so often he would casually drink his beer or join in on the conversation, but the entire time his dick remained brick hard. And anytime I would make the slightest movement, he would tighten his grip and hold me right in place. I swear, the crazy part about it all was that between the alcohol, his jumping dick, and the virile scent of his cologne, my center was soaking wet and throbbing so badly. I was pretty sure I'd made a mess of the seat of my panties.

"So all the wives get together at least once a month, sometimes more," Lisa said, looking at me.

After taking a second to realize what she had just said, I shook my head. "Oh, no. I'm not his wife. Just a friend."

"Dis my la' baby right here," Jorell interjected with that Alabama accent of his, his words rolling effortlessly off his tongue.

I rolled my eyes at that, 'cause God only knew what these people were now thinking about me. Probably thinking that I was some jump-off or groupie. Both of which couldn't be further from the truth. Although we'd shared a kiss a couple of months ago, I hadn't had sex with him in almost a year. I hadn't even talked to him in weeks, the last time being the day of his graduation.

"Matter of fact, let me holla atchu for a minute, shawty," Jorell said, taking my drink out of my hand. He gave my glass and his beer to one of the waiters before taking me by the hand.

With long swaggering strides, he pulled me through the crowd. Being that I was so short, my feet were moving overtime as I scampered behind him like a rag doll. When we finally reached the other side of the room, he pulled me into a small corridor. It was a dark, narrow space near the restrooms, and from what I could tell, he and I were alone. Without warning, Jorell pushed me up against the wall and pressed his body into mine. When his hand reached for my right thigh and slithered beneath my dress to caress the curve of my hip, I stopped breathing.

He leaned down, closing the space between our mouths. "You miss me?" he whispered.

My head shook vigorously from side to side, but this was an act of deceit. I actually missed his ass like crazy,

thinking about him every morning, noon, and night, but
there was no way I could admit that. Jorell must have
sensed that I was lying, because he reached around to
gently squeeze my bare ass before lifting my leg around
his waist. My hands immediately went to his chest, and
I released the breath I had been holding. With my heart
racing wildly inside it, my chest heaved up and down.

Slowly, he leaned down to kiss me. I could feel his
hardened muscle grind into me ever so subtly. And then
it happened—I fucked up and moaned.

"Ahh."

He pulled back, a cocky smirk on his face. "You sure la'
baby don't miss me?" he asked, lifting his brow.

Biting down on my bottom lip, I lied and shook my
head again. Yes, I missed him, and I was horny as hell,
but there was no way I was going to play his games.
During the time I'd known him, Jorell had proven to be
a true player. He was inconsistent, nonchalant and, more
than anything, liable to break my fucking heart. *Again.*

"I gotta pee," I told him. Gently pushing him off me, I
sucked in a deep breath.

After pulling down my dress, I slipped by him and into
the nearest bathroom, which was around the corner. I
didn't need to pee; I had lied about that too. I just needed
a moment to get myself together, because Jorell was not
about to ruin my night. There were too many tall, fine
single men walking around here for me to be stuck up
under one for the rest of the night, not to mention the
free food and drinks.

Taking in a deep breath, I glanced at myself in the
mirror. Realizing that I liked what I saw, I fluffed my hair
with my hands and fixed my earring before blowing a
kiss to myself. Jorell had better go sit down somewhere, I
thought. Once I had washed my hands and dried them, I
started for the door. But as soon as I opened it, I ran right

into Jorell, who was holding one side of the doorframe. Instead of letting me out, he pushed me back inside the bathroom.

"Anybody in here?" he asked. He ducked his head down to check the stalls as he gripped me by the shoulders.

"What are you doing in here?" I asked, looking around, although I knew we were alone. "Stop! We need to go," I said, protesting.

"Nah. I need to talk to you right quick." His arm circled around my waist as he led me to the farthest stall. He pulled me inside it.

I looked at him like he had lost his mind when he closed and locked the door. "Jorell, stop playing. Let's get out of here," I said again.

Pinning me against the bathroom wall, he looked down at me. "Shawty, why you acting like that, huh? You don't miss a nigga?"

"Clearly, you don't miss me, either," I told him.

His eyebrows gathered in confusion. "Whatchu talkin' 'bout?"

"You don't call me, and you don't text . . . not even after what happened at your graduation with Meechie—"

Jorell leaned down and ceased my rant with a deep kiss on my lips.

"No!" I shoved him back and shook my head. "I'm not doing this with you."

"Shawty, you know I miss you," he admitted, then licked his lips.

"I don't know shit!"

"Stop talking crazy, gul." He tried lifting my chin, but I jerked my face away. "What? You don't love me no mo'?" he asked, grabbing my chin again, but this time firmer, forcing me to look him in the eye.

I didn't want to lie about that and tell him no, so instead, I said nothing. Just stared up into his overly handsome face and into those piercing dark brown eyes. *Shit*.

"What do you want from me, Jorell?" I asked breathily, already tired of the back-and-forth. "You already know I love you, but you fucked that up, remember? You lied and cheated on me."

"Shawty, I know what the fuck I—"

"You broke my fucking heart, Jorell!" I cried. I had been fighting back my emotions all this time. I'd promised myself that I would never, ever let him see me cry, but now my heart was at its breaking point.

As a lone tear trickled slowly down my cheek, I could see his eyes softening. "Damn," he muttered. "Don't do this to me, la' baby. You know you my heart, shawty."

I shook my head. "All I know is what you show me," I said weakly.

With a look of humility, he nodded his head. "I'm gon' do better," he promised, then made his way back to my lips.

With my chin pinched softly between his fingers, he leaned down and kissed me again. This time I was too fragile to fight back, so I closed my eyes and allowed his tongue to part my lips. His large hands began roaming up my thighs, and unexpectedly, he lifted me off my feet. I held on to his neck, feeling the kinkiness of his locs beneath my hands, as my legs naturally wrapped around his waist. That all too familiar steely muscle of his below made its presence known once again.

But when his hands started tugging at my lace thong panties, I freaked. My eyes popped open wide, and I looked at him. "I'm scared, Jorell," I confessed through a whisper.

"You afraid of me? Don't you know I love yo' ass?"

That was Jorell's very first time telling me that, and in that moment it was all I needed to hear to keep going.

Instantly, I planted my hands at the sides of his face and brought him to me. I kissed him so deeply and passionately that my body began to heat up all over. When Jorell's fingers finally found my center, I could feel him smiling against my mouth.

"Why you acting like you don't miss me, gul, when you sitting here wet as fuck?"

"I do miss you," I admitted softly before kissing him again.

As we kissed, I could feel Jorell suddenly fumbling with his pants. And when his mouth gradually made its way to my neck, I heard my labored breathing, which had tripled in speed. My nipples had hardened to stone, and my centered ached relentlessly for this man. Without warning, he gripped my hips and plunged his lengthy dick inside me.

"Uh," I moaned.

It seemed that as soon as he took that first stroke, we heard the bathroom door open. I could've sworn it was Perri out there, mumbling something to herself, but when Jorell covered my mouth with his hand and slowly pumped inside me, I lost all train of thought. My head leisurely fell back against the wall from the amount of pleasure I was experiencing. Jorell was the last guy I'd had sex with. Exactly eleven months, three days, and eighteen hours ago. My body was long overdue.

"Damn. I miss this li'l pussy," he whispered in my ear, drilling in and out of me with such precision and ease.

Hearing him talk dirty to me, with someone right outside the door to the stall, started to send my body over the edge. "Ooh," I moaned through his fingers, which were still cupped over my mouth.

"Shh," he whispered in my ear.

When he released his hand from my mouth, I kissed his lips and bucked my hips against him. We were in the thick of passion when, all of a sudden, I heard Mia out there, talking shit. I knew Perri could handle her own, so I stayed put. I allowed Jorell to hoist my legs up higher and plunge deeper inside. That minor maneuver shot a wave of tingles through my core, and within a split second, an intense orgasm exploded between my thighs. I bit back the sounds of extreme bliss that threatened to spill from my lips as my body trembled from the release.

As I grew limp against the wall, feeling boneless and fatigued, Jorell continued to plow into me. Suddenly, the sound of a hard slap could be heard. It came from the other side of the door to our bathroom stall.

"You bitch!" I heard Mia yell.

Listening to all the commotion out there, I was just about to tell Jorell to put me down, but then this nigga gripped my throat with his hands and rolled his hips up into me. *Fuck.* He had started that grinding shit, which he knew would make me absolutely weak. And that was all it took to get me to a second wind. I started kissing his neck—that spot right beneath his left ear—as his hand roughly squeezed my ass.

"Mmm," he grunted lowly.

From the way his muscles flexed against me, I knew he was cumming, so I moved my hips in a circular motion. Given all the commotion in the rest of the bathroom, there was no need for us to be quiet at this point. I didn't care about our heavy panting or the sounds of our bodies colliding against one another. When I reached down and grabbed Jorell's ass, forcing him to penetrate me deeper, he fucking lost it.

His body froze in place, and his eyes rolled to the back of his head. "Fuck," he groaned, releasing his fluid inside me.

"Somebody's in here fucking, Ma. Let's go." That was Derrick. Not even a second later, we heard the bathroom door open and close.

"Damn, shawty. I swuh to Gah, you got the best pussy in the whole wide world," Jorell finally uttered, breathily.

I just laughed and shook my head. After a few seconds of silence, reality hit, and I could feel my facial expression turning into a more serious one. He was still holding on to me, and my trembling legs were folded around his waist. I looked him directly in the eye. "Don't make me regret this, Jorell."

Instead of responding, he brushed my hair back with his fingers and gave me a gentle kiss on the lips.

Chapter 10

Jorell

For the past two months, I'd been traveling between Alabama and LA, trying to get my housing situated. With my first check from the NBA, I had rented a two-bedroom condo out in Malibu. It wasn't anything fancy, but it wasn't too far from Staples Center and was near the beach. I'd also been putting some financial things in order for my mother and Meechie, and this entailed linking bank accounts and making shared custody arrangements. Truthfully, the goal was to get Jornelle out in LA full-time with me, but for now, she would be coming out during the off-season.

Plus and I were now back in Maryland, packing up our old apartment before the start of training camp. He also had to attend Perri's graduation tomorrow. Since she'd dropped out for a semester to run off to Miami with ole boy, she hadn't graduated on time. She'd actually had to spend most of her summer taking classes at Georgetown.

"What about this?" Perri asked, holding up a dusty old pair of Plus's headphones, which had fallen behind the sofa.

"Nah. Throw them shits away," Plus told her, filling a large bag with more trash.

"So, Jorell, have you talked to Nika?" Perri asked.

I was sitting on the floor, packing up the game system. I craned my neck around. "Nah." I shook my head.

Feeling an instant wave of guilt wash over me, I turned back to wrap the cord around the controller.

After Nika and I had fucked that night in the bathroom, I had kept in contact for a while. We had talked just about every day over the phone until the moment came when I had to go out to LA. That was when reality sank in. I had to scramble to find an apartment, Meechie already had her hand out for some of that NBA bread, and training camp was just around the corner. Again, I was back to thinking that Nika couldn't be a part of my world. I just had too much shit going on, and I refused to drag her into it.

"She said she's been trying reach you for the past couple of weeks. I think she even asked your mama to have you call her, yo," Perri went on to say.

I sighed, because I knew I'd been avoiding Nika like the plague. "Yuh, I'ma call her. She gon' be at your graduation tomorrow?"

"Yeah, she is."

"What time's y'all flight on Monday?" I asked, switching subjects.

Plus, Perri, and Camille were all moving out to LA together as a family, and to be honest, I envied them for that shit. Meechie could never be to me what Perri was to Plus, so there was no way I'd ever even consider moving her out to LA with me. Meechie was still in her feelings about me, and making her an offer like that would only confuse things between us after I'd already made shit crystal clear.

"Our flight's at ten," Plus answered.

Suddenly my cell phone vibrated next to me on the floor. It was an incoming text message. I looked down and saw Brenda's name appear on the screen. I read her text.

Brenda: Hey, boo. Y haven't I heard from u?

Me: I been out of town. Back in Alabama and to LA.

Brenda: Oh yeah. I forgot. You dat nigga now. ☺

Me: What's that supposed to mean?

Brenda: Nigga, don't play shy. You in the NBA now. Big-time.

I laughed out loud.

"Fuck is you over there smiling for, yo?" Plus asked.

I shook my head. "Shawty crazy," I muttered.

Me: I'll be here for two more days.

Brenda: Well, I hope to spend at least one of them with you.

Me: I'll see what I can do.

"Plus, this girl is calling again," Perri snapped behind me. I turned around to see her holding Plus's vibrating cell phone in the air, and the look on her face wasn't a pleasant one.

"Well, answer that shit, then, shorty. Fuck you want me to do?"

Perri softly sucked her teeth before answering the phone. "Hello." She paused, waiting for a response. "Hello?"

Whoever it was must not have said anything, because Perri hung up and made a growling sound, like she was frustrated. "I swear, these simple bitches gon' make me hurt them, yo."

My eyes went over to Plus, who just shook his head as he continued sweeping the floor.

"Breh, who was that?" I asked.

Plus snorted out a little laugh. "Brianna," he said.

"It's not funny, Ahmad!" Perri said, raising her voice, on the other side of the room.

"I didn't say it was! You making a big deal outta nothing, P," he said.

"Jorell, this bitch has been calling Plus's phone non-stop for the past couple of months. I'm talking late-night hours and all." Suddenly the room went silent, and I could see the wheels spinning in her head. "What kind of relationship did y'all even have?" she finally asked as she looked over at Plus.

"Ugh!" he groaned, swiping his hand down over his face. "We've already been over this shit, like, a million fucking times, Perri. I used to tutor her. That's it!" he yelled.

Perri's jaw tightened momentarily before she abruptly flung his phone down on the couch and stormed out of the apartment.

When the metal door slammed behind her, Plus muttered, "Shit. Let me go fix things with her ass."

"Damn, breh. I can't believe Perri's ass jealous like that."

Scratching behind his right ear, Plus shook his head to correct me. "Nah, Brianna been doing way too much, yo. Shorty came to the last few games of the season, wearing my jersey and shit. Even showed up here one night while you were down in Alabama. Had wine and flowers in her hands, all 'at."

My eyes ballooned. "And Perri was here?" I questioned.

Plus nodded his head. "Yeah. Her and Camille."

"Damn, breh. You ain't tell me all of that. Fuck shawty want?"

He sucked his teeth. "Talking 'bout she wanted to say goodbye and hoped we could still be friends once I moved away. Perri ain't say shit but was mean mugging the hell out of her ass the entire time. And now . . . it's like the chick just won't stop calling me."

"Wow. I thought li'l Bri Bri was cool. But she on some straight stalker shit, mane."

"Tell me about it," he mumbled, heading toward the door. "But look, let me go holla at her. I'll be right back."

***

The August sun was relentless as we stood around the perimeter of Georgetown's Healy Lawn. Perri had just crossed the stage, graduating with a bachelor's degree in sports management, and now we were all outside waiting for her to come out. Her entire family was in attendance, including Nika's pretty ass. As soon as I had seen her, I had tried to go over and speak to her, but she had simply waved at me like a mere stranger and had kept to herself.

Something was clearly wrong. Throughout the entire ceremony, I had noticed that she kept getting up from her seat, and no matter what I said or did now, she wouldn't make eye contact with me. Usually, I could say a few words, flash a winning smile, and charm the panties off the muthafucka, but today it just wasn't doing the trick. If I didn't know before, I damn sure knew now that Nika was completely pissed off. And after the way I had fucked her in that bathroom the way I did, only to dodge her calls in the end, I honestly couldn't blame her.

Instead of coming over and waiting with the rest of us, Nika decided to stand alone on the lawn and wait for Perri by herself. After about ten minutes or so of suffering in that heat, I saw her go back inside, and then the two of them finally came running out together. Both of them were smiling from ear to ear, like two kids in a candy store. Of course, my la' baby looked as pretty as ever in a coral-colored maxi dress, with those gold bangles jingling on her arm. As I stared at her as she came toward us, her curly brown hair blowing back in the wind, I became mesmerized. So much so, my dick began twitching in my pants. *Damn.*

When everyone went over to congratulate Perri, I went up behind Nika and grabbed the back of her arm. She turned around, and when she saw it was me, her nose flared. I had never seen her look at me that way, with such disgust. That shit instantly bothered me. Instead of trying to rap to her like I wanted to, I took the hint and held my hands up in surrender. Slowly, I could see the harshness in her face subside, like she really didn't mean to hurt my feelings. I could tell that she wanted to say something, but it was like there was also something inside her fighting back.

Feeling my phone vibrate in my pocket, I backed away from Nika and the small crowd that had quickly formed around Perri. "Aye, breh, I'll be right back," I told Plus, with a nod of my head.

As I walked onto the sidewalk, I looked down at my phone. It was a text from Brenda.

Brenda: Where u at?

Me: Graduation, remember?

Brenda: Look to your right.

Feeling confused, I glanced over to my right and saw Brenda driving along the curb in her mother's rusted-out Oldsmobile. I was beyond irritated when I saw her behind the wheel. Sure, I had told her last night that I was going to Perri's graduation and that afterward I would try my best to swing through, but that didn't mean it was all right for her to pull up on me. Shawty was tripping.

When the car came to a stop alongside me, she reached over and rolled the window down. Controlling my temper, I clenched my jaw and walked closer to her car. I ducked my head down in the window and rested my arms on her car door. "What's good, shawty? What you doing out this way?"

"I told you that I wanted to see you before you left. And I figured that if I didn't come see you, you might try to skip out of town on me again," she explained, flipping back the long braids from her neck.

"But, shawty, I told you I was hanging with the fam today and shit. Didn't I say I'd hit you later?"

"Yeah, but I know how you do. Come sit with me," she said, motioning me with her long hot-pink fingernail.

Hesitantly, I walked around the front of the car, reached through the open passenger window, and pulled up the lock before opening the car door. I couldn't even get situated in the seat before Brenda started trying to hug and rub all up on me. It annoyed me, but then my eyes raked over her body. I had to admit that shawty looked damn good in the biker shorts and sports bra she was wearing. If I didn't know any better, I would have thought her lazy ass had just left the gym.

"What's good witchu?" I asked, looking over at her in the driver seat.

She leaned over the console and placed her hand on my chest before gazing up at me. "I missed you, boo," she said. When she put her hand on my face, I jerked slightly in place.

"What you doing?" I asked as she tried to kiss me.

Then I heard my name being called. "Jorell!"

I turned and looked out my window and saw Nika staring down the street to her right. It was obvious that she was looking for me, but in that instant I felt temporarily paralyzed. I was a few feet away, sitting in Brenda's car, while Nika was searching around for me. Snapping out of it, I reached to open the car door. Nika's gaze finally locked on mine, and she started walking toward me. *Fuck!*

"I need to talk to you before you leave . . . ," Nika called. Her voice trailed off when her eyes shifted behind me and landed on Brenda. I didn't know why, but in that moment I felt like I'd just gotten caught. And, of course, Brenda just had to be so damn extra about everything. She was hanging on my back like an unwanted item of clothing, her chin resting on my shoulder and her hand wrapped around my arm, like we were legit together. I sent a hard glare back at her over my shoulder, then shrugged her off of me.

When I turned back to face Nika, I noticed that she was shaking her head, as if she was disappointed in me. "What's up, shawty?" I asked as I climbed out of Brenda's car.

"Nothing," she said lowly, backing away, with her hands up. "I—I made a mistake." And with that, she turned around and began to jog away.

Chapter 11

Nika

As I ran back to Perri and the rest of her family, I quickly cupped my hand over my mouth. It was the only thing holding back the cry I so desperately wanted to release. For the past month, I'd been trying to reach out to Jorell, because I needed to let him know that I was pregnant. But leave it to Jorell to be the same inconsiderate, inconsistent bastard I'd known for the past three years. He'd been dodging my calls and ignoring every last one of my texts.

Oddly enough, I had been keeping in touch with his mother. But each and every time we'd talk, I'd feel guilty for keeping such a big secret from her. Truthfully, I had wanted to talk to her about my pregnancy, but something in the back of my mind had kept saying that I had to tell Jorell about it first. I'd known I'd finally see him today, I had decided that I was going to pull him aside and let him know what was up.

During the entire graduation ceremony, Jorell had kept trying to capture my attention. He had kept trying to talk to me while everyone else was around, but I didn't want that. I needed to talk to him in private, not suffer his immature attempts at flirting, or hear all the excuses in the world as to why he hadn't call or shown up, or listen to how I was still his li'l baby, blah, blah, blah, bullshit. *No!* I needed to have a real adult conversation with him so that we could figure out what we were going to do.

For the past month, I'd been scared out of my mind, sick, and feeling all alone. And the one day I actually felt hopeful about getting some relief by possibly having him in my corner, he was out there entertaining another bitch. No, Jorell and I weren't together, so I didn't expect much, but *my God*, he was taking me on an emotional whirlwind. The last time we were together, this man actually came out of his mouth and told me that he loved me. He impregnated me and made me promises that he knew damn well he wouldn't keep. Now here I was, nine weeks into carrying his unborn child and about to lose my natural mind.

When I went back to join the rest of the crowd, I immediately spotted Perri through my blurred vision. Ms. Tonya, Mr. Phillip, and the rest of the family were all gathered around her. And from the distance, it appeared that the only person that was missing was Plus. After taking a few more steps, I noticed that Perri's eyes were cast down toward the ground and her trembling fingers rested delicately on her bottom lip. That was when I realized that Plus was kneeling down in front of her. Swallowing back my own emotions, I walked up and listened as he professed his love.

"Perri, not only are you my best friend and the mother of my child, but you are my entire heart and soul. The first person I think about in the morning and the last person I dream about at night. For all the years that I've known you, you've accepted me as I am. No false pretenses or facades, just a nerdy-ass kid from Millwood that could ball," he croaked, staring up into her watery eyes. "And, bae, I swear that's all I ever want to give you in return. If nothing else, I want you to always know that I love you just the way you are. You're beautiful, from the top of your head to the bottom of your feet. And I swear, you got the biggest heart, shorty . . ." Choking on his own words, Plus paused for a moment and shook his head to gather himself. When the tears started to fall from Perri's eyes, they simultaneously fell from mine.

With one hand holding hers and the other over his chest, Plus went on to say, "Perri Daniels, will you do me the honor of being my wife?"

Everyone around them gasped softly when Plus reached down in his pocket and pulled out a small black box. When he opened it, a brilliant princess-cut diamond twinkled.

"Will you, P?" he asked again, almost appearing timid as he peered up into her eyes.

After Perri sucked in a huge breath of air and cast her amber-colored eyes up toward the sky, she faintly bowed her head. "Yes," she whispered and gave a soft cry. Looking down at him, she nodded her head as confirmation. "Yes, Ahmad, I'll marry you."

Before Perri even had a chance to catch her breath, he rose to his feet and wrapped her in his arms. Seeing that one lone tear slip from the corner of Plus's eye made me cry that much harder. It seemed as if this moment was all too bittersweet for me. I was bearing witness to the ultimate love. No, it wasn't that Perri and Plus's union was perfect, but the love they had for one another was just that. I'll admit that a tinge of envy invaded me as I stood there wishing that the father of my unborn child felt just an ounce of what Plus had shown. Not only was I about to separate from my dearest friend, losing her to a state almost three thousand miles away, but not a single person knew that I was pregnant. Inwardly, I was distraught.

Sniffing back my tears, I walked over to Perri and Plus and put my arms around both of them. I was happy and sad all wrapped in one. When Perri pulled back from me, she surveyed my face.

"Are you okay?" she asked, her nose cherry red from sniveling, as a look of concern took over her expression.

Doing my best to assure her that I was fine, I nodded my head. "Yes. I'm just so happy for you guys. You already know I'm gonna miss you."

"I'm gonna miss you, too, but I promise we'll still see each other. We'll keep in touch," she assured me.

Not feeling 100 percent certain about that, or about anything, for that matter, I gently squeezed her shoulder and gave her a soft smile.

After a long, sentimental day, I pulled up the driveway and parked my car in front of Grandma's home. Taking a moment to gather my emotions, I rested my hands on the steering wheel and took a long, deep breath. Grandma could always read me like a book, so I wanted to get myself together before I walked in the house. I stepped out of the car and looked down the lonely block, where the streetlights had just come on. It was a little past eight on that summer night, and the sky had just started to turn gray.

As I climbed the porch steps, I could hear the living-room TV playing loudly inside. Poor Grandma was going deaf in her left ear. When I let myself in the screen door, which was already unlocked, I saw her sitting on the sofa, eating from a bowl of grapes in her lap. Although the house was dark, the end-table lamp beside her was on.

"Hey, baby," she offered, her eyes still pasted to the flashing screen. She was watching a rerun of *Family Feud*.

"Hey, Grandma," I said, feeling my cell phone vibrate inside the little purse I had hanging on my arm. Paying it no mind, I stepped farther inside the house and tossed my purse on the recliner chair. I already knew it was Jorell calling. He'd been blowing my phone up nonstop ever since I'd left the graduation.

Watching the show, Grandma patted the seat next to her on the couch before tossing a grape in her mouth. With heavy feet and a heavy heart, I trudged over and plopped down beside her.

"Well, if that ain't the dumbest answer," she mumbled, shifting the bowl onto my lap.

Just as I put one of the grapes in my mouth, she looked over at me. "So tell me. How was the graduation?" she asked.

"Oh, it was great, Grandma," I said, forcing a chipper sound from throat. "Plus actually proposed."

"Hmm. Well, good for them. I know you're gonna miss her."

After releasing a low, weepy breath from my lungs, I gulped back my sadness. "Yes, ma'am. Very much so."

Grandma remained silent for a second. She was probably sitting there and overanalyzing my every expression and movement. She was just observant and intuitive like that, especially when it pertained to me. "Was that knuckleheaded boy there?" she suddenly asked.

Scrunching my brows, I glanced at her. "Who?" I asked, playing stupid.

Her eyebrows rose from the top of her glasses as she pursed her lips to the side. "Oh, you know who. Ya' li'l boyfriend."

I couldn't help but roll my eyes at that. "Yeah, he was there," I huffed.

"Um, so what was he talking 'bout? Heading off to LA and being a basketball star?"

Staring off at the other side of the room, I shook my head. "No. I didn't really get a chance to talk to him much this time, Grandma."

"So, what? Y'all not even friends no more?" she questioned, disgruntled.

"I really don't know what we are anymore," I whispered.

"Well, you talk to the boy's mama just about every damn week. That's gotta mean something!" She fussed so much that she began wheezing.

I gently patted her on the back until her breathing calmed. "Grandma, it's fine, really. I probably won't ever see him again."

For just that brief second, I wanted so desperately to be a little girl again. The same little girl that would crawl up into my grandmother's lap for her to hold me. From the time I was four years old up until I turned eighteen and moved in with her full-time, I would stay here with her during the summer. Over the years we had learned each other and connected through the soul.

She turned to me and asked, "Is everything all right?"

Tears welled in my eyes. No matter how hard a task it was, I knew I was going to have to tell her about my pregnancy. I just didn't want her to know by whom.

"Grandma, I'm pregnant," I confessed lowly. Not even able to look her in the eyes, I stared down at the bowl of grapes in my lap.

Grandma turned the TV down real low and just kept quiet for a while. As the sheer white curtains in the living room blew softly from the night's warm air, I could hear the sound of cars riding by in the distance.

"Does he know?" she asked knowingly.

I shook my head, with a deep swallow. "And I don't think I'm going to tell him, either," I admitted before holding my breath. Feeling totally unprepared for her reaction, I slowly cut my gaze over in her direction.

"Well, baby . . ." She let out a deep, heavy sigh and grabbed me by the hand. "Whatever it is that you want to do, know that I always got you."

Chapter 12

Perri

It had been three whole weeks since we'd moved out to Malibu. Plus had rented us a small two-bedroom house on the beach. It wasn't even a third of the size of Tez's place, but, man, was it beautiful. It had these sparkling white marble countertops in the bathrooms and kitchen and whitewashed wooden floors throughout. Leading out onto a terrace overlooking the ocean were these large double French doors that let in an enormous amount of light. Although I should have known better with a three-year-old running around, I couldn't resist decorating the entire house in white. For some reason, it made the space feel more serene, and to me, it signified a brand-new start for our little family.

Plus had been away at training camp for the past two weeks, but today he was finally coming home. While Camille played in her room, I sat on the living-room floor, looking at bridal magazines. *Ugh!* Between Ms. Tonya and Myesha constantly calling me about this wedding, I was about to go insane. It hadn't even been a good month since Plus proposed, but our family already wanted to know the date. I was far from a *girly* girl, and in recent years, whenever I had had to face these kinds of situations, Nika had been right by my side to help me along the way. I missed my friend dearly.

Upon hearing her little feet pad down the short hall into the living room, I looked up and found Camille carrying two naked Barbie dolls in her hands.

"Mommy, which one you like?" she asked, holding them out for me to see.

I took both of them and pretended to study their little features. Truthfully, each doll had seen better days. The white one with blond hair and blue eyes had red marker scribbled on her face, while the black doll's hair was tangled and sticky. Though their skin, eyes, and hair were different hues, their facial attributes were practically identical.

"Hmm . . ." I shrugged. "I don't know. I like them both, Mille," I told her, attempting to give them back.

"Well, I'll let you play with this one," she said, shoving the white doll back and taking hold of the black one.

She quickly spun around on her toes, making her pink tutu twirl, and then headed back toward her room. I released a soft chuckle and tossed the Barbie doll on the floor. No matter how much of a tomboy I was, Camille was a prissy little princess at heart. Not to mention she was growing up so fast. Her curly hair was already past her shoulders, and her speech surpassed that of most children her age. I knew that had a lot to do with Ms. Tonya, because even when Camille was just a little baby, she would talk to her like she was an adult. I swear, those two were tighter than a pressure cuff. And judging by the calls each and every night, when they'd say their prayers together, I knew they missed each other awfully bad.

Suddenly I could hear my cell phone ringing, and based on the Rihanna "Rude Boy" ringtone, I knew who it was. *Speak of the devil.* In recent days that number had been Ms. Tonya's favorite song, so I had programmed it into my phone with her name. After lifting myself up a tad from the floor, I reached over and grabbed my cell phone from the back of the couch.

"Hey," I answered.

"Hey, baby. What you doing?" She was bored.

I shook my head and smiled. "Nothing."

"Oh, well, have you and Ahmad picked out a date yet? Me and Aria got time on our hands, and we want to start planning now," she said.

"Plus doesn't even get back from camp until later today, remember? I haven't gotten a chance to talk to him about it yet."

"Well, you been talking to him on the phone, right? I thought we would know something by now." She gave a little chuckle. "What? You scared?" she teased.

"Yo, chill out. We haven't even been engaged a whole month yet," I told her with a little laugh. "I don't see y'all pressuring Myesha and Tez like this."

"That's 'cause Myesha ain't my child. Besides, I'm tired of all the back-and-forth with you and Ahmad. Now that he's in the NBA, he needs stability. You can give him that," she explained.

"So how's Aria?" I asked, changing the topic.

"She's getting there. Lost most of the feeling in her right side, so they're working on getting that back now. Just taking it day by day." She sighed.

I truly felt bad for Aria. Instead of going to prom or graduating with the rest of her senior class, she'd been held back. She'd been in the hospital so much after the fire occurred that she hadn't been back to school since it happened. But next week she would finally be going back to school.

"She ready for school?" I asked.

"Chile . . . just ready to get it over with," she replied.

"Y'all still coming out for his first game, though, right?" I asked before taking my finger in my mouth to bite off a hangnail.

"Yeah, we're all coming. Aria said she wouldn't miss that for the world."

All of a sudden, I heard keys jingling in the lock on the front door. With the phone still up to my ear, I craned my neck and saw Plus plodding in, with a large duffel bag over his shoulder. I couldn't get to my feet fast enough.

"Bae," he called out to me.

As I eagerly walked toward him, I could feel a wide smile spread across my face. "Aye, Ms. Tonya? Let me hit you back. Plus just walked through the door," I said into the phone.

Upon hearing my voice, Plus's eyes immediately locked with mine before he subtly licked his lips. I didn't know if I was just horny or what, but he looked so damn good standing there in the entryway. I could see the swell of his muscular chest in that gray T-shirt he wore. Flexing those strong arms and revealing their cuts, he dropped his bag down on the floor. He actually had on the same Nike basketball shorts as I did, only his sported a big, healthy bulge in the front. *Damn!*

"Okay, tell him to call me later. And don't forget to set a date," Ms. Tonya replied all in one breath.

Without even saying goodbye, I hung up and made my way over to where Plus still stood by the door. Neither one of us spoke; we just stared intently into one another's eyes. And when I was finally there in front of him, and we were standing almost chest to chest, he reached around and grabbed a handful of my ass.

"Mmm," he groaned, bringing his mouth to my neck. "I missed you," he said, his voice just above a whisper. His erection jutted out at me.

"I missed you too, *honey darling*," I teased.

He let out a light chuckle before sucking on my neck. "You smell good," he mumbled against me.

Enjoying the feel of his wet tongue slithering across my flesh, I closed my eyes. "I'm wearing your favorite." I whispered, my hands softly caressing his muscular back. "Lever 2000."

Pulling back, Plus sucked his teeth. "See, you got jokes, yo. Where my princess at?"

He gave me a hard slap on the ass before stepping farther into the house. "Camille," he called.

Not even a split second later, I heard Camille running back down the hall. "Daddy! Daddy!" she yelled.

The way he scooped her up in his arms and she locked her arms tightly around his neck, you would have thought these two hadn't seen each other in years.

"You miss me?" he asked knowingly. Then he watched as she nodded her little head in an exaggerated fashion. "Daddy missed you too, princess."

"Can we go out on the beach?" Camille asked sweetly, almost sounding whiny, and then she poked out her bottom lip and batted her bright amber-colored eyes.

She'd been asking me to take her out to the beach all day long, and I had consistently told her no. I had explained that we would go tomorrow, once her father got home and was settled back in. Now here she was, clearly testing me and going above my head. And in dramatic fashion at that.

"Sure we can go out to the beach. Give Daddy a minute to change his clothes," he said, putting her down.

"No! I told her that we would all go tomorrow, since you're just getting home today."

"It's fine, P. I want to spend some time with y'all."

Now, I know my daughter was only three, but the cunning smile she gave me as she looked up was one of a full-grown woman.

"Go put her bathing suit on," Plus said, smacking me on my behind again.

I looked at him and rolled my eyes.

"What?" he asked, his eyebrows wrinkled in confusion.

"See, this is why she's spoiled now, yo. Between you and your mama, boy, I swear," I fussed, shaking my head.

"We ain't gon' be out there long, bae," he said, softening his tone when he put an emphasis on the word *bae*. Then he subtly wet his bottom lip with his tongue, as if he knew that this would make me fold.

Nigga knew he was sexy, I thought.

"Whatever."

With a little attitude, I took Camille by the hand and walked back to her room. After changing her into her bathing suit, I went down the hall to the bedroom I shared with Plus. He had just finished unpacking his bag and was now pulling his shirt over his head. From the way my body began to heat up all over, you would have thought it was my very first time seeing his bare chest. I took a deep swallow and went over to my dresser to pull out my white one-piece. The first week we moved out here, I had tried wearing the bikini Derrick bought me, but Plus had made me throw it in the trash. He didn't understand that the bathing suit held no connection to Derrick for me. It was just something I simply felt sexy in. *Oh well.* We'd ended up at Point Dume Plaza, a mall, that day, and Plus had bought me five brand-new bathing suits.

As I wiggled my naked hips and bare breasts into the bathing suit, I caught Plus giving my body a full sweep with his eyes. "What?" I asked.

He bit down on his bottom lip and shook his head. "Nothing."

"What's wrong?" I said. But then my eyes dropped down to the swelling that had formed in the front of his trunks. "Oh, no!"

"What?" he said as a wholesome smirk pulled at his lips.

"That!" I pointed at his crotch. "That's gonna have to wait, Ahmad. You've already promised Camille."

Tilting his head to the side, he looked at me with pleading eyes. "Shorty, I can't even get five minutes? She ain't gon' know. Shit, she's in there playing." He shifted his gaze toward the door.

"Later tonight, *honey darling*. I promise."

Plus twisted his lips to the side. "Honey darling, huh? You laying that shit on mighty thick."

Making my best attempt at sex appeal, I strutted over with an extra-hard swish in my hips. After lifting myself up on the balls of my feet, I wrapped my arms around his neck and looked up into his warm brown eyes. "Tonight, Mr. Taylor, I want to hear all about training camp. About how you crossed them niggas over. Tell me how they liked your fadeaway and that crazy-ass jump shot you got," I said, sliding one hand down the smooth plank of chocolate pecs. "And then," I said, holding up my right hand, "I promise you can have your way with me. Okay?"

He offered a sexy smirk, then winked his eye at me. "I'ma hold you to it," he said before leaning down to place a soft kiss on my lips. As soon as his lips connected with mine, Camille came bursting through the door. She stood in a sparkly pink and gold two-piece bathing suit that revealed nothing but her protruding belly. The oversize shades resting on her face and that one hand she had placed on her tiny hip made me do a double take.

"Daddy, let's go!" she said, having the nerve to wag her head.

Hearing how bossy she was made Plus scrunch up his nose.

"See there? You created that little monster. Now go do what the diva says," I teased through a whisper.

I laughed when I heard him mutter something under his breath as he staggered over to take her by the hand. While they went ahead without me, I grabbed three beach towels from the linen closet, then dipped into Camille's room to get her bucket of beach toys. Just as I was about to head out through the double French doors, I heard the doorbell chime. After setting everything down in the single chair in the living room, I walked over to the door and looked out the peephole. It was a UPS delivery guy, so I quickly opened up the door.

"Ms. Daniels?" he asked.

"Yeah, that's me."

"Okay, just sign here please," he said, passing me a clipboard.

After I signed my name, he passed me a package neatly wrapped in brown paper. Right away, I noticed that there was no sender's name, only a New Mexico address. As far as I could remember, I hadn't ordered anything, and I damn sure didn't know anyone from New Mexico. Puzzled, I brought the package into the house and set it down on the kitchen table. I quickly unwrapped it to find a shoe box of sorts inside. I didn't think anything of it, nor did I hesitate to open it up. But when I did, chunks of vomit rose to the back of my throat. There was a bloody chicken's head inside, and it wreaked. Lying beside it was a folded white sheet of paper smeared with blood. Carefully, with a trembling hand, I reached in and grabbed it with the tips of my fingers. When I opened it up, there was brief note, harshly written in black permanent marker.

A Chicken's Head for the Chicken Head. He'll never be happy with a manly bitch like you!

Chapter 13

Nika

Four months had passed since I last saw Perri. Although I talked with her just about every other day, things were just not the same. I hadn't even told her about my pregnancy, and the guilt of it all was starting to eat me to pieces. Every time we spoke, I felt like I was living a lie. But what was my alternative? I knew without a doubt that Perri would tell Plus. He was her best friend, and she confided in him about everything, and if Plus found out, I knew the news would eventually get back to Jorell.

When Perri had invited me out to LA for the Lakers' first game of the season a couple of months ago, I had made up an excuse about having to study for midterm exams. The truth was, I just hadn't wanted any of them to see me pregnant. As of late, Perri's calls had been about their upcoming wedding, which was set for April. My due date was the first week of March. I didn't know exactly how, but I was determined to make the scheduling work. Perri was my girl, after all, and she wanted me there as her maid of honor. If I had to face Jorell on that day, so be it. I refused to let her down.

The last time I had spoken with Jorell was the day of Perri's graduation. He had called and texted me several times on the days that followed, but each and every time, I had forced myself not to respond. I had decided to just let him live his life. Grandma had said that she would have my back with this baby, and we had decided that we would raise him or her together. I knew it wasn't an ideal situation or the fairy tale I'd been dreaming about most of my life, but I'd convinced myself that it could work. *It had to.*

As I sat in the passenger seat of Ms. Bernadine's Lincoln town car, I stared blankly out the window, taking in all the familiar highway signs and exits. I rested my elbow against the glass. Clarence was driving us all down to a megachurch convention in Mobile, Alabama. At first, I'd worried about being in the same state as Jorell, but then I'd remembered that he was now living permanently in LA.

Surprisingly, Clarence had become a good friend to me. He was a good listener at times, and he hadn't seemed to judge me when he found out that I was pregnant. Clarence had become more confident in himself over these past few months, especially after he'd gotten his first accounting gig at Providence Hospital. He had been leaving the high-water polyester pants at home and had even started wearing contact lenses instead of his regular glasses. Even with all that said, I still wasn't physically attracted to him, but I was happy for him.

"How much longer, Clarence? I've got to use the bathroom, baby," Ms. Bernadine said from the back.

Clarence turned the gospel music down on the radio, then looked through the rearview mirror. "We should be there in about fifteen minutes, Grandma. You want me to stop?" he said.

I could hear Ms. Bernadine huffing and shifting in her seat behind me. "No. That's fine. I'll just wait," she replied.

Clarence must've had our ride calculated down to the minute, because in exactly fifteen minutes we were pull-

ing into the parking lot of the Hampton Inn. No sooner
had he put the car in park than Ms. Bernadine bolted out
and ran inside the hotel lobby. Clarence and I looked at
each other and fell out laughing.

"I told Grandma to pack her Depends, but she's stubborn like that, ya know," he said, pulling the key out of
the ignition.

"Bernadine gon' get you for tellin' all her gahdamn
business," Grandma Pearl mumbled behind us.

After the three of us got out, Grandma Pearl went
inside while Clarence and I got the bags out of the
trunk. Although the sun was shining brightly, it was still
chilly—near sixty degrees—outside that day. Dressed in
an olive-green turtleneck and light blue skinny jeans, I
was fairly warm. I also had a brown leather moto jacket
on top, with the knee boots to match. Luckily, I could
still fit in them at five and a half months pregnant. I'd
purchased them at a discount last summer in New York,
when Perri and I went to the NBA draft.

"Say, you wanna go over to the mall later, while they
rest up?" Clarence asked, rolling a suitcase behind him as
we walked up to the front entrance.

"Yes. I definitely could go for some retail therapy right
about now."

His eyes traveled down to my round, pregnant belly.
"Yeah, maybe you could buy some things for the baby,"
he offered with a little smile.

"Yeah, maybe." I shrugged.

Not even two hours later, Clarence and I were shop-
ping over at Springdale, an outdoor mall. He was on
the hunt for more work clothes, while I was just looking
for anything that caught my eye. After going from store
to store, we decided to stop at Jos. A. Bank. I selected

three pair of pants for Clarence to try on, and when he disappeared inside one of the little dressing rooms, I started skimming through the racks.

"Nika? You still out there?" Clarence called from his dressing room a few minutes later.

"Yeah, I'm here. Come on out," I said.

When Clarence opened up the dressing-room door and appeared in the doorway, I had to admit that he looked very nice. He had paired the black dress pants I'd picked out for him with a light green button-up shirt and a fancy tie to match. Although he didn't even have on his shoes, he stood taller somehow, perhaps because his shoulders were pushed back. When he turned around and twisted his body as he looked himself over in the mirror, I could tell that he liked what he saw as well.

"Sharp. You should get it," I said.

"You think so?" he asked, with his eyes still glued to his reflection.

"Yes. And there's no need to try on the other two pairs of pants I gave you, because they're the exact same, just a different color."

"Yeah, but I want to try them on with the shirts I picked out."

I sighed. We'd been in this store longer than my patience would allow. "Fine," I said. "I'm about to go to Tropical Smoothie. Just meet me down there when you're all done."

"All right. I'll call you on your cell when I'm on my way."

The cool air blew against my face as I trekked over to Tropical Smoothie, just two doors down. Luckily, my hair was up in a messy ball at the top of my head, or else the wind would have it blowing wild. As soon as I walked in, I went straight up to the counter.

"Hmm," I muttered, looking up at the menu.

"Ma'am, are you ready to order?" asked a pretty Asian girl behind the counter. She had a Tropical Smoothie visor on her head.

"Uh, yes. Let me get a Thai Chicken Wrap and a Mango Magic Smoothie."

"For here or to go?" she asked.

"For here."

"That'll be thirteen, eighty-eight," she said.

I pulled a twenty from my purse and passed it to her.

"I thought that was you," I suddenly heard behind me.

I turned around to see Ms. Annette standing there, holding Jornelle's hand. My mouth immediately went dry when her eyes fell to my very prominent belly. "H-Hi, Ms. Annette," I said, giving a guilty smile, followed by a little wave.

"I—I . . . ," she stammered and then shook her head. "I didn't know you were pregnant."

"Uh, yes, ma'am. Almost six months," I admitted. Then I glanced over at Jornelle. "Hi, pretty girl," I cooed, waving my fingers at her.

God, if she isn't the spitting image of Jorell. From her deep chocolate skin to that dark set of wide eyes, she was truly his twin. Even from a mile away, anyone could see that she was a beautiful little girl. She had two long pigtails neatly styled in her hair, and small gold hoop earrings in her ears. Looking her over, I even had to give Meechie her props. Jornelle was dressed perfectly in a heather-gray peacoat and fitted blue jeans. On her feet were a pair of tan leather riding boots that closely resembled the ones I had in my own closet. Jornelle looked like the perfect little woman.

She waved her little hand back at me and said, "Hey, I know you."

"You do?" I asked, elevating my voice and widening my eyes. I was always animated like that with kids.

She nodded her little head. "Yeah, you're my daddy's friend."

A huge gush of air was released from my lungs when I sighed. "Yes. And your grandma's friend too," I said. I shifted my gaze back to Ms. Annette, whose mouth was still partially open. "Well, are you guys eating?"

"Ah, y-yes," Ms. Annette said.

"Okay. I'll join you."

While Ms. Annette and Jornelle walked back over to their table, I stood back from the line and waited for my order. I already knew what Ms. Annette was thinking—that I was carrying Jorell's child. And although I didn't want to lie to her, I felt I had no other choice. Once I got my tray of food, I headed over to join them. As soon as I sat down at the table, Jornelle hopped up from her seat and came around to sit right next to me. I thought it was sweet.

"So what brings you all the way down here?" Ms. Annette asked, pushing up her glasses.

"My church is having a convention this week, and I drove down with my grandmother," I explained. Taking a small bite of my wrap, I allowed Jornelle to play with the bangles on my wrist.

"Well, does Jorell know you're in town?"

I swallowed back my food, then dabbed the corner of my mouth with a napkin. "Ms. Annette, remember? I told you that Jorell and I don't talk anymore. I haven't spoken to him in months."

"Well, does he know you're pregnant?" she asked in a blunt tone.

I cleared my throat and looked her directly in the eyes. "It's not his child," I lied.

A quick look of relief washed over her face before she smiled. "Right. I just didn't know if you two still kept in touch or not."

"No. Jorell is living his life, and I'm living mine," I told her straight out.

She nodded her head. "Well, you two aren't the only ones. It seems . . ." Her voice trailed off before she cut her eyes down at Jornelle. Then, silently, she mouthed the word "Meechie." "Is living her life too," she went on to say. "Running behind some thug, thinking it'll make my son jealous. Every week she's dropping this one here . . ." She nodded her head toward Jornelle, who wasn't paying her any attention. "Off with me for days at a time. I swear, between her and my son, they're gonna drive me crazy. I'm too damn old to be raising other people's children, ya know?"

"Wow," I let out. It was all I could think to say.

"Ms. Nika?" Jornelle patted me on the arm. "Me and Grandma are gonna watch *The Princess and the Frog* tonight. You wanna come?" she said. Looking at me with those pretty dark brown eyes, she waited for an answer. "Grandma bought ice cream and popcorn," she added.

"Uh . . . I don't know, Jornelle. Maybe nex—"

Then I heard someone call my name. "Nika!" I looked up to see Clarence walking toward our table. "You didn't answer your phone," he said when he reached us.

I reached down in my purse, pulled out my phone, and realized that not only was my phone on vibrate but that I'd already missed three calls too. "Oh, my bad," I told him.

Clarence's eyes bounced from Ms. Annette over to Jornelle. "Oh, I'm so sorry for interrupting," he said.

"Clarence, this is a good friend of mine, Ms. Annette," I said, introducing them. Then I placed my hand on the top of Jornelle's little head. "And this here is her granddaughter, Jornelle."

As soon as I said Jornelle's name, Clarence's eyes doubled in size. Over the past couple of months, I'd been confiding in him about the happenings of my life. And I'd mentioned Jornelle's name a few times in tandem with her father's.

"Guys, this is Clarence . . ." I hesitated. I bit down on the corner of my lip. "*My boyfriend,*" I added.

Clarence's neck whipped back, and his eyes shot over in my direction. "I . . . I'm—" he stuttered.

If Ms. Annette hadn't been staring me dead in the face, I swear, I would have rolled my eyes at him. Clarence was going to mess this all up for me.

"Clarence, sit down," I said cutting him off. I pointed to the seat next to Ms. Annette and directly across from Jornelle.

As soon as he sat down, Ms. Annette turned in her seat and studied him. "Oh, so you're the father to be?" she asked.

Clarence now had beads of sweat the size of peas coming from his brow, and his lower jaw was practically sitting on the floor. He was stupefied to silence.

"Yes!" I said, speaking up for him.

Clarence took a hard swallow and closed his eyes dramatically, like he couldn't believe what I'd just said.

"So will you?" Clearly saving the day, Jornelle tugged on my arm.

"Will I what, baby?"

"Will you come over to Grandma's house and have movie night with us?" she asked.

Not that I had any other plans, since the convention wasn't until tomorrow afternoon, but I had to turn down her offer. I mean, it was one thing to talk to Ms. Annette over the phone, but actually bringing a lie like this into her home was another thing altogether. Let's face it. I was carrying her grandchild and keeping it a secret, for Christ's sake.

"Please," Jornelle pleaded, already on the verge of tears.

Shit.

A miniscule sigh was released from my lips. "Sure. What time is everything starting?"

"I think we'll start the movie about seven, that way I can have her in the bed about nine," Ms. Annette answered.

"Oh, her mom isn't coming to get her tonight?" I asked.

Ms. Annette pursed her lips to the side, as if to say, "Yeah, right.".

My eyes then shifted toward Clarence, whose nerves were readily apparent. Judging by the tension lines in his face and his rigid posture, he was about to break. "Clarence, you'll drop me off, right?"

With a disappointed look in his eyes, Clarence said, "Sure. I'll take you."

We all ate our food, and then I gave Jornelle and Ms. Annette a hug before we went our separate ways. As soon as Clarence and I got inside the car to drive back to the hotel, he went off on me.

"Why would you tell that lady that I'm your baby's father, Nika? Jeez!"

I looked at him and rolled my eyes. He was so damn corny.

"Because it was obvious that she thought this was Jorell's baby. Now she's not worried about it."

"But you lied on me!" he shouted, pointing to his chest.

"Who cares? It's not like you're ever gonna see her again. Chill out."

With a clenched jaw, Clarence drove back to the hotel in silence. Now I felt even guiltier than before. In my mind, I was battling with the fact that my baby would never know the other side of his or her family. Jornelle would actually be my child's sister, and Ms. Annette would be his or her grandmother. Reality was starting to set in, and if there was one reason to finally tell the truth, that was it.

Why does Jorell have to be such a jackass? I thought.

Rubbing my swollen belly, I sat contemplating whether or not I should reach out to him again. After pulling my cell phone out, I scrolled through my contacts until I found his name. I stared at it for a few minutes, thinking about all the different ways I could possibly go about this. Hell, I was almost six months pregnant at this point, and I already knew how that would look. He was an NBA rookie with money now, but it was not like I hadn't tried to tell him before. The entire summer I had tried calling him nonstop, but to no avail. I had even tried to tell him at Perri's graduation, but my jealousy and resentment had gotten the best of me that day.

As if my finger had a mind of own, it unexpectedly hit the screen. My stomach was literally quivering inside as I nervously pulled the phone up to my ear. After the third ring I could no longer take the pounding in my chest, and I was about to hang up.

But then I heard the remote sound of a woman's laughter. "You so stupid, babe." Her voice, upbeat, seemed to be getting louder in the distance, and then I could hear her adjusting the phone at her mouth. "Hello."

My heart immediately sank, and I panicked and abruptly ended the call.

Chapter 14

Plus

I was more than halfway through my first season in the NBA, and I was already averaging twenty-four points a game, seven assists, and three rebounds. My stats were higher than those of any other rookie this season, and it made me a strong contender for the Rookie of the Year Award. I'd signed with one of the best sports agents in the game, Marcus Droby, I already had a few endorsement deals lined up on the table. With the money I'd be bringing in this time next year, I was almost certain my family would be set for life.

Jorell, on the other hand, rode the pine most games, and I could tell it was taking a toll on him. Not only had he been drinking more than usual, but his spending had become excessive as well. These days he practically lived in the strip clubs and would spend five to ten racks each and every time he went. I'd also noticed that he'd been slack when it came to practice and being on time for important team meetings. Georgetown had prepared us better than what he was giving, and I knew that I would eventually have to pull my boy aside for a serious conversation. But since we had just beaten Boston 130–127, today just wasn't going to be that day.

It was a little after eleven o'clock that night when our entire team headed over to Synn Gentlemen's Club to celebrate our victory. We rolled up in six black Escalade limousines and pulled alongside the curb one by one. When the driver opened up the door to the truck I was in, I could hear the bass of the loud music thumping from inside the club. I climbed out behind our power forward, Raheed, and Jorell came out after me. After we walked inside the club, we were all escorted to a private VIP area in the back.

The secluded space had a nice view of the main stage, and a personal bar was set off to the side. I could see that several bottles of liquor and champagne were already being chilled on ice. It seemed not even five minutes after we all sat down and got settled with a drink in our hands that the strippers started filing in. There had to be at least fifteen of them, and they were bare breasted and all different shades.

Surprisingly, Perri hadn't seemed to mind when I'd told her where we were going after the game. She had just asked that I make it home safe before telling me that she loved me. I guessed I had been earning her trust these days, and I was truly grateful for that. Truthfully, I didn't even plan on staying out late tonight. I just wanted to show my face for the team, and then I was going to bounce. The only thing I ever wanted to do after a game was lay up under Perri. She would climb on my back and massage my shoulders while I ran down each play of the game. Then I would listen to her tell me all the shit I'd done wrong and what she thought I needed to work on. Any other nigga's ego might've been bruised by that, but Perri was my best friend. Not only did she know basketball like the back of her hand, but her advice came from a place of love too.

As I sat next to Jorell, I took in the pretty, light-skinned girl who was shaking her large jiggly ass in his face. She had on a red thong, with matching red lipstick on her lips, and her feet were in a pair of clear stiletto sandals.

Jorell took a big gulp of Hennessy from his glass before pulling her down into his lap. His hands rubbed between her thighs as she leaned back into his chest and allowed him to whisper in her ear. Although I couldn't hear what he was saying, I was pretty sure that they were discussing the events of their upcoming "after" after-party. I let out a quiet snort of laughter and shook my head. My boy was wild.

"Hey, handsome. Can we offer you a dance?" asked a stripper with blond hair and blue eyes. She was standing next to a dark-skinned beauty with a long black weave hanging down her back.

I shrugged. "Do your thing, shorty."

As the beat dropped to Jeremih's "Birthday Suit," the two of them started dancing to the down-tempo rhythm. Sensually grinding, they dipped down low between my legs and worked themselves up with a slow flip back of their hair. When they began getting reckless with their hands and shit, reaching for my crotch, I gently pushed them away and leaned up in my seat.

Jorell raised his empty glass up at me. "Aye, breh, do me a favor and get me another."

I guessed he figured that I was on my way to the bar. After slipping a hundred-dollar bill in each of the girls' G-strings, I took his glass and went over to get myself another drink. While most of our crew was drinking Henny and Cîroc, I had settled on Patrón for the night.

"Lolli?" called out one of the big bouncer dudes by the velvet ropes.

The light-skinned girl sitting on Jorell's lap strained her neck and looked in his direction.

"You up next, Mama," he told her.

When she stood up and was about to walk off, Jorell gently grabbed her by the arm. "Shawty, don't forget about me after your set," he told her, winking his eye.

After a few more minutes, I heard Lil Wayne's "Lollipop" blaring from the club's speakers. From where I stood at the bar, I could see the girl Lolli sauntering her way down the main stage. The way niggas all gathered around with wads of cash in their hands, I figured shorty had to be the main attraction. With her long red fingernail placed teasingly between her teeth, she meandered sexily to the edge of the stage. She dropped down low and dramatically popped her thighs open wide, giving the audience a nice view. I had to admit that shorty was bad as fuck. She hadn't even taken off her thong yet, and niggas were already making it rain.

"Lolli's something else, huh?" I heard someone say behind me.

I looked back to see my sports agent, Marcus, standing there. He looked to be almost in a trance as he ogled Lolli as she danced on the stage. He kept pushing his glasses up the bridge of his nose every so often as he tilted his head to the side, like he was trying to get the best view. Marcus was a funny-looking guy with thinning dark brown hair and a big nose. Although all his clients were well over six feet tall, he was short, reaching only five feet, seven inches. He was in his midthirties, and till this day I don't think I'd ever seen him in anything other than a suit.

"Yeah, shorty's definitely a bad one," I agreed, nodding my head.

Without removing his eyes from Lolli, Marcus suddenly cleared his throat. "So did you ever get a chance to look into the security firms I sent you?"

In addition to the money I was getting, I'd been getting a taste of fame. Last month I was on the cover of *ESPN The Magazine*, and the month before it was *Sports Illustrated*. Both had featured me as one of the most promising players of the year. And it was all good, until it became harder and harder just to walk down the street. It wasn't nothing for me to get ambushed at the mall or at a restaurant by fans that simply wanted an autograph or a picture taken. Not to mention the fact that Perri had started getting hate mail. For whatever reason, people didn't think that Perri should be the woman on my arm. The shit had got so bad, to the point where that the gossip magazines had dug up some pictures of her from high school. Even had had the nerve to put them in their paper, with the headline YOUNG NBA STAR CHOOSES HIS HOMELY CHILDHOOD SWEETHEART.

"Yeah, I looked over them, but I think I may end up going with someone else," I said as I looked to him.

"Oh yeah?" he replied, clearly distracted, as he wagged his head from side to side to match the bounce in each of Lolli's ass cheeks.

"Yeah. My brother owns a security firm back home, and he's thinking about expanding his business," I lied. Tez hadn't mentioned anything about growing his firm, but in my mind, the plans had already been laid.

Finally, that seemed to get Marcus's attention. His eyes shifted to me over the top of his glasses. "You'll need an experienced security team, Taylor. Not some homeboy hookup from the hood, because I already see that's where you're headed."

Cocking my head to the side, I narrowed my eyes. "Marcus, do I pay you, or do you pay me?"

"Well, you pay me, but it's—"

"Exactly! Now shut the fuck up and finish watching shorty shake her ass!" I barked, pointing toward the stage.

There was no doubt that Marcus was the best at what he did, or else I wouldn't have hired him. He could negotiate a contract like nobody's business, and his connections reached far. But what I didn't care for was the subtle racist remarks he'd throw out there sometimes, not to mention the mere fact that he thought a nigga was stupid. My IQ was 130, so I was definitely far from that.

Marcus's teeth clamped down tight, and his jaw flexed with frustration.

"I'll send you the information on my brother's security firm as soon as possible," I told him.

Leaving him standing there, I walked back over to my seat. Jorell was gone, so I set his glass of Hennessy next to his chair and sat down. As soon as I put my glass up to my lips, another stripper was headed my way. The strong scent of her perfume actually met me before she did. I looked up to find a decent-looking girl in a neon-green bikini. Her milk chocolate skin was covered in body glitter and tattoos, and her short hair was styled in a smooth bob.

"Can I dance for you, Ahmad?" she asked. Trying to be seductive, she twisted her body from side to side and batted her doe-like eyes.

Caught completely off guard by the fact that she had just called me by my first name, I frowned up my face. "Nah. I'm good."

With an attitude, she whipped her neck back before she placed her hand on her hip. "You good?" she asked, sounding shocked.

"That's what I said, yo. I don't want all that glitter and shit all on me."

Rolling her eyes, she sucked her teeth, then turned to walk away.

Suddenly I could hear Raheed laughing on the other side of me. "Damn, homie. You be giving these stripper hoes a hard time," he said.

Taking another sip of my Patrón, I shook my head. "Man, let me just get the fuck up outta here. You see where Jorell went?" I said.

"Somewhere in the back," Raheed said, gesturing with a backward nod of his head.

I got up and started to make my way in that direction. Along the way, I had to pry a few strippers' hands off me, which only irritated me further. Truth be told, I really just wanted to hurry up and get home to Perri. A nigga was pussy whipped like a motherfucka, and I was missing shorty some kind of bad.

Before I could turn the doorknob to the private room in the back, I heard a woman's soft moans coming from inside. I gave a quick, hesitant knock on the door before going into the room. Jorell was sitting back on a velvety purple couch, with his pants down to his ankles. It was obvious that he and Lolli were fucking, given the way she rocked her hips as she straddled his lap. Next to them on the end table was what appeared to be lines of coke on a mirror. I prayed that shit was Lolli's and not his.

"Yo, I'm out," I hollered over the music.

Jorell gripped Lolli's ass in place and looked at me over her shoulder. "A'ight, breh. Be safe," he said.

"Nah. Yo, you be safe." I nodded toward the coke on the end table. "And strap up."

"Fa sho'," he said.

Once I got outside, I stood in front of the club and asked one of the drivers to take me home. It took us just under an hour to get there. Seeing all the lights out in the house, I climbed out of the limo and made my way up to the front door. Hearing the waves in the ocean crash against the shore in the background, I put my key in the lock. As expected, the alarm went off, disrupting the silence throughout the house. I quickly disarmed it, then reset after locking the house up.

Quietly, I walked down the short hall and peeped inside Camille's room. Lying on her back, she was dead to the world, with a pink sleep mask covering her eyes.

I smiled, then softly closed her door and made my way down to the master bedroom. Other than the light that strained through the blinds, our room was completely dark. I made out the lump underneath the covers and quickly realized that Perri was fast asleep.

Trying to keep quiet, I went inside the en suite bathroom and turned the shower on. Although victorious, it had been a long, grueling day, and I needed something to relax me before I went to bed. After I stripped down, I opened the glass shower door and stepped inside. Instantly, I inhaled the heat and steam. I pressed my body against the front shower wall and allowed the hot water to flow down my back. That was when I heard the shower door suddenly opening behind me, and I felt an unexpected cool breeze hit my backside.

I looked over my shoulder to see Perri standing there, completely nude. After turning around to face her, I took in the sight of her heavenly body. She was toned from being an athlete, yet she still had hips and an ass from giving birth to Camille. I knew that my opinion was biased, but I swear, those stripper hoes at the club didn't have shit on P's natural beauty.

"Congrats, *honey*," she said, her amber-colored eyes sparkling back at me, as she stepped farther into my space. "I missed you."

I didn't respond. My arms just went out, circled her waist, and brought her to me. Placing her hands on the sides of my face, she lifted herself up to kiss me gently on the lips. And just like that, my dick became solidified, and I could hear myself involuntarily groaning into her mouth. She reached down between us and stroked my length with her hand.

"I guess this means you missed me too," she said, pulling back.

Without warning, I scooped her up so that her legs were wrapped around my waist.

"Oh," she gasped.

I carefully positioned her body up against the cool shower wall and stared into her pretty, bright eyes. "I missed the fuck out of you, bae," I confessed through a whisper.

As her warm entrance hovered over my erection, I could hear her breathing become more and more intense. "You love me?" I asked, already knowing the answer, as I tightened the grip my palms had on her ass.

She bit down on her bottom lip and slowly nodded her head. "Yes," she breathed.

Without delay, I lowered her trembling body down onto my length and plunged deep inside her. I watched as her mouth slowly dropped open from pleasure and her head collapsed back against the wall.

"I love you too, P."

Chapter 15

Jorell

No thanks to me, we had just won our first game of the New Year. Instead of going out to celebrate with the team, I decided to head straight to the crib. As I cruised down the highway in my brand-new Lamborghini Murciélago, I toked on a fat blunt. Although I knew the league gave out random piss tests, this chronic shit seemed to be the only thing getting me through these days. As of late, I had felt like my life was a never-ending battle.

Adding to the fact that I wasn't getting any play on the court, Meechie consistently had her hand out for money. And it didn't matter that my mother kept Jornelle three, sometimes four days out of the week; Meechie somehow thought that she was entitled to more child support. I was already paying her five thousand dollars a month, but she kept saying it wasn't enough. She didn't give a fuck that I wasn't getting the big endorsement deals like Plus; she just wanted her money, or her "back pay," as she'd often called it. I knew that all her recent antics were just to spite me for hurting her. She was a woman scorned.

In addition, there was big-booty Brenda from DC. Shawty was now claiming to be pregnant with my baby and was already asking for money to help with her pre-natal care. Off the top, I'd strapped up every single time I'd fucked with Brenda, so I didn't even believe her ho ass when she said the baby was mine. And secondly, what kind of prenatal visits cost three to four thousand dollars a pop? I was like, "Shawty, yo' ass ain't got no muhfuckin' Medicaid, bruh? The fuck!" But she claimed she didn't have any health insurance, so I'd been dealing with that.

As if shit couldn't get any worse, my cousin Nard got locked up last week. Apparently, he was pulled over for reckless driving, and the cops ended up searching his car. He had his Glock on him and five ounces of weed inside the glove compartment. At first, my aunt called me, asking for bail money; then I was hit with Nard's lawyer fees too. Nard was like a brother to me, so it was the least that I could do, but *gahdamn*, it just seemed like everyone in my life had their hand out. Not only was my money dwindling fast, but the shit was starting to get old too. I was starting to feel used.

After I pulled into the parking garage, I hopped out and tossed the remains of my blunt on the ground. Once I stepped onto the elevator and pressed the button for the top floor, I allowed my head to fall leisurely back against the wall. Closing my eyes, I felt both physically and emotionally drained. It had been a long day. As soon as the elevator doors chimed and opened, I got out and started down the long hall that led to my apartment door. In the distance I could already see a strange man standing in front of my door.

Oblivious to my approach, he just stood there, turned to the side, talking to himself. As I got closer, I could feel my eyes squinting, as I was trying to see if I recognized him. He was a tall man, standing just an inch or two shorter than I did. His limbs were long and lanky, and his skin was dark as coal. I scrunched up my nose when I got a good look at the oversize Sean John getup he had on, along with the off-white Reebok Classics on his feet.

Purposely trying to scare him, I walked up real close. "What you need, breh?" I asked with a bit more bass in my voice than normal. Since I'd moved into this apartment building, I hadn't had any problems. No stalking-ass Lakers fans, nothing, and I wasn't about to start now.

His eyes widened as he turned to look at me. "Oh, uh . . . yes, um, I . . . I . . . ," he stammered.

"Why you in front of my door, mane?" I asked, with a scowl on my face. I noticed the small specks of silver facial hair, which contrasted with his darkened complexion, as he blinked nervously.

"My name is Jerome Walker," he said, his voice deep and shaky, with a hint of an island accent. The man was so on edge that I could literally see the thick lump he swallowed back as it traveled down his thin neck.

Raising my brow, I looked at the man as if he were crazy. "Okay?"

Removing the oversize Yankees cap resting on his head, he sighed before clearing his throat. "I'm . . . your father," he said just above a whisper, eyes everywhere except for on me.

With a sudden jerk of my neck, I narrowed my eyes instantly. "What?" I asked, desperately needing him repeat himself.

"Jorell," he sighed. A shaky breath was released from his lungs before he squared his shoulders and finally looked me in the face. "I'm your father."

It didn't take but a split second for a swirl of anger to spiral from the pit of my stomach. My head cocked back dramatically from both rage and masked confusion. "Nigga, if you don't get the fuck on away from aroun' my doorstep . . . I ain't your fucking son!" I barked.

"Let me explain—" he began.

"Nah, mane, you don't need to explain shit!" I could practically hear the blood rushing through my head as spit flew from my mouth. "Take yo' black ass back from where you came from!" I yelled, pointing down the hall.

The man held his hands up in surrender, then looked at me with pleading eyes. "Call your mother," he said. I don't know if it was the convincing tone of his voice or the softening look in his eyes, but I took another look at him again. I saw that the bone structure of his face matched my own. Even his wide nose and the dips and curves of his dark brown lips were like mine.

Slowly, he reached down into his pocket and pulled out a business card before handing it over to me. I looked down at it and saw an orange logo with TURNER CONSTRUCTION on the front, the name and number of a Wallace Reed typed right below. "Oh, my number's on the back," he said.

I flipped over the business card, and sure enough, handwritten in black ink was the name Jerome Walker, with a phone number scribbled underneath. Running my hand over the top of my head, I sucked my teeth. "Mane," I let out slowly. There was nothing else that I could say.

"Just call your mom. She'll tell you," he urged one last time. Then he turned and walked away.

I felt like the wind had just gotten knocked out of me: my breath suddenly hitched, and my posture grew limp. It took everything in me to open up that apartment door. I trudged all the way into the kitchen and pulled a cold beer from the fridge. Leaning back against the edge of the counter, I turned up the bottle and guzzled down more than half of the beer. With my mind still racing and my hands trembling like a fiend's, I grabbed my cell phone and dialed my mother's number.

"Hello," she answered.

"Ma?"

"Hey, baby. I saw your game," she said in a cheery voice.

Closing my eyes, I drew in a deep breath. "Ma, who's Jerome Walker?"

The other end of phone line remained silent. The suspension seemingly growing as the seconds rolled by, I could hear my heart practically beating through my ears.

"Ma?" I called again.

"How do you know that name, Jorell?" she asked, her voice suddenly low and weighty.

"Is he my father?"

"Jorell—"

"No, Ma. Just answer the fucking question! Is that nigga my father?" I slammed my fist down on the counter.

A gasp of air was released hesitantly from her lips. "Y-yes. He is," she admitted softly.

Struggling to stand on my own two feet, I closed my eyes. "Ma," I breathed.

"How did you find out about him?"

I shook my head. "Nigga just showed up at my door."

"He only wants money, Jorell."

For some reason, hearing her say that shit hurt me to the core. I mean, it was one thing to know it, but to actually listen to my own mother come out of her mouth and tell me the ugly truth brought tears to a nigga's eyes. I wasn't stupid by far. Why else would he come and find me after twenty-two, almost twenty-three years? But even knowing the truth of it all didn't lessen the pain.

"I know what the fuck he wants, Ma. Fuck!" Exasperated, I swiped my hand down over my face. "I'll handle it," I said, then hung up the phone without even giving her a chance to respond.

After finishing the rest of my beer, I sent Lolli a text message and told shawty to swing through. My mind was all over the place, and I needed something to ease my troubles fast. It was like shit kept being dumped on me, and I was slowly drowning inside. No one knew about my financial burdens. No one knew about Brenda and this baby. I was carrying the load all on my own. And tonight, of all fucking nights, my deadbeat father showed his face after twenty-three years. I didn't know how much more weight on my shoulders I could take until I finally broke.

Ignoring my mother's back-to-back calls, I jumped in the shower. Not even ten minutes after I got out, a hard knock sounded on my door. After pulling my boxer briefs up around my waist, I walked to the front of my apartment. As I looked out the peephole, ensuring that it wasn't that Jerome nigga again, I saw Lolli standing there, with another girl by her side.

"Sup, shawty?" I said, pulling open the door.

"Hey, baby," Lolli cooed, coming in for a hug. "I brought a friend. Is that all right?"

I glanced over at the brown-skinned girl standing in the doorway. She was decent enough in the face, and from what I could see through the tight little minidress she wore, her body was banging. She had a long honey-blond weave down her back, and each of the dimples on the sides of her face were pierced. "Yeah, she straight," I told her. Then I invited both of them in with a nod of my head.

Once they slipped out of their shoes and left them by the door, they followed me down to my bedroom. While I rolled up a blunt, they stripped out of their clothes. Since Lolli had been to my place a time or two before, she went over to cut some music on. Wearing nothing but their bra and panties, they both jumped on my king-size bed and started dancing to "BedRock," by Young Money. I sat back against the headboard and smoked my blunt, just watching the two of them act silly.

As the song continued to play, they started to kiss and feel on each other. The way ole girl was gripping Lolli's fat ass made me jealous inside. Letting a thick swirl of smoke escape from my lips, I grabbed Lolli by the ankle. When she looked down at me, I chucked my chin up at her, telling her to come here. While she hopped down to her knees beside me, I took another pull from my blunt. Then I grabbed the back of her head, pulled her face to mine, and blew a shotgun between her lips. That eventually led to a deep kiss.

All of a sudden, the brown-skinned girl hopped down from the bed and padded across the room. "I got something even better," she said, digging inside her purse, which was sitting on the floor. She pulled out a small vial filled with coke.

"Yes!" Lolli exclaimed, watching as the girl came back over to pour it on the nightstand.

As the other girl cut the white powder into straight parallel lines, Lolli pulled my boxers down to my thighs. Just having her that close to my crotch made my dick instantly swell. She wasted no time licking the tip before putting me fully inside her mouth. My abs tightened from the immediate sense of pleasure, and my head to fell back against the headboard.

"Shit, gul," I hissed, hearing the sounds of ole girl snorting beside me, as I closed my eyes.

"You want some?" I heard her suddenly ask.

Without delay, Lolli's head lifted up from my lap, and she reached to take the small straw from ole girl's hand. Reaching over me, she hastily leaned her face down toward the nightstand and snorted one line, then two. As she rubbed and tweaked her nose, sniffing back the remains of the residue, she handed me the small straw. I hesitated, then shook my head.

"Nah, shawty. I'm good."

Ole girl was still standing beside the bed, but now she slowly peeled her bra straps down her shoulders. "You sure? It'll make tonight a lot of fun," she said. After exposing her full, perky breasts all at once, she let her bra drop sexily to the floor.

After thinking about it for only a split second, I reached to take the straw from Lolli's hand. While she went to put her face back down in my lap, I leaned over and snorted my very first line of cocaine *ever*. The initial burn up my nose seemed to dissipate quickly, as a euphoric feeling began to settle in. The brown-skinned girl then got on the bed and straddled my other leg, joining Lolli.

Somehow the sensation on my dick became magnified as the two of them alternately sucked and licked my length. But my mind, however, was a different story. It went completely numb. No longer was I thinking about my money problems or that deadbeat nigga Jerome. I was purely anesthetized . . . *straight gone.*

Chapter 16

Nika

"Push, Nika! Push!" the midwife coached as she leaned down between my trembling thighs.

Holding my breath, I bore down so hard, it felt like I was ripping in two. "Ugh!" I groaned.

For the past seven hours I'd been at UM Prince George's Hospital, in full-blown labor. It was the first week of March, and as planned, Grandma was right there by my side. She kept telling me that everything would be all right as she rubbed a cool cloth across my forehead. I was scared and in extreme pain, but Grandma was my rock. She kept reminding me of the sweet little boy that I'd soon be holding in my arms.

When another contraction hit, I knew it was time for me to push again.

"Push down, Nika. Hard!" the midwife urged.

Squeezing Grandma's hand, I pressed my chin down against my chest and pushed with all my might. "Ugh! Fuck!" I cried out. I started breathing heavily, and tears ran from the corners of my eyes.

"That's it. Just one more like that," the midwife said.

Looking over at Grandma with a weary expression on my face, I noticed tears on the rims of her eyes. "He's almost here, baby. Just one more," she told me, smoothing back my hair with her hand.

Too exhausted even to speak, I simply nodded my head. I was beyond tired, and my arms and legs were completely weak. I didn't even think I had enough strength in me to push one more time, but not wanting to waste any more energy, I declined to say it out loud. After a few short moments of reprieve, I felt the onset of another hard-hitting contraction.

Gritting my teeth from the pain, I pushed one final time. I gave it everything I had inside me, all in hopes of finally hearing the my son's first cry.

"That's it, Nika! Push! He's coming," the midwife said excitedly.

"Argh!"

"Push, baby, push!" Grandma cheered, looking down between my legs. "Oh my God," she gasped a moment later.

That was when I heard his little squeal. It was loud enough for me to know that his lungs were strong, but you could also tell that the sound was coming from something very small. I looked up just in time to see his tiny, blood-covered body being lifted in the air. The umbilical cord was still attached, but to me, he was the picture of perfection.

After Grandma cut his cord, the nurses took him away to get him cleaned up. "You did great, baby," Grandma said, and then she gave me a closed-lip smile.

When the nurse brought my son back over to me, he was bundled in a powder-blue blanket. As she placed him in my arms, I looked down to get a good glimpse of his face. It didn't even surprise me when I saw the spitting image of Jorell peering back at me. His dark eyes were already open wide, as if he'd been here many moons before. I was, however, caught completely off guard by his lack of hair. With as much hair as both Jorell and I had, I was shocked to see that my baby was damn near bald. He had only a few fine hairs slicked down on the crown of his head. Nevertheless, he was absolutely beautiful.

"My Lord," my grandmother uttered breathlessly. "He's so perfect, Nika. What are we gonna call him?"

Kissing the top of his soft little head, I closed my eyes. "Nicholas. His name is Nicholas Turner."

It had only been six weeks since I'd given birth to baby Nicholas when I found myself on an airplane headed to Alabama. With each day that had passed, pangs of guilt had worn steadily at my conscience. I couldn't believe that I had kept such a huge part of my life from Perri. She was such a good friend, and honestly, she didn't deserve the way I'd been shutting her out of my life. Her wedding was next week, and I planned on telling her everything then. It would be a clean start before I started my new job the following week as a radiology tech.

Then there was Ms. Annette, whom I was currently preparing to face. I didn't know what I was going to say or even what her response would be, but I knew I had to tell her about her grandson. I was already expecting her to be mad at me, because that much I deserved. The only thing I could hope for was that she didn't deny my child.

Baby Nicholas was curled up against my chest, and I looked down and kissed his sleeping face. *There is no way she can refuse this precious angel here*, I thought.

After almost a four-hour flight, our plane landed, and I was off to the baggage claim, with my baby strapped across my breasts. Once I had grabbed my luggage and his car seat from the carousel, we caught a cab straight to Ms. Annette's. With every passing mile on the ride over, my nerves grew more and more intense. Silently, I kept cursing myself out for not taking Grandma up on her offer. She had wanted to come along on this trip and give me support, but I had told her that I needed to handle this all on my own.

When we finally pulled up in front of Ms. Annette's, I let out a sigh of relief upon seeing her car parked in the driveway. Thankfully, she was home, because it wasn't like I'd told her I was coming. Inhaling a huge breath of air, I shook off those last-minute jitters. I unlatched Nicholas from the car seat, then made my way up to her front door. Luckily, the cabdriver was nice enough to carry my luggage up the driveway for me.

I knocked twice before the front door opened. Instead of Ms. Annette, I was greeted by Jornelle. "What are you doing opening up the door?" I asked with a smile.

"Ms. Nika!" she said excitedly, opening the door all the way.

As I walked in, struggling to get all my things inside, Jornelle took off in the direction of the kitchen.

"Grandma, Grandma! Ms. Nika's here," I could hear her say.

Wiping her hands with a kitchen towel, Ms. Annette walked toward me, a surprised expression on her face. "What are you doing all the way down here?" she asked, looking at the suitcase down by my side. "And who's this little fella you brought here to see me?" She cooed at baby Nicholas, a smile on her face, as she bent down to touch him in his carrier.

"Ms. Annette." I swallowed hard, letting my eyelids flutter shut. "This is your grandson, Nicholas," I said all in one breath.

"Say what now?" she said as she stood up straight. Cocking an eyebrow from surprise, she threw the kitchen towel over her shoulder.

I couldn't even look the woman in the eye. Instead, I hung my head real low and shifted my eyes down to the floor. "Baby Nicholas . . . is your grandson," I confessed just above a whisper.

"My grandson? But you said . . ." Her voice trailed off as the realization sank in that I'd told the biggest lie ever. "Does Jorell know? About the baby?" she asked lowly.

With just the mere mention of his name, I immediately burst into tears. "No," I cried. Covering my face with my hands, I shook my head.

She reached down and lifted Nicholas's carrier from the floor. "Come on in here, chile," she told me, then turned and started walking back toward the kitchen. "Witcho' lying ass," she mumbled under her breath.

Wiping my face, I followed behind her and allowed Jornelle to take me by the hand. She was being sweet and was trying to soothe me. When I walked into the kitchen, Ms. Annette already had Nicholas out of his carrier. She was cradling him in her arms and rocking him softly from side to side. Sniffing back my emotions, I took a seat at the kitchen table across from them.

"Yep, this is definitely Jorell's son. Got those same little Chinky eyes. And that nose," she said, peering down at his face.

Hearing her claim my child gave me some small dose of comfort and brought a little smile to my face.

"So when are you going to tell him?" she asked, still looking down at the baby.

"I'm going to LA next week for Perri and Plus's wedding. I promise I'll talk to him then."

"Uh-huh. So why did you lie?"

Shamefaced, I shifted in my seat. "Jorell's not ready for another baby, Ms. Annette." I cut my eyes over at Jornelle, who was standing beside me, playing with my hair. "You know it, just like I do," I said.

"That doesn't give you the right to hide something like *this* from him. This is his child, Nika. He's missed your entire pregnancy and the birth of his firstborn son. Precious weeks of his life," she said, shaking her head. "Does this have anything at all to do with you and him?"

"No, well . . . yes, but . . ." Feeling frustrated, I placed my hand on my forehead. "I tried to tell him, Ms. Annette. I really did. But he slept with me and just cut me off. Wouldn't even pick up the damn phone for me." I sighed.

"Well, then, why didn't you come to me, baby?" she asked, softening her tone. A motherly look of pity suddenly appeared in her eyes.

Overcome by it all, I shrugged my shoulders. "By then I just said to hell with him. But then after I came down here and saw you and Jornelle, I started feeling guilty all over again. I wanted her to know her brother," I explained.

"Brother?" Jornelle asked unexpectedly.

Not realizing that Jornelle had even been paying us any mind, I shifted my gaze to her. "Yes. Baby Nicholas," I said, pointing over at my son. "That's your brother."

Confused, Jornelle wrinkled her eyebrows as she scrunched up her little nose. "I have a baby brother?" she asked.

Feeling a closed-lip smile suddenly creep across my face, I nodded. "Yep, you have a little baby brother."

"Well, you know she's gonna tell Jorell, right? If not him, her mother," Ms. Annette interjected.

I lifted my shoulder. "It's fine. I'll just have to deal with it."

As the day went on, our emotions seemed to finally settle down. Jornelle kept asking me to do things with her, such as taking her to go get some ice cream. When I explained that I didn't have a car, Ms. Annette gladly volunteered hers. For some odd reason, I thought she wanted me to get out of the house so that she could bond with her grandson all alone.

The last time I'd been in Alabama, I'd promised Jornelle that I would get her a mani-pedi, so before we went to get ice cream, I pulled into the nail shop around the corner. It was hood as hell, located in a shoddy strip mall, but those were usually the best ones. As soon as we got out of the car and walked in, they put us in spa chairs. While our feet were soaking, Jornelle was talking my ear off.

"When I go back to school, I'm gonna tell everybody that I have a baby brother." Jornelle looked at me, then placed her finger on her chin. "Can I call him Nicky?"

"Well . . ." I said, dragging out the word.

"Yes, that's what I'll call him. Baby Nicky. Are you gonna teach me how to change his stinky diapers?"

I released a light snort of laughter and nodded my head. "Sure. As soon as we get back to the house, I'll show you."

"Thanks, Ms. Nika. You're the best." When she looked up at me with those same dark eyes as my baby's, I couldn't help but smile. At five years old, Jornelle was adorable, and her sweet personality was infectious.

"You're gonna be a wonderful big sister, you know that?"

Instead of answering the question, Jornelle tilted her head curiously to the side. "Are you my daddy's girlfriend?"

My eyes instantly bugged out from my being caught off guard. Drawing in a sharp breath, I softly shook my head. "No. I'm just your brother's mom," I told her honestly.

"Okay. Well, I still love you," she said, turning back to kick her feet up in the water.

I had thought that seeing Ms. Annette hold my baby for the first time made this trip worth the while, but this moment here with Jornelle had truly topped all others.

"I love you too," I told her.

Then suddenly, out of nowhere, I heard someone yell, "Jornelle! No, fuck that! Jornelle!"

Hearing all the commotion, I looked toward the front of the shop and saw Meechie rushing in, with another girl behind her. A scowl graced her pretty, fair-skinned face, and her big lips were twisted up in a frown. When she got to where Jornelle and I were sitting in the back, she shot me a venomous glare. A quiet groan came from the back of my throat as I rolled my eyes.

"Jornelle, what are you doing here?" she asked, looking directly at me.

"Me and Ms. Nika came to get pedicures. Right, Ms. Nika?" Jornelle said innocently, glancing at me for reassurance.

My chest rose as I took in a deep breath. Trying to calm myself so that I could speak calmly to Jornelle's mother, I tucked my hair behind my ears. "Yes, Ms. Annette allowed her to come with me. We just stepped out to get our nails done before heading over to get some ice cream," I explained.

"So she just lets any and everybody take my baby." Meechie rolled her eyes and pulled out her cell phone.

"Let's just go," said the girl who had come in with Meechie. Then she gently grabbed Meechie by the arm.

"Nah, fuck that! Ms. Annette thinking I'm playing with her ass." After dialing a number, Meechie placed the phone up to her ear. "And get your behind over here, Jornelle!" she snapped.

Poor Jornelle hopped up from her seat and trekked over to her mother with bare, wet feet and all. Judging by the scared look on her face, she didn't even know what was going on as she stood by her mother's side.

"Oh, so now this heffa don't want to pick up the gah-damn phone," Meechie huffed, then ended the call. Then she looked down at Jornelle. "Go get your shoes, little girl. We leaving," she fussed.

As soon as I heard that, I dialed Ms. Annette's number on my phone, but just like Meechie's, my call went un-answered. When Jornelle came up beside me to get her shoes, she placed her little hand delicately on my arm. "Give my brother a kiss for me," she said softly. Her voice was so low, as if she knew her brother was being kept a secret. After nodding my head, I gave her a discreet little wink.

"Let's go, Jornelle! Now!" Meechie shouted, with a snap of her fingers, before heading back up front. At this point, she was putting on a good show, and everyone in the nail shop was looking at her as if she'd completely lost her mind.

It literally broke my heart to see Jornelle amble slowly behind her, looking so sad, but there was nothing I could do. Meechie was her mother, and it was clear that she absolutely hated me.

Chapter 17

Jorell

"How the fuck you gon' have that bitch around my child, Jorell!" Meechie shouted in my ear.

Dramatically pulling the phone back from my ear, I wondered who the fuck she thought she was talking to. "Fuck is you talkin' 'bout, shawty?" I asked.

"Oh, you know what the fuck I'm talking about! I'm talking about ole girl, who you *claim* you don't have no dealings with no more. She's been toting around my gahdamn child like she's hers!"

"Ole girl?" I was completely confused.

As Meechie sucked her teeth, I could only imagine her rolling her eyes. "Yeah, that fake Curly Sue wannabe bitch!" she spat.

Right then I knew that she was talking about Nika, because she was the only chick I'd ever messed with that had naturally curly hair. What I didn't know was why Nika would be around Jornelle. "Aye, let me call you back," I told her, then abruptly hung up the phone.

I immediately dialed my mama's number since she was the one keeping Jornelle more days than not. I also knew that she still kept in contact with Nika, so I figured she would help me get to the bottom of this shit. As I sat at my kitchen table, listening to the phone ring, I cut the lines of coke down in front of me. What started out as something minor and fun I did with Lolli from time to time had ended up being a daily habit of mine.

"Ma," I said when my mother picked up.

"Jorell?"

"Hey, what's all this craziness Meechie talking 'bout with Nika and Jornelle?" I asked.

"Well, you know how crazy your baby's mama is. I let Jornelle go with Nika to get her nails done and for ice cream earlier, and, well, Meechie saw them out together and had a damn hissy fit. Child even had the nerve to come back here to the house and tell me that I can't see my own granddaughter no more, since I wanna let her go off with strangers."

"So wait," I said, my mind racing with multiple thoughts. "Nika's down there?"

"Yeah, she's here."

My eyes narrowed into slits. I didn't have a clue as to why Nika would be in Prichard. "For what?"

"She came here to see me and Jornelle. Came a couple of months ago too."

Damn. I missed the fuck out of shawty.

Smoothing down the corners of my lips with my fingers, I sat there, deep in thought. "Oh, fa real? Shawty ask about me?" I finally said. Just the thought of Nika's little sexy ass had my dick twitching in my pants.

"Uh, not exactly," my mother muttered with an attitude. "But you definitely need to call her. Has she tried reaching out to you?"

"Not in a good li'l minute. I hit her up a few months back, but I think she blocked my number," I said, with a scratch behind my ear.

"And why would she do that, Jorell?" my mother asked, like she just knew there was more to the story. And truth be told, there was. I did my la' baby all wrong last year by giving her a false sense of hope for us. I fucked her, then told her I loved her, which was all true. But then I made a promise I knew damn well I couldn't keep. I promised to be there for her, when I could barely be there for my damn self. Hell, other than sending a monthly check, I wasn't even there for my own daughter. I was finally in the NBA, supposedly living out my dreams, but my life was a fucking disaster.

"I 'on' know, Ma," I lied. Pinching the tip of my nose and sniffing, I looked down at the rolled-up dollar bill and the white powdery substance before me. This habit of mine was getting out of control, but I swear, it was the only thing getting me through these days. "Let me call you back."

"Fuck!" I spat, hitting the steering wheel out of frustration, as I sat at a red light.

Three days had passed since Meechie called me about Nika, and today I was running late for practice. After a long night of partying with Lolli and two other strippers from the club, a nigga was hungover to the max. I was supposed to be at practice by ten, but since I'd woken up late, it was now going on eleven. Coach was gonna have my ass.

By the time I finally made it through the thick LA traffic and into the parking lot of the UCLA Health Training Center, it was almost noon. Before I got out of the car, I took one last sip of my detox cleanser and sat it back in the cupholder. The chances of a random piss test were slim, but anytime I showed up for practice these days, I drank a detox cleanser that would make my urine clean. It was some high-priced off-the-market shit that a teammate of mine had suggested. He was a cokehead who stayed in the clubs.

I climbed out of the car and immediately felt that California sun beating down on me. After pulling my Nike duffel bag over my shoulder, I slammed the car door shut and headed inside. As I passed by Plus's brand-new Benz, I frowned. Seeing it parked right up front somehow caused a surge of jealousy to wash over me. Not because he had a new Benz, because, shit, I had a Lamborghini. It was just that night after night, Plus was doing his thing on the court, and as a result, he now had more paper than he could count. At one point in time, I had felt like he and I were on the same level. Two "ain't shit" niggas from the hood who could ball like no one else. But over the past few months, something had drastically changed. Plus had been getting his shit together on and off the court, while I seemingly had been failing miserably at life.

After entering the building, I peeked my head inside the gym first just to make sure practice was still going on. Since everyone was still on the court, I dropped my things off in the locker room and headed right to the gym. Suddenly I could hear the sound of several rubber soles screeching to a halt. I didn't know if was that white girl that had a nigga so paranoid or what, but it felt like I had a million eyes on me as I walked to the center of the court.

"Jorell, what the fuck, man!" Coach Jackson snapped. Flailing his arms in the air, he shot me a venomous look.

I gripped the back of my neck and let out a deep sigh. "I know, Coach. I know. A nigga got stuck in traffic," I tried to explain.

"Traffic, my ass! Just for being late, you owe me a hundred suicides, and I'm fining your ass twenty thousand."

My eyes damn near popped out of my head. "Twenty thousand!" I was floored. Did this nigga forget how much I was making? "Coach . . . breh, come on," I damn near begged through a sigh.

When Coach ignored me, turned back around, and blew his whistle, I knew there was no changing his mind. Mumbling a slew of obscenities beneath my breath, I jogged toward the back wall. While everyone continued to play a scrimmage game on the court, I started my suicide drills off to the side. A nigga felt like he was still in high school, being reprimanded in front of other niggas on my team.

After a whole hour had passed, I was still only a fifth of the way through the drills. Once Coach blew his whistle, I bent over to catch my breath. In my peripheral, I could see Plus trotting over in my direction, with a water bottle in his hand. Still breathing heavily, with sweat pouring from my face, I stood up and placed my hands on my waist.

"Damn, yo," Plus said, tossing the bottle at me.

I caught it just in time and squirted a stream of water in my mouth. "Thanks, mane."

After chucking up his chin, his mouth partially open, he glided his tongue to the back of his molars. "So . . . since when do you show up late for practice?" he asked.

Plus was my boy through and through, but hearing that nigga talk to me like I was one of his kids instantly had me heated inside. Coolly, I took another shot of water before looking Plus right in the eyes. "I said I was stuck in traffic," I told him evenly.

"Yeah, but you been fucking up a lot lately. What's up wit' you?"

Shocked by his stern voice and blunt choice of words, I threw my head back. "*Fucking up*? Nigga, just 'cause I ain't getting as much play time as you or getting the endorsement deals don't mean I'm fucking up!"

Immediately sensing that I was angry, Plus tried to place his hand on my shoulder. "Hey, man, I ain't trying to come at you on no disrespectful-type shit—"

"Shit! I can't tell," I barked, cutting him off, and gave a hard shrug of my shoulder.

Pinching the bridge of his nose, Plus let out a small sniff of frustration. "Look, yo," he sighed. "All I'm saying is that you've been moving mad different lately." He put both of his hands up and took a small step back. "I don't know what's going on with you, but if there's anything I can do to help, or if you just need somebody to talk to, I'm here."

After taking in everything that he said, I nodded my head. Part of me felt like I could really use a friend, but the other part of me had too much damn pride. I knew that if I told Plus about my money problems, he would offer to help me out financially, and as a man, I just couldn't have that. When Plus walked up and held his hand out to me, I hesitated at first. I was still mad, but just not at him; I was mad at myself. After dapping him up, I pulled him in for a brotherly hug.

"You're still coming to the final fitting tomorrow night, right?" he asked, lifting his brow. Given that his wedding was only a few days away, he planned to meet with all his groomsmen tomorrow for the final tux fitting and then go out for a few drinks with them.

"Yeah, I'll be there."

Doing a slow backward jog, Plus chucked up his chin. Then he turned around and headed for the locker room. After tying my dreads up in a tight knot behind my head, I took a deep breath and went back to running my suicides. It took me almost another three hours just to complete them all. My body was so sore and weak afterward that I could barely walk straight when I left the gym. By the time I hit the shower and exited the building, the sun was already setting in the sky.

I quickly called Nika, but she didn't pick up, and I left no message. I was just lifting my eyes from my cell phone when I spotted that Jerome nigga standing next to my car.

"Shit," I muttered. Chest was burning with anger as I quickened my pace. "Breh, what the fuck? You stalking me now?" I snapped.

He smiled. "No, son—"

Son? This nigga had totally lost his fucking mind. My eyes then shifted to his right hand, which was planted on the rooftop of my car. "Mane, if you don't get yo' greasy-ass hands off my muhfucking car!" I barked, feeling my nostrils flare.

His hands instantly shot straight up in the air, as if he thought I was the police. "Oh, my bad. My bad."

Feeling myself about to spin out of control, I inhaled a huge breath of air. "Look, what is it that you need, mane?" I asked, trying to keep calm.

"Did you talk to your mama yet? Did she tell you who I am?"

A quiet, sarcastic snort escaped me. "Yeah, she told me that you're my sperm donor. So what that mean? The fuck you keep coming around fa?"

Slipping his hands into the pockets of his pants, he cleared his throat and squared his chest. "I—I know I don't have a right to ask anything of you, but . . ."

"Then don't," I said dryly.

Slowly, he shook his head. "I'm desperate," he confessed. "I lost my job last year, and I'm all the way out here on my last dime. My car has already been repossessed, and now they're getting ready to take my home. I'm asking . . . No! I'm begging you for help, son."

This nigga here . . .

Completely unmoved by this man's story, I casually reached for the car door handle. "Sounds like a personal problem to me, breh." I yawned. "Good luck, though."

Just as I opened the door, I felt his hand grip the back of my arm. I instantly reacted.

"Nigga, if you don't get yo—"

"Wait, man. Just wait!" he yelled. I turned back to see a man in utter despair. Tears had already begun to form in his eyes, and his lips were quivering slightly.

Feeling a shred of compassion, I pushed out a breath of air. "Aye, look. I'm sorry for ever'thang you going through," I told him, looking down into his eyes. "I really am, but it's not my problem, mane. In all my twenty-three years of living, I ain't never even laid eyes on you. Then you wait until a nigga finally get into the NBA and get some bread in his pockets to come see about me? Nah." I shook my head. "Fuck that! I haven't needed no Daddy this long, and I damn sure don't need one now. Whatever you gotta do to work that shit out . . ." I dismissively waved my hand in the air. "Go do it. But you gon' stop coming around, before I get an order put on yo' ass."

"What about your brother and sister?" he asked, making one last hopeful attempt. "They'll be homeless too."

I knew he was trying to pull a nigga's heartstrings and all, but hearing that shit only made me hate his ass more. "Brother and sister?" I quipped, arching my eyebrow in his direction.

He nodded his head and took a deep swallow. "Yeah. Jermaine and Jessi," he said with a wide-eyed expression.

All of a sudden, I could feel my eyes squeeze into tapered slits, and my jaw clenched so tight that it literally hurt. "So you mean to tell me that you out here trying to get money from me to help save Jermaine and Jessi's ass, huh?" I said through gritted teeth, pointing to my chest. "To make sure them niggas can eat?" I cocked my head to the side, waiting for a response.

Fully aware of his actions, he suddenly dropped his shoulders in defeat. "Well—" he started to say.

I didn't even let the remaining words fall from his lips before I caught him completely off guard with a stiff punch to his face. After seeing Jerome's body fly back to the ground, I opened my car door and hopped inside. I slammed the car door shut so hard, I thought my window would shatter.

After rolling the window down, I sent a shot of spit in his direction. "Don't bring yo' ass back around me, muthafucka, or I'ma put a hot one in yo' ass!" I spat.

He didn't even respond, just continued to lie sprawled out on the pavement, holding on to his jaw.

Once I put the car in reverse and backed out of the parking space, I sped off so fast that my tires screeched and created a gray cloud of smoke. My heart was pounding overtime in my chest, and my hands were trembling so bad, I could barely control the steering wheel. At the first red light I hit, I quickly dialed Nika's number. I needed *her*—anything to help calm me down. But, of course, she didn't answer. Ever since my mother had told me that Nika came to visit, I'd been trying to reach out to her nonstop, but she hadn't ever picked up the phone. Once I saw the light flash green and heard the customary fourth ring, I hung up and removed my foot from the brake to continue my drive back home.

Chapter 18

Perri

In just two more days I would officially be Mrs. Ahmad Taylor. I couldn't even have conceived of this way back when we'd been just two raggedy kids from Millwood, but over the years I'd come to realize that Plus and I were destined to be together. He was as natural to me as breathing. He and I were like green on a blade of grass or a family of birds living in a tree. No matter how many storms seemed to pass, the love Plus and I shared always persevered. Unbeknownst to us, I was his and he was mine from the very beginning of time.

Since our home was so small, Plus had rented out an entire estate in Holmby Hills, an affluent neighborhood in LA. Everyone, including us, was staying there for the wedding. Plus and I had already arrived and got settled in. The massive mansion had panoramic views of all that Southern California had to offer. From the east wing of the house, you could see the skyscrapers of the city, and from the north side, there was a view of the hills. And from the master-bedroom window, there was nothing but a breathtaking view of the beautiful blue ocean.

A whopping fifteen grand a night, the estate boasted thirty-two thousand square feet, seventeen bedrooms, and twenty-two baths. Not only were we staying for the next few days, but we were also going to be married right out there in the courtyard—surrounded by lush palm trees and one hundred guests, and not too far from the pool. Everything was going to be perfect. And the very day after our wedding, Plus and the Lakers would take on the Miami Heat in the final game of the season. Plus and I would then take a short trip to Saint-Tropez for our honeymoon and would return in time for the playoffs. It had all been planned out.

"Bae, what you in here doing? You know everyone will be here within the next hour," Plus said after walking into the master bedroom.

I was sitting down on the floor in front of the TV, playing a game of *NBA 2K11*. Call me crazy, but I had packed up my PlayStation and had brought it with me. "I'll cut the game off when everyone gets here," I told him, eyes glued to the screen as my fingers tapped swiftly across the controller.

Plus sat down next to me on the floor and nudged me over slightly. "Restart it and reset it for two players," he said.

"Nah, I'm about to whup the Hornets' ass, yo," I told him, hitting the keys twice on the controller. "Booyah! That's what I'm talking 'bout!"

"Shorty, put that game away. Everybody's on their way," Plus all but whined.

I cut my eyes over at him, with a smirk. "You just told me you wanted in. Now I gotta put the game away 'cause everyone's coming over?"

He licked his full brown lips. "I just—"

"Want some damn attention," I said, cutting him off.

He let out a light chuckle. "You damn right." Plus leaned over and began softly kissing me on the neck.

I was still trying to finish out the game, but having his wet mouth connect with my flesh was making me horny. Slowly, Plus reached over and pinched my nipple through the sports bra I was wearing.

"Mmm, stop," I moaned, suddenly feeling hot and flushed all over.

"Nah, I ain't stopping shit till you put this game down." He snatched the controller from my hands and thoughtlessly tossed it to the side. After leaning in to kiss my lips, he began easing his fingers beneath the waistband of my basketball shorts.

As much as I wanted to finish that damn game, I wanted Plus's body more. That all too familiar aching started to flare up between my thighs, and my heart rate began to pick up speed. When Plus rose to his knees, with his lips still attached to mine, I began yanking up his shirt. Feeling the hard lumps of his abs beneath my palms, I couldn't help but moan with urgency.

Once he pulled the shirt all the way over his head, exposing that simple gold chain around his neck, he flung it carelessly across the room. Plus's smooth chocolate body was cut to perfection. Wide pecs and arms carved like a God's. Slowly, I trailed the tip of my tongue down the length of his neck, then onto his sculpted chest. I kissed and teased his skin, feeling his big, strong hands gently squeeze my ass.

"Mmm," he groaned. "Take that shit off, P."

Just as I straightened up to remove my sports bra, the house speakers chimed. "Mr. Taylor, one of your guests has arrived," Roy, the butler, announced. The house was so massive that you had to communicate through an intercom system.

"Fuck!" Plus groaned. He quickly pecked me on the lips, then stood and went over to grab his shirt off the floor. As he walked across the room, my eyes followed the large bulge in his pants.

"Stop looking at my dick, yo," he said, slipping his shirt back on. "Let's go."

We traveled down the long hall for what seemed like minutes just to get to the staircase. Halfway down the steps, I saw Nika standing in the foyer, with her suitcase by her side. She looked to have gained a little weight, but she was still beautiful. Her curly hair framed her pretty face like a lion's mane. An involuntary smile spread across my face. I hadn't seen my girl since the end of last summer, and I missed her like crazy. Although I had sworn it wouldn't, distance had put a strain on our friendship. We were in two different time zones and barely even talked or texted on the phone these days. And the times we did, it seemed like there was always something pulling her away.

"Nika!" I squealed, greeting her like a *girly* girl would do. Arms open wide, I ran over to give her a big hug. "I feel like I haven't seen you in forever."

She squeezed me back so tight, you would have thought we were long-lost sisters or some shit. Then she touched the big fluff ball on the top of my head. "Girl, what have you been out here doing with your hair?" she asked, with her nose turned up.

I shrugged. "Nothing."

"And that's exactly what it looks like too," she muttered.

I quickly socked her on the arm.

"Ow." She laughed, grabbing her arm.

"What up, Nika?" Plus chimed in and gave her a hug.

"You ready for the big day?" she asked him.

"You know me. I stay ready." He looked over at me, then winked.

"Well, you definitely outdid yourself with the house. It's beautiful," she said as she looked around.

When Plus reached down to grab her suitcase, I placed my hand on his shoulder. "No, *honey*. I got it. I'm gonna show her up to her room. You just wait out here, in case anyone else shows up," I told him sweetly.

He dropped her luggage to the floor and pecked me on the lips. "A'ight, bae."

Nika's head whipped back and forth from me to Plus. "Honey? Bae? Y'all, please don't tell me y'all doing this cheesy-couple shit now."

"Nika, shut the fuck up and come on." I picked up her suitcase and started for the stairs. "Matter of fact, here." I turned around and shoved the bag in her hand. "Take your own shit," I told her.

"Shoo!" She wiped her forehead dramatically. "For a second there, I thought you came all the way to Cali and changed up on me, girl."

I pursed my lips to the side before letting out a chuckle. Nika always did know how to make me laugh.

As she followed me up to her room, I looked back at her over my shoulder and saw the pretty teal sundress she wore, with gold sandals and earrings to match. It was a stark contrast to the black sports bra, basketball shorts, and Nike slides that I was wearing, but Nika knew me. She had accepted me from day one, and I loved her for that.

When we got to her room, I could immediately tell that she was impressed. Her eyes lit up as she looked everything over from left to right. The entire room was decorated in a pale shade of blue, including the comforter on the king-size bed. We had chosen to put her in the rear of the house, in a room with a balcony that overlooked the pool.

"So where's my Camille at?" she asked, dropping her bag onto the tiled floor.

"Taking a much-needed nap. MJ's gonna be here soon, and I already know that together, they can be a handful."

With a reluctant expression on her face, Nika tucked a wispy piece of hair behind her ear and took a seat on the edge of the bed. "Perri, I need to tell you something," she said softly.

Her mood had suddenly shifted, and I wasn't quite sure why. "Okay?"

She released a sharp breath from her lungs before placing her hands nervously on her knees. "But first, I need to know that you won't be mad at me."

"Why you acting like we twelve years old, yo? Just spit that shit out. I can take it. What? You don't wanna be in the wedding?"

"Oh, no! I feel honored that you asked me to be in your wedding."

"Oh, good, 'cause I thought that since you gained a little weight—"

"Perri!" she shrieked. "I'm going to be in the wedding. And, for your information, I gained only ten pounds."

"Whatever, yo." I shrugged. "So what is it that you need to talk to me about?"

Nika a took a hard swallow, then dropped her head down into the palms of her hands. "I had a baby," she mumbled.

My head dipped forward, in her direction. "Say what now?"

Peering up at me with regretful eyes, Nika blew out a big breath. "I had a baby, Perri," she confessed.

My eyes ballooned, and my jaw instantly dropped. "Get the fuck outta here!"

She nodded her head. "You heard me right. I had a baby."

"When? By who? Why didn't you tell me?" I had so many questions that I was hitting her with them all at once.

"You remember the night of the NBA draft?"

"Yeah," I said.

"And the rooftop party?" She continued when I nodded. "Well, while you were in the bathroom, arguing with Mia, I was in one of the stalls . . ."

My mouth fell open again, and I covered it up with a slap of my hand. "I knew it!" I yelled loudly. "You fucked Jorell in the bathroom, didn't you?"

Shamefully, Nika nodded her head before shielding her face with both of her hands.

"But wait, I don't get it. Why didn't you tell me? Or why didn't Jorell tell us? I see him all the time." I was totally perplexed.

When Nika finally uncovered her face, I could see that she was emotionally overwhelmed. She even had tears in her eyes. "Jorell doesn't know, Perri. I didn't want you or Plus to end up telling him about the baby, so that's why I kept it a secret from you guys too," she admitted with a shrug. "I mean, at first, my plan was to just go ahead and tell him. All last summer long I tried, but he kept dodging me. You know how Jorell does."

I nodded, knowing exactly what she was talking about. As much as I loved Jorell's crazy ass, he was real wishy washy when it came to women and relationships. At one point, he and Nika would be all hot and heavy; then the next, he would turn cold and just straight ignore her. As of late, it wasn't nothing for me to see him with a different woman every time he came around. I just chalked it up to him being single and not ready to settle down, but the more I thought about it, the more I had to admit that he was a hard one to figure out.

"So is it a boy or a girl? Do you have pictures of my godbaby?"

As soon as I asked about her baby, a smile formed in her eyes and her disposition changed. She pulled out her cell phone and started scrolling though some pictures before handing it over to me. "His name is Nicholas," she said pridefully.

"Oh, Nika," I cooed, looking down at a picture of this little chocolate baby who looked so much like Jorell, it was ridiculous. "He's so precious."

"Thank you."

"So where is he?" He looked too young to be separated from his mother.

"Grandma's here with him at the hotel, and so is a friend of mine, Clarence."

"Clarence?" I made my eyebrows bounce up and down, just to be silly. "Is that your new boo thang?"

"Girl, please." She shook her head. "No, Clarence is just a friend. He's actually been there a lot for me over these past few months. He's been my rock," she said lowly.

Instantly, I felt bad because someone else had been there for her when I couldn't. "I'm sorry you had to go through your pregnancy alone."

She shrugged. "It's okay. I did it to myself. Besides, Grandma's been amazing. I think she loves that little boy more than she loves me," she told me, then gave a little pout.

"Yeah, that's how it goes. Daddy and Ms. Tonya love Camille more than they love us." I shrugged. Then suddenly a thought occurred to me. "So are you ever going to tell Jorell? You know he's in the wedding, right?"

"I know, and I planned to tell him after the wedding. I don't want to ruin y'all's special day with all my drama."

"Thanks for that, because I have a pretty good feeling he's not going to take that shit too well."

"Well, I tried to tell him. It's his own damn fault!"

I placed my hand on her shoulder to calm her down, but she shrugged me off.

"No, Perri, I'm serious! He's the one that fucked me and told me that he loved me. The nigga said that he would finally get his shit together, but no, what did he do? He . . ." She couldn't even get it all out before she broke down and cried.

"It's gonna be all right, Nika." I rubbed her on the back. "I promise."

Leaving Nika to unpack her things and get her feelings in order, I headed back downstairs. The whole family had arrived, even Aria. I was so happy to see her living life again. On the night of the fire, her whole world had flipped upside down, and she was trying to get things back on track. She had lost not only her father but also her childhood home and, temporarily, the ability to walk. Now she was back in school, finishing up her senior year of high school.

"There she is," my father said, holding his arms out for a hug.

I ran to him and hugged him tight. Then I placed my head on his chest and inhaled his scent, my eyes closed. I had never really considered myself a daddy's girl until I had to live away from him on the opposite side of the country. I had missed my father terribly.

"Ooh, chile, we gotta lot of work to do before this wedding," Ms. Tonya said, referring to my hair and bushy eyebrows. I'd definitely been slacking on the "beauty routines." I'd just been living the hippie life with Plus and Camille by the beach, trying to stay out of the limelight.

I went over to give Ms. Tonya a hug, then Myesha, who had MJ on her hip. "Yes, girl, we're about to give you a whole transformation," she said as I leaned in to give MJ a kiss on the cheek.

"Damn. Y'all act like I look bad."

"You look beautiful to me, baby," Plus interjected, slinking his arms around my waist.

"Aw, thank you, *honey*."

"The fuck?" Tez asked, with a befuddled look on his face. Then he pulled me away from Plus and put his hand up to my forehead. "Nigga, is you feeling a'ight?" he asked me, with his head cocked to the side.

I punched him in his chest, making him laugh. "Boy, shut up," I said.

Tez then pulled me in for a bear hug and kissed the top of my head. "Yo, I been missing the fuck outta y'all two knuckleheads." His eyes quickly scanned the room. "This shit is fly, yo. My nigga making that NBA bread. That's what's up."

"What about me, Uncle Tez?" I looked behind me to see Camille standing there, rubbing her eyes. She must had just woken up.

"I missed you more than all them other chumps, squirt," he told her, lifting her high up in the air.

"Uncle Tez," she giggled.

Once he set her back down on the floor, she and MJ took off for the next room, with my father and Ms. Tonya following behind them.

"But, yeah . . ." Tez's eyes roamed the room once more as he nodded his approval. "This shit here is real nice."

Plus was humble, so he didn't even respond. He just shook his head and fought against a smile.

Not even two seconds later, the doorbell suddenly chimed. All our eyes shifted toward the front door as the butler made his way over to open it. When the door opened, Jorell was standing there, with Jamal and Shivon behind him. Although I didn't care too much for Shivon, Jamal was like family, and she was his plus one. They'd been together forever, so it was expected that she would show.

"Whaddup, whaddup, whaddup!" Jorell swaggered into the room dramatically and immediately dapped up Plus, then Tez. He had his freshly twisted locks pulled back from his dark, chiseled face, and a Jesus piece swung from his neck. I had to admit that he looked good, even with that flash of gold in his mouth. I knew that if Nika was down here, she'd be swooning inside right about now.

When he went to hug me, my entire body seemed to tense up. It was a natural reaction from someone who was keeping a very important secret, one that directly affected him. I didn't want to be involved in their mess at all. I could only hope that when Nika finally told him the truth, he would take the news well and step up to the plate.

"H-hey, Jorell," I stammered, pulling back from his embrace.

"Shawty, you good?" he asked, narrowing his eyes, with a smirk on his face. "You ain't getting cold feet, are you?" He chuckled.

I sucked my teeth, then pursed my lips to the side. "Nigga, please."

He laughed again, then said, "My mama and Jornelle going to fly in on Saturday for the wedding."

"Okay. Cool."

He then turned to Plus, who was greeting Jamal and Shivon. "So what we getting into tonight, fam?" he asked.

"Just chilling by the pool, with food and drinks tonight, yo. All the girls going out, though," Plus answered.

Jorell glanced down at the flashy Cartier watch on Plus's wrist, then turned back to Myesha. "Well, y'all need to hurry up and start getting ready. It's gon' take all night just to get Perri's look together," he joked.

"Shut the fuck up. See? You starting already," I told him.

He held both of his hands up. "I'm just speaking facts, Baby Mama. Them eyebrows look like they 'bout to connect," he said, pointing to my face.

I rolled my eyes, then looked over at Myesha. "If Nika does my hair, you gonna do my eyebrows?"

"Yeah, I got you, girl," she said.

"Oh, so Nika's here?" Jorell asked, licking his lips.

"She's my maid of honor. Of course she's here. She's upstairs resting," I told him.

"Where my room at? Next to hers?" he asked, with hint of humor in his eyes.

I shook my head. "Not even close, yo. We put you in a whole 'nother wing."

Then my gaze shifted over to Shivon, who was standing sheepishly off to the side. She didn't have Tasha here to fuel her mean-girl spirit, so I hoped that her attitude would be a positive one this weekend. Or else we'd have major problems. "Shivon, you gonna roll with us tonight? It's gonna be like my unofficial bachelorette party," I said.

"Minus the strippers," Plus noted.

"Fuck, nah," Tez muttered, shaking his head.

"Sure, I'll go," Shivon said.

"All right. Come on, y'all. Let's go get ready," I urged.

Plus and I had been in California for almost nine months, and I still didn't have any friends here. Although some of the other basketball wives had tried to invite me out, I didn't really fit in with them, and I hated acting phony. So tonight, as we rolled out to the club in my brand-new Porsche Cayenne, it was just the four of us: Nika, Myesha, Shivon, and I.

After pulling up to Lure, I had the valet park my car, and then we all headed inside. I wore an all-white Herve Leger bandage dress, with silver heels and accessories. Nika had styled my hair in big, pretty curls and had pulled the top half back off my face. Myesha had waxed each of my bushy eyebrows into a perfect arch, and she had even done my makeup for tonight. I had on dark, smoky eye makeup and soft pink lipstick. They both did their thing.

Nika wore high-waisted black leather pants and a sheer white cropped blouse. Like mine, her makeup was flawless. She had dark eyes and red lips. Her curly brown mane was pulled up to the top of her head, with only a few soft tendrils hanging down on each side of her face. Myesha had gone for a more natural approach. She sported a strapless beige jumpsuit from Bebe, with Louboutins on her feet. Her curly black hair was styled in a semi-Afro that perfectly framed her pretty face. And then there was Shivon, who wore a red catsuit that was sheer at the top. Her makeup was similar to Myesha's: organic hues of brown, gold, and bronze.

The club was completely packed when we entered, and the music was thumping loud. Plus had made sure to reserve us a private section in the VIP for the night. After linking hands, we made our way through the thick crowd. Along the way, I looked out onto the dance floor and noticed a few players from the Miami Heat. It wasn't unusual, given the fact that they were playing against the Lakers this Sunday. That immediately made me think of Derrick. *Is he here tonight?*

"How you doing, beautiful?" some guy said, tugging on my arm. I pulled away and continued walking through the crowd, with the girls behind me.

"Damn. Look at her eyes, bro," another one said.

"All them bitches bad, homie."

I swear, niggas could be so disrespectful at times, but considering that we were in a dark nightclub full of young single people, I shouldn't have expected much more. Once we got into our section, I ordered two bottles of Ace, because the girls all wanted champagne. While we waited, dancing a bit in our seats, I looked out into the crowd.

"Oh, shit. This my song," Myesha said. She hopped up as "Dance (Ass)," by Big Sean, blared throughout the club.

While Shivon and I sat back, Myesha and Nika danced in front of us. They had the undivided attention of so many niggas as they dipped and rolled their bodies stripper-style.

"Come dance with me," Nika said, reaching for my hand.

I shook my head and crossed my legs.

"Still being shy, I see," I suddenly heard over the music.

I looked up and saw Derrick standing beside our section. When we made eye contact, he bit down on his bottom lip. I'm not even going to lie. The nigga was still sexy as ever to me. He was standing there with his hands tucked in the pockets of his pants and his shirt clinging to the muscles of his chest. He had his signature Yankees baseball cap on his head and sparkling diamonds in each of his ears.

"How you been doin', Ma?" he suddenly asked, then licked his full dark pink lips.

Nika, Myesha, and even Shivon cut their eyes over at me. I swallowed back my nerves and said, "Oh, hey."

The timing couldn't have been any better when the cocktail waitress strolled over with our champagne. I removed a single flute from the tray and downed the champagne all in one swallow. That was just how uneasy I now felt in Derrick's presence. This was the second time since our breakup that we'd actually seen each other, and neither Plus nor Mia was present this time around. I figured he would want to talk.

Derrick stepped in close enough for me to smell his Tom Ford cologne, then leaned down and whispered in my ear, "Can I talk to you for a minute?"

Fuck.

Everyone's eyes were still glued to me as they waited for my answer. "Sure," I said, nodding my head. "I'll be right back, y'all." I quickly reached for another glass of champagne and tossed the bubbly to the back of my throat.

A look of disappointment was etched across Myesha's face as I stood up from my seat. However, she had absolutely nothing to worry about. I loved Plus and would never disrespect him. As Derrick and I started to make our way through the crowd, I didn't know which was beating louder, the music or my heart. There were so many people in the club that Derrick and I got separated a bit. Suddenly he wiggled his fingers next to mine, inviting me to take his hand. Reluctantly, I took ahold of it and followed him into a private corner booth on the opposite side of VIP.

When we sat down, we took a silent moment to study each other faces.

"I swear, you're still the most beautiful girl I've ever seen, Ma," he said finally, his freckled face and piercing dark brown eyes staring back at me.

No longer could I look him in the eye; I had to turn away. "Thank you," I said, tucking a piece of hair behind my ear.

"So I hear you about to change your last name this weekend."

Unable to speak, as my mouth had suddenly gone dry, I nodded my head.

"Plus is a very lucky man," he commented. Although I wasn't looking directly at him, I could feel his eyes on me. "So tell me . . ." He paused, moving in closer so that I could hear him whisper. "Are you happy?"

That got my attention. My eyes slowly shifted toward him, and I could feel my left eye beginning to twitch. "Very," I said, cocking my head to the side.

He held both of his hands up in surrender. "My bad, Ma." He removed his hat from his head and ran his hand over his head. "I'm bugging. I wasn't trying to be disrespectful. I just needed to know."

I took a deep breath and turned to face him in my seat. "Look, I'm sorry for leading you on all that time," I said, cutting to the chase. "I've been in love with Plus practically my entire life, and when I thought he had rejected me, I forced myself to try to move on."

"I was the rebound guy. Got it!" he said, flexing his jaw.

"No," I replied, shaking my head. I reached over and gently touched his hand. "I loved you."

It was subtle, but his head jerked back when he heard that. "You loved me?"

"I did. Very much so."

"Just not as much as you love him?"

I let out a deep sigh. "I don't know how to explain it, yo. It's like no matter how much I loved you, no matter how much I forced myself to move on, I couldn't stop loving *him*. I tried. I really did. There were so many nights when I didn't want to love him, because it hurt so bad. I even prayed not to, but—"

"'Cause he's Camille's father? Your first," he mused, trying to rationalize my conduct.

I shook my head. "It's more than that. He's . . . the one." I gave his hand a gentle squeeze. "I know that's probably not what you wanted to hear."

He licked his lips and shook his head. "Nah, Ma, that's what I *needed* to hear. I needed closure . . . just me and you. No family, no boyfriends, no fighting, just me and you. You feel me?"

I nodded.

"And now that I know you happy with that nigga, maybe I can move the fuck on, too, and stop thinking about your pretty ass," he said before letting out a light chuckle.

"But I thought you were with Mia."

He shook his head, indicating that they weren't an official couple.

"But don't y'all have a baby?"

"Yeah." He flashed his dimply smile and pulled out his phone. He scrolled through the screen before passing the phone over to me. "That's DJ."

"Derrick, Jr." I said. "He's adorable," I added, looking at the cute little baby boy with deep dimples and curly jet-black hair. "How old is he now?"

"Nine months old."

Placing my finger on my chin, I tilted my head to the side. "Hmm, so I wonder when you got her pregnant?" I asked sarcastically.

With a guilty smirk, Derrick scratched behind his ear. "Yeah . . ." He sighed. "I fucked up."

I shrugged. "It's all good. You had history with her, just like I had history with Plus. We both cheated, and we both hurt each other." I placed my hand on his shoulder and looked him right in the eyes. "I'm so sorry for hurting you, Derrick. I truly am."

"Me too, Perri." When he leaned over and kissed my cheek, my eyes closed involuntarily, because I knew it would be my last time touching him like this.

He stood up and reached for my hand before helping me to my feet. Then he escorted me back over to the girls, who were all dancing, drinking, and seemingly having a good time. Even Shivon, who had a lit blunt in her hand.

"I'ma check you later, Ma," he said, with a single nod of his head. I gave him a little wave, then watched him saunter out of our section.

"Girl, so what the hell was that about?" Nika asked.

"Just closure. Something I think we both needed."

"Well, good, because I did not want to have to snitch on your ass when I got back home," Myesha said jokingly. "Come on. We ordered shots," she added, leaning down to pick up one of the small glasses sitting on the table.

I grabbed a single shot glass filled with clear liquor and raised it up high in the air. Shivon and Nika followed suit, both grabbing a glass and raising it up to mine.

"To my first and only true love, Ahmad Taylor," I said.

"To Ahmad Taylor," they all cheered in unison.

We tossed the shots back with ease and reached down for another one. I didn't know if it was my talk with Derrick, the shots, or the champagne, but I was starting to feel real good. I even started dancing . . . well, as best I could, at least. Tonight was going to be a great night, and the only thing I could think about was getting back home and fucking the shit out of my soon-to-be husband.

Chapter 19

Nika

Last night we had the best time at the Lure. We got drunk and danced until they shut down the place. The only problem was that someone had slashed all of Perri's tires. We had to call Plus and Tez to come and get us. Perri was so upset that she damn near cried. On the ride home, Plus explained that Perri had been receiving hate mail for quite some time. He said that he and Tez had been putting together a plan to get them both security full-time.

Now, today was the day before their actual wedding, and the plan was for everyone to hang out by the pool. While everyone was eating breakfast, I slipped out and drove over to the hotel that Grandma, Clarence, and baby Nicholas were staying at. When I entered Grandma's room, she was lying back on the bed, watching TV, with my baby sleeping peacefully next to her.

Smiling, I immediately went to go touch him. "Don't you wake that baby up, Nika," Grandma said, stopping me in my tracks.

Pouting, I sat gingerly on the edge of the bed. "But I haven't seen him since yesterday morning."

Grandma looked at me over the rims of her glasses. "He's fine. I know what I'm doing," she said curtly.

"I know you do, or else I wouldn't have left him with you." I rolled my eyes.

"Uh-huh," she muttered. "So what y'all got going on over there today?"

"They're doing a pool party or something. But I think I'm just gonna stay here and chill with Nicholas today."

"Chile, if you don't go on and have you a good time while you can . . . And take Clarence with you. He's been cooped up in here while you been out partying and having fun."

She was right. I had invited Clarence all this way just to be my plus one for the day of the wedding, and now he was stranded here at the hotel. Truth be told, I had invited him only in case Jorell showed up with Meechie or had another one of his bitches on his arm. I didn't want to feel like an outcast, the way I had been made to feel at Perri's graduation, so Clarence had agreed to come with me. Since I'd arrived, Jorell and I had crossed paths only once, and based on the fact that we had only said hey to one another in passing, I assumed both Ms. Annette and Jornelle had kept my secret. There was definitely tension between us, and the reality that I was keeping such a huge secret from him only made it that much harder for me to look him in the eye.

"Fine," I sighed. "Does he have enough milk and diapers?"

Grandma pursed her lips to the side. "Well, you the one that packed. So you tell me." She was being sarcastic, because I had packed enough diapers and formula to last a whole month.

I peered down at baby Nicholas and watched his chest rise and fall as I admired his sleeping face. Every day his features seemed stronger, and I had to admit that he looked more and more like Jorell. Even Ms. Annette had agreed when I sent her pictures of him this past week. Hovering over him, I carefully leaned down and placed my lips on the soft curls of his head. He stirred a bit but, thankfully, didn't wake up, or else Grandma would've had my ass.

After calling down to Clarence's room and telling him to get ready for the pool party, I hung around with Grandma for a bit.

"So . . . ," she said from a chair in the corner, her old hands working a ball of blue yarn and two long silver needles.

"Yes, Grandma?"

"Have you finally told that boy about him?" She nodded toward Baby Nicky's crib.

I drew in a frustrated breath and shook my head. "Not yet. But I will."

"When? 'Cause the longer you wait, the harder he's gonna take it. Every day that passes by without him knowing that Nicholas is his son is another day he misses seeing him grow. Another day he won't get to see his smile or hear that tiny laugh that you and I love. No matter what he's done, Nika, you gotta tell him."

I took a hard swallow, feeling a sudden wave of guilt wash over me. She was right. Nicholas had been growing steadily each day. And when he smiled, if you looked really closely, you'd see these faint little dimples in his cheeks. I was robbing Jorell of all those precious images—taking away his natural right to bond with his child. "I'll tell him after the wedding, Grandma. I promise."

"Mmm, you better." She made a quick adjustment to the ball of yarn on her lap and kept knitting.

Once Clarence was finally ready, we met down in the hotel lobby. He had on a pair of neon-green swim trunks that were a few inches too short for my taste. The white T-shirt he wore exposed his round belly, and there was a pair of white rubber flip-flops on his feet. Although this getup wouldn't have been my choice for him to wear, over time I had learned to just let Clarence be. How he looked or dressed no longer phased me, because he was just my friend. *And a damn good one at that.*

It took us forty minutes to get back over to Holmby Hills. As soon as we got through the security gate and pulled up around the circular driveway, I could see a few more cars lined up that weren't there when I left. When we stepped out of the rental, I smelled barbecue smoke drifting in the air. I had forgone breakfast, so my stomach instantly growled.

"This place is amazing," Clarence said, observing the grounds as we walked up to the front door.

After we rang the bell twice, the butler came to the door and let us in. From the foyer, I didn't see anyone in the main rooms, so I led the way out back. Sure enough, everyone was out by the covered pool, listening to music while the food was being cooked on the grill. Plus, Tez, and Jamal were already in the pool and were swimming with the kids. There were a few more people around, whom I quickly recognized as Plus's aunts, uncles, and cousins from out of town, ones that I'd met a time or two before. Thankfully, from what I could tell, Jorell wasn't out there.

Upon entering the pool area, I spotted Perri, who was lounging in her bathing suit beside Myesha and Shivon. I walked up and called, "Hey, y'all," before glancing behind me. "This is my friend Clarence. Clarence, this is Perri, Myesha, and Shivon," I said, introducing them.

Clarence shook each of their hands, then sat down in a nearby lounge chair.

"Girl, Jorell is going to have a damn fit," Perri said under her breath.

I scrunched up my nose. "Why?"

Instead of responding, she just shook her head.

"I'm going to head up and put my bathing suit on," I told them. Then I looked over at Clarence, who was lying back, with his feet crossed at the ankles. "You gonna be all right?" I asked.

He nodded and placed his hands behind his head, looking even more relaxed.

Hurriedly, I walked back inside and went straight up to my room to get dressed. Since I'd gained a little weight in my midsection after having the baby, I chose a powder-blue one-piece that was trimmed in gold and had a sweetheart neckline. I pulled my hair up into a high ponytail and slipped on a pair of gold flip-flops to match. Once I was all dressed, I headed back downstairs.

Of course, before I could even get to the bottom step, the first person to meet my eyes was Jorell. Bare chested, he was standing by a small table at the back door. He didn't think anyone could see him sneaking grapes and popping them into his mouth. I had to admit that he looked delectable as ever with his smooth dark skin, which seemed to have this natural glow about it. But knowing his cocky ass, he probably rubbed baby oil on himself just to show off. He had on a pair of Gucci board shorts, with matching Gucci slides on his feet, and around his neck was the thin gold chain that I'd seen him wear at least a dozen times. His sculpted upper torso seemed to have broadened over this past year, and I must say that he looked good. *Real good.*

Taking a nervous swallow, I tried to just walk past him and head out back. But just as I reached for the doorknob, I heard him say, "Shawty, you ain't gon' speak?"

My eyes closed as I inhaled deeply before turning around. "Hey, Jorell."

"Do we got a problem? Some shit you need to get off yo' muhfuckin' chest?" he asked before popping another grape in his mouth. His cocky, nonchalant demeanor made my blood boil, but he was getting me hot at the same time.

"Oh, there's a lot we need to talk about, but now's not the time or the place." Rolling my eyes, I spun back around on the balls of my feet and reached for the doorknob again. This time, I knowingly gave him a full view of my thickened ass and hips. "I'll let you know," I tossed over my shoulder.

I was playing it cool, but deep down I was nervous and could hardly breathe. The time for me to tell him about Nicholas was winding down, and I didn't know how he would react. Not to mention the dreadful fact that I was still attracted to him. The entire time I stood next to him there, my pussy throbbed between my thighs. *Ugh.*

As soon as I entered the indoor pool area and inhaled the scent of the warm chlorine, I walked over toward Clarence and the girls. I took a seat at the end of Clarence's lounge chair, by his feet.

"What's wrong?" Myesha asked, most likely noticing the frown on my face.

I shook my head. "Nothing. Just Jorell's crazy ass."

Not even a second later, I caught sight of Jorell, with Gucci shades covering his eyes. He strode toward us, but then he stopped abruptly, like something had caught him off guard. Dramatically, he removed the shades from his face and began shaking his head. "Hell to the nah," he muttered, loud enough for us to hear.

"Jorell, don't come over here starting no shit, yo," Perri warned.

I looked back and forth between the two of them, because I didn't know what they were talking about. Then Jorell walked up to where I was sitting with Clarence and stood directly in front of me. "So this the shit you doing now, shawty?" he asked. He curled his upper lip, to show off that gold grill, as he wrung both of his hands together.

"What are you talking about, Jorell?" I was completely confused.

"So this yo' nigga?" His eyes cut sharply to the person seated behind me on the lounge chair.

"And? If it is?" I asked, with a sudden attitude. No, Clarence wasn't my man, but that was none of Jorell's business. He hadn't laid an eye on me in well over eight months, and it had been even longer than that since the last time we were physical together. He had no claims on me.

Clarence put his hands in the air. "Aye, brother, I'm just—"

"Aye, brother," Jorell mocked. "Mane, if you don't shut yo' fat ass up," he growled, then looked at me. "Shawty, where the fuck you find this clown at?"

The sounds of Plus and Tez laughing from the pool weren't making things any better. I swear, they could be so damn immature at times.

"Stop being so disrespectful. Who I bring around is none of your damn business!" I snapped.

"You gon' always be my business," Jorell said, grabbing me up by the arm.

It seemed that at the exact same time I was being lifted to my feet, Clarence shot up from the chair and got in Jorell's face.

"Get your hands off of her, man," Clarence told him.

With me still in his grasp, Jorell shot Clarence a furious glare, then allowed his eyes to roam him up and down. "This what the fuck you want, Nika? Some fat, coochie-cutter, flip-flop-wearing muthafucka?"

Before I even knew what was happening, Jorell shoved me back down in my seat and grabbed Clarence up by his collar.

"Get off of him, yo," Perri yelled, finally standing to her feet. "Ahmad, come get your boy," she said. But as the seconds rolled by, it seemed like Plus just couldn't get there fast enough.

"I'm not even with her," Clarence croaked out at last. He sounded every bit like a scared, wounded animal as he rapidly blinked his eyes.

I stood up and tried my best to pry Jorell's hands off him, but I was no match for his strength. "Get off of him!" I screamed.

"And this is what the fuck you want?" Jorell asked me again. With a tight grip on Clarence's shirt, he shook him and leered at me.

"Just stop, Jorell. Please," I begged, placing my hand on his shoulder in a desperate attempt to calm him down.

Before I even realized what was happening, Jorell flung Clarence's thick body into the pool like a rag doll.

"Jorell!" I screamed. His ass had taken things way too far. We weren't even together.

Then, like a madman, he leaned down and violently flipped my lounge chair over with his hands. "Get the fuck out my face, breh, fo' I toss yo' li'l ass in there too!" he spat, pointing his finger in my face.

As if my body had a mind of its own, I hauled off and slapped him hard across the face. "Fuck you, Jorell!"

He grabbed his jaw, then gave me a dazed look.

"And stay the hell away from me. I mean it," I warned. Leaving poor Clarence and the rest behind, I stormed out of the pool area and went back inside the house.

Chapter 20

Jorell

"I swear, I don't know what she sees in you," Clarence's bitch ass mumbled, rolling his eyes. With the clothes on his back completely soaked with water, he trudged out of the pool, carrying his flip-flops in his hands.

"Nigga, shut yo' gap-toothed ass up," I spat.

"I swear, you get on my damn nerves, Jorell," Perri fussed as she went to get Camille out of the pool. "You lucky you dealing with Nika, and not me, 'cause I would've whupped your ass."

Sucking my teeth, I gave her a dismissive wave of my hand before putting my shades back on.

While she and Myesha took the kids in the house, I took a seat on the pool ledge and placed my feet in the water. Plus, Tez, and Jamal were still in there playing with a kiddie basketball and hoop, acting like shit just hadn't gone down.

"You pissing my wife off, yo. Don't make me have to put your ass out of the wedding," Plus threatened, with a little chuckle.

"Whatever, mane. It ain't me. That's Nika's dumb ass. She knew I was going to be here."

"But wait, you and shorty ain't even together, is y'all?" Tez asked, his eyes narrowed, clearly confused about the whole situation.

I shrugged. "Nah, but shawty know how we rock anytime I come around."

"And that's the problem," Jamal's roach-looking ass interjected.

"Mind ya business, breh," I told him. That was Plus's boy; he didn't know me like that.

"Nah, but he's right, yo. When's the last time you even talked with Nika?" Plus said.

Stroking my chin with my hand, I thought about his question. "Um, I think it was Perri's graduation."

"Damn! That shit was, like, a year ago," Tez said.

"Yeah, and I was with Brenda," I replied.

"Brenda from DC?" Plus asked.

"Yeah," I sighed. Just thinking about Brenda and this baby situation made me want to smoke or snort something. She was due any day now and was expecting me to be at the hospital when she delivered. "She claim she's pregnant by me," I confessed. I felt the weight from holding in that secret for so long finally being lifted off my shoulders.

"What? How you get her pregnant all the way from out here?" Plus asked, with furrowed brows.

"Nah, she's, like, eight months. I smashed the night Perri graduated, and she claim I got her pregnant. She's been hitting me up for money ever since." I shook my head.

"Damn," Plus muttered. "Why you ain't say nothing?"

I shrugged. "Shit's just been catching me at every angle. I ain't feel like talking to nobody. But she's the least of my worries, because I think she's lying. I know I strapped up."

"Well, take the test, then, and get that shit over with. I just had to do the same thing," Tez admitted.

"With who? MJ?" Plus asked.

"Fuck no! I wish Myesha would. Shayla had a baby last year and claimed that I was the daddy. I took the test and wasn't the father."

A baffled expression crossed Plus's face, but he didn't say anything else, I guess because Jamal and I were there.

"Yeah, fa sho', I'ma take the test. Then I gotta figure out what to do about Meechie and Jornelle."

"What's going on with Meechie?" Plus asked.

I gripped my forehead and let out a deep breath. I was getting this shit all out today. "Meechie been leaving Jornelle with my mama for days at a time, and now she's trying to take me to court for more child support. I'm, like, breh, what the fuck for? My mama say she keep Jornelle four, sometimes five nights a week, but Meechie want me to give her more money."

"If you don't mind me asking, how much you giving her now?" Plus asked.

"Five racks, breh," I answered, shaking my head.

"Damn. Y'all niggas got some money," Jamal said casually, slamming the ball in the hoop.

"Nah, *them* niggas got money." I pointed toward Plus and Tez. "Then you remember my cousin Nard?" I asked Plus. "He got locked up on some bullshit, so now I'm paying for his lawyer." I sighed.

"Damn, yo. When it rains, it pours," he said.

Then there were a few moments of silence, as everyone took in all the bullshit I was going through, I guessed, before Plus finally chimed back in.

"So what you gon' do about Nika?"

"Just give shorty the dick. She'll be all right," Tez said, completely unfazed. Then he started making his way out of the pool, as if this was the end of the discussion. "I'm going to get me some food," he threw over his shoulder.

"Shawty has gotten a little thicker," I mused, thinking of her newly thickened framed. La' baby had always been beautiful as fuck, but those few extra pounds she had packed on had made my dick twitch at first sight.

"Yo, just leave her alone until you get your shit together," Plus advised. "Besides, I need this wedding to run smoothly tomorrow. I don't need Perri beating yo' black ass down on her big day." He laughed.

"Yeah, right. But check it, I'ma go holla at shawty to see if I can at least apologize."

"Yeah, you did throw dude in the pool for nothing," Jamal's instigating ass said.

I glared hard at him without so much as a blink. "Again, mind ya business, breh."

I dapped Plus up, then took my feet out of the pool to dry them off. Then I headed to the house. When I made my way up to where I thought Nika's room might be, I heard voices coming from behind a cracked door.

"That man is nothing but a thug, Nika. You can't tell him," I heard the guy named Clarence say.

"She has to! He's Nicholas's father, yo." That was Perri. "Wouldn't you want someone to let you know about your son?"

"Son?" I whispered aloud to myself, thinking about what they might be talking about.

"Yes, but *I* know how to act. There's no way that the man I just saw out there could be a responsible father to your child," fat ass said.

"That's just it. He wasn't acting like himself. I've never seen that side of him before. Normally, he's very sweet and funny." I could practically hear the smile in Nika's voice when she spoke.

"Nika, now is not the time to be swooning over Jorell's crazy ass," I heard Myesha say suddenly.

Hearing my name immediately caused my ears to perk up even more. What the fuck were they talking about? I wondered.

"But he is a good father to Jornelle. He could be a good father to Nicholas too, right?" Nika declared.

Nicholas?

"Nika, I don't mean to come down on Jorell, 'cause you know he's my boy . . . ," Perri said, then let out a deep breath. "But his fathering skills with Jornelle are very questionable. He hasn't seen that girl in months. Now, I don't agree with keeping Nicholas a secret from him, but just know that Jorell's not perfect. He's got a lot of growing up to do before he can be this *ideal* father figure you're expecting him to be to your baby."

Baby?

With muddled thoughts racing through my mind, I plodded through the huge mansion to my room. I kept thinking back to the last time Nika and I had actually had sex. *Draft night in the bathroom.* Then I remembered her blowing up my phone for several months after that night. *Fuck!* It was all making sense now, even her reaction to seeing me with Brenda after Perri's graduation.

But my la' baby wouldn't keep no shit like that from me, would she?

Beyond the point of stress, I locked my bedroom door and pulled out a small bag full of cocaine. Careful not to make a mess, I spread the powdery white substance across the small mirror I had set on the dresser. For the past hour, my nostrils had been itching for a taste, but now that it was right there in front of me, within arm's reach, my hands were literally trembling, and I could hardly keep the rolled-up dollar bill steady between my fingers.

I ended up snorting ten lines that night, by far the most cocaine I had ever done.

The bright light of the morning sun came glaring through my bedroom window and caused my eyes to flutter open. With my legs hanging halfway off the bed, I was lay back atop the covers. My swim trunks and gold chain were still on from last night. I had gotten so fucked up between the Hennessy and the cocaine that I could barely even remember last night. Wiping the crust from my eyes, I rolled over to grab my cell phone off the nightstand. Staring me back in the face was a digital clock that read 10:58 a.m.

"Fuck," I muttered, realizing that I had overslept. The wedding was starting at two o'clock.

When my eyes finally settled on my phone, I saw that I had seven missed calls and a few unread text messages. Scrolling through, I saw that two of the missed calls were from my mother, one was from Meechie, one was from Lolli, and *four* were from Brenda. I listened to Brenda's voice messages.

Brenda, at 1:08 a.m.: "I'm starting to have contractions. Call me back ASAP."

Brenda, at 2:01 a.m.: "My mother's taking me to the hospital now because I'm already five minutes apart. Call me."

Brenda, at 3:48 a.m.: "I'm in labor. Call me back please!"

Brenda, 8:57 a.m.: "Jorell Jr. was born at seven fifty-four this morning. Seven pounds, eight ounces, and twenty-one inches long. Call me back, Jorell!"

Jorell Jr. . . . Fuck!

A sudden wave of nausea hit me all at once, and my head was spinning to the point where I could barely see in front of me. After struggling to stand up on my own two feet, I woozily staggered to the bedroom door. Upon hearing voices on the other side of the door, I quickly unlocked it and opened it, using only the doorframe for balance. I leaned my head out to see Jamal and a few of Plus's cousins walking up and down the hall.

"Hey, man, where you been at? Everybody's getting ready," Jamal said, his bare bird chest exposed and a white towel draped around his waist.

I swiped my hands over my face in an effort to focus my blurred vision. "Where's Plus at?"

"He's in the room down there, getting ready." He pointed. That was the plan for everyone. All the men were to stay in this wing of the house, while the women stayed in the other wing.

"All right, I'm jumping in the shower now," I told him, with a sniff of my nose.

Just as I had told him, I hopped in the shower. I ended up staying in there, under the hot water, for every bit of thirty minutes, trying to get some relief from the hangover I was experiencing. Anything I could do to soothe the pounding headache that accompanied all the depressing-ass thoughts I had floating around in my head. Had I really fathered three children by three different women? Had I already failed at my NBA career before it had even got started? Would I be able to survive financially another six months, the way I was going?

Once I got out of the shower and got all dressed in my tux, I decided to snort a few more lines on the dresser. Without it, I honestly didn't think I would make it through the day. And although I knew I needed to call Brenda back, I didn't. I didn't want to add to the stress I knew I would be facing with Nika here. Instead, I headed downstairs to be with the rest of the wedding party.

The whole first floor seemed to have been transformed since yesterday. There were now huge bouquets of pink roses strategically placed around the living room, and all the living-room furniture had been cleared out and re-placed with these fancy-ass pub tables, which had flutes of champagne sitting on top of them. Soft instrumental music was piped through the speakers all around the house, and in addition to Plus's and Perri's families being there, a few more people affiliated with the Lakers had arrived.

As I looked out the window by the front door, I spotted Plus in an all-white Armani tux. He looked anxious and kept slipping his hands in and out of his pockets. I stepped outside and walked up behind him.

"Whaddup, playboy?" I called. When he turned around, I dapped him up and brought him in for a brotherly hug. "You nervous?" I asked, placing my hand on his shoulder.

"Hell nah. But there's paparazzi and reporters lurking all around the damn house, and the photographer should have been here an hour ago," he explained.

"Oh, I thought you was getting cold feet on me, breh." I chuckled.

"Nah, shorty's definitely the one for me. I just don't want muhfuckas ruining her day and shit."

"Didn't y'all hire somebody to worry about shit like that for y'all?"

"Yeah, the wedding coordinator, Donna." He chucked his head in a backward nod as we stepped back inside the house. "She's out back, still trying to get shit situated out there," he said.

From the corner of my eye, I caught sight of Nika quickly approaching us. Although she had a frown etched on her face, when I turned to get a full view of her, I swear, shawty had never looked more beautiful to me. She wore a long, strapless pink gown that clung to her newly wide hips and full breasts. With each stride she took toward us, I could see the bell-like bottom of her gown sweep lightly over the marble floor. Her curly hair was pinned up off her shoulders and loosely held in place by what looked to be a piece of sparkly jewelry. Her lips were painted a pearly pink and looked like candy. La' baby was looking sexy as fuck. *Damn.*

When she got in front of us, she planted her feet in a wide stance and placed her hand on her hip. In the other hand was a small box. "Plus, this shit is getting out of hand," she said, handing the box over to him.

Plus's eyebrows wrinkled in confusion. "The fuck is this?" he asked as he turned the box in his hand.

"Just open it up. She thought it was a present from you before the wedding," Nika replied.

Plus slowly removed the top of the box to reveal a small plastic baby covered in what appeared to be blood. "The fuck!" he muttered.

"Look at the note," she told him, then pursed her lips.

Plus pulled a yellow sticky note from the top of the box and read it out loud in a low mumble. "May your marriage be just like the baby you couldn't have. Dead!" He closed his eyes and let out a deep sigh before clenching his jaw. "Fuck," he groaned.

"She's upstairs crying, and you know Perri don't even be crying like that."

Plus didn't say anything else before he took off for the staircase.

"Wait!" Nika called out. "She doesn't want you to see her!"

Plus glanced back at her over his shoulder and nodded his head. "I know. I got it."

As Plus climbed the second set of stairs on the other side of the house, I walked up behind Nika and placed my hand on the small of her back. Her head whipped around with an attitude before her eyes looked me up and down.

"Don't touch me, Jorell." She narrowed her eyes. "And what is that shit all on your nose?" she asked.

Immediately, my hand went up to cover my nose and pinch the tip. Grateful that I didn't have to come up with a lie, I stood there and watched her hips swish away from me.

Chapter 21

Plus

"Perri!" I knocked on the bedroom door.

"Just leave, Plus. I don't want you to see me," Perri said. I could hear her sniveling on the other side of the door.

Hating the sound of my girl crying, I placed my forehead against the door. "Then just come to the door so I can talk to you. Please."

After a few moments passed of what sounded like her shuffling around the room, I could suddenly feel her presence near me. "P?" I called through the door.

"Yeah, I'm here," she said lowly.

"You all right?"

She sighed loud enough for me to hear her through the barrier between us. "I guess," she said.

"I've already talked to Donna, and we're gonna start tightening up our security, bae. Checking the mail, the cars, all that," I told her. For a few seconds, I waited for a response, but I got nothing. "P?"

"Yeah. I'm here."

"Shorty, you don't sound happy. Is everything else okay?"

"I'm just . . . *I'm scared.*"

That admission immediately sent a sharp pang through my chest.

"Not of marrying you, Plus," she added, clarifying the matter, as if she could hear my innermost thoughts. "I'm just scared that there's someone out there that won't let us be happy. Like . . . who did I fuck with for them to come at me like this? And on my wedding day," she croaked. I swear, the sound of tears in her voice was enough to make a nigga cry right then and there.

"Baby, I'm gonna fix it, I promise. I'm gonna find out who keeps fucking with you, and I'm gonna fix it. Okay?"

From the other side of the door, I could hear her sniffing back more tears before she finally whispered, "Okay."

"Do you still wanna marry me?" I asked. Although I knew she loved me, with each second that passed, my heart was damn near beating farther out of my chest. Finally, she answered.

"Yes, *honey.*" Finally, I could hear a tiny smile in her voice.

I pressed my palms flat against the door, then rested my forehead in between them. "Well, then, I'll meet you at the altar at two o'clock?"

"I'll see you there at two o'clock," she replied. "Plus?" she called out, like she was trying to catch me before I left.

"Yeah, P?"

"I love you."

A corny-ass smile spread across my face. "I love you too."

Exactly one hour and twenty-two minutes later, I was standing outside, in the courtyard, waiting for Perri to finally walk down the aisle. It was a perfect seventy-five-degree day, with low winds and a brightly shining sun. I had to admit that in the final hour, our wedding coordinator had actually come through. As cheesy as it sounds, everything was perfect, down to all the fancy pink and white flowers and the cameras that were rolling off to the side. We had a little over one hundred guests in attendance on this day, all of them sitting just above the green lawn, in the stark white chairs.

Behind me was my brother and best man, Tez, and behind him was my only other groomsman, Jorell. Back when I was younger, there wasn't a person alive who could've told me that TK and Jamal weren't going to be the ones by my side on this day, but as the years had rolled by, the three of us had somehow grown apart. And although Jamal and I were still pretty tight, Tez and Jorell were like my brothers. Across from me stood Nika, who was Perri's natural choice for maid of honor, and behind her was Myesha, Perri's other bridesmaid. Bishop Solomon from the megachurch Abundant Life of Christ was there to marry us. He came highly recommended by a few people from the Lakers' front office and had even agreed to counsel us after the wedding. I know most people did it in reverse and went to premarital counseling, but rarely did Perri and I ever do things like most people.

All of a sudden, I saw my princess, Camille, appear down at the other end of the aisle. She wore a fluffy white dress that bounced as she walked in my direction, and in her hand was a white basket full of pink rose petals, which she sprinkled along the way. Her curly dark hair, which was usually styled in a ponytail, was loose today and hung just past her shoulders. And on top of her head sat a silver mini-crown that sparkled from the sun. My baby girl lived for *girly* shit like this, so I knew that she was over the moon. But no matter how tickled I got at that, there was no denying how absolutely beautiful she was. As the light bounced off her amber-colored eyes and flickered back at me, my lips couldn't help but give in to a proud smile. Once she was all the way down the aisle and next to me, I gave her a little wink, just to let her know that she had done a good job. She tried to give me a discreet thumbs-up in return, but of course, the crowd noticed and erupted in laughter.

When the music suddenly changed the song to "Heaven," by Jamie Foxx, my heart took off inside my chest. It was the song that Perri and I had carefully chosen for its double meaning. While she just wanted to feel like her mother was there with her on her wedding day, I wanted to let her know that she had truly been an angel in my life. With my emotions already causing me to choking up, I kept my eyes fixed on the end of the aisle. I swear, it felt like eternity before she finally appeared.

In a long, smooth white gown that framed her breasts like a heart, Perri literally stole my breath away. As her father guided her down the aisle, tears quickly formed in my eyes. *Shit.* Tez must have noticed, because he placed his hand on my shoulder. Once they were finally here, standing in front of me, I got a glimpse of Perri's teary amber eyes behind the veil.

"We are gathered here today before the grace of God to unite Ahmad Taylor and Perri Daniels in holy matrimony. A union that is not to be entered into without deep consideration, but rather reverently and soberly. Into this holy estate, these two persons present come now to be joined. If anyone can show just cause why they should not be lawfully wed, let them speak now or forever hold their peace," Bishop Solomon said.

With the exception of the birds chirping outside, there was complete silence.

"Who giveth this woman to be married to this man?" the bishop asked.

"I do," Mr. Phillip answered, with a bit of authority in his voice. Then he placed Perri's trembling hand in mine before taking a seat next to my mother.

"Let us bow our heads and pray. Lord, we thank you for gathering everyone here today. We ask that the strong love Ahmad and Perri share for one another on this day forever remains present in their hearts. We asked that you bind their spirits and souls only to your liking, Lord, creating a union of fortitude that shall never be divided. May their love continue to increase their faith and trust in you. Bless their marriage with everlasting peace and happiness, both here on earth and in eternity. Amen."

"Amen."

When Bishop placed his hands on each of our shoulders and turned us to face one another, Perri and I finally locked eyes. "At this time, Ahmad and Perri will exchange their own vows," he announced.

I cleared my throat and took both of Perri's hands in my own. "Perri, one of the very first memories I have of you is when we were both about five years old back at Millwood. You were sitting on your stoop and . . . I was sitting on mine just two doors down. Both of us eating our freezie cups that we had just bought from around the corner, at Miss Erma's house. Then Fat Mike from down the block rolled up on that little-ass tricycle . . ." I glanced over at Bishop as the crowd chuckled. "Fat Mike pulled up on that little bike and tried to punk me. You remember that?" I asked as I looked at her.

A natural smile eased into the corners of her lips as she nodded her head.

"He was, like, three years older than us and tried to come over and take my freezie cup away. Man, that nigg . . . I mean dude, almost had me in tears. Mushing me all in the face, tryin'a pry that cup from my hand." I shook my head at the memory. "Then you walked over, lips all red, with that half of a Styrofoam cup still in your hand, and was like, 'Why 'on' you just leave him alone, yo?'" I chuckled, and so did she, at the sound of me mimicking her young voice. "Then out of nowhere you shoved Fat Mike to the ground. Man, I wouldn't have believed it myself had I not witnessed it with my own eyes, but Fat Mike jumped up so fast and hopped back on his bike, like he was really scared of you."

Everyone laughed again.

"I know those aren't traditional vows or what you would probably hear at most weddings. Hell, most men would be too ashamed to even tell that story." I let out a light snort of laughter. "But I said all that to say, shorty, you have always been my guardian angel, my best friend, and the defender of my heart. Since the dawn of time, I could always count on you to have my back. Over the years you have been there for me mentally, physically, and emotionally in more ways than I can count. And when I envisioned the woman that I wanted to spend the rest of my life with, the woman that I wanted to bear all my children, I promise . . ." Hearing my own voice suddenly crack with emotion, I closed my teary eyes and shook my head, unable to speak.

"Tell it," said someone in the crowd. "You got it!"

Sucking in a huge breath of air, I opened my eyes and allowed the tears to finally fall. "Shorty, I promise it has *always* been you. Not only are you tough in life, but you're tough in love too. In my eyes, you are the most precious, most beautiful creature on this earth, and for all the days that follow today, I vow to remind us both of that."

When Perri reached up with her manicured hands and began thumbing away my tears, all our family and friends let out a series of aws from the crowd.

"Perri," Bishop Solomon said.

"Ahmad, not being able to share my life with you would be considered unnatural, because over the years we've shared just about everything. After I lost my mother, at just six years old, you openly shared your mother with me," she said as tears pooled in her eyes. "Then, when we started middle school, we both shared our love for basketball. You made the boys' team, while I made the girls'. And then right out of high school, we brought a precious baby girl into this world together. We were both so scared and didn't know how we would make it all work, but . . . somehow we did." She closed her eyes and took a breath. "But through it all, you know what we shared? An unwavering friendship. I know that most people think marrying your best friend is for fairy tales and movies, but with you, Ahmad, it's the real deal. You are *truly* the love of my life. I vow to be your lover and companion, your biggest fan and toughest adversary. I promise to love you in sickness and in health all the days of our lives. I love you and won't ever stop, until death do us part."

"The rings?" the bishop asked.

By the time we slid the rings on each other's fingers and said, "I do," I was so anxious that I could hardly wait to pull back her veil. When I finally did, her eyes and nose emerged, red from crying, but she was still the most beautiful bride. Her hair was pulled up off her neck, and her skin looked like the creamiest shade of caramel. Before Bishop Solomon could even pronounce us husband and wife, I took her in my arms and rushed to kiss her lips. At first, I thought she would protest or maybe even laugh, but Perri was just as eager for me as I was for her. Her hands slid across the back of my head as she closed her eyes to deepen the kiss. I tightened our embrace when I felt her body press into mine. We didn't care about Bishop standing there or our family and friends watching from afar. It was just me and Perri in that moment, *together*.

Chapter 22

Nika

"That's a wrap," the photographer said after snapping his final shot.

Although the ceremony had been over for an hour, the entire wedding party had been held hostage in the house for a photo session. With aching feet, and stress from the long day already tightening my shoulders, I headed back out to the reception to find Clarence. It was only seventy-five degrees that day, but the sun was at its peak and was shining brightly outside. The wedding planner had a huge white party tent planted in the backyard, with a dance floor and a DJ set up in the middle. It was nice.

Before I could make my way over there, I spotted Jornelle rushing full speed ahead toward me. "Miss Nika, Miss Nika!" she called out, with her arms spread wide.

I took in how pretty she looked in her peach-colored dress, which popped against her dark brown skin. She had this perfect little bun that sat right on top of her head, with a matching peach ribbon tied around it. Although she was very much a big girl, and not a baby, the only word that came to mind whenever I saw her was *precious*.

When she finally got in front of me, she gave me a hug, then took me by the hand. "Miss Nika, I like your dress," she said.

I looked down at her and admired her from up close. "I like yours more. Who did your hair?"

"Grandma." She pointed back toward the party tent, where I could see Ms. Annette headed our way. She, too, looked lovely in a fitted lavender pantsuit with some sort of beading on the lapels. Her dreads were pulled back off her face in a simple ponytail, showcasing the sharp angles of her cheeks.

"Hey, baby," she said when she reached us. After lifting her glasses and resting them on the top of her head like they were shades, she gave me a hug. "Where's my noodle?" she asked right away, referring to Nicholas.

"He's back at the hotel with Grandma," I replied, with a wide smile. Just the mere mention of my son's name always had that effect on me.

Feeling a little tug at my hand, I glanced down to see Jornelle's big brown eyes. "Am I gonna get to see my baby brother again?"

"Baby brother, huh? So y'all knew about this the whole time and ain't say shit!" I froze in place and my eyes immediately snapped shut at the sound of Jorell's voice booming behind me. "Y'all some disloyal muthafuckas, breh, I swuh to Gah," he griped.

Instead of turning around to face him, I opened my eyes and shifted my gaze to his mother. Rather than displaying a look of shock or guilt, Ms. Annette's face was twisted in anger. "Now, you watch your mouth in front of my grandchild," she warned him through gritted teeth, eyes glaring at Jorell, who still stood behind me. "If you want to go in that house and talk about this . . . *like adults*, then we most certainly can do that. But all this fussing and cussing shit you're on, I'm not doing that with you out here in . . . front of all these people," she told him.

"Nah, fuck that! Since y'all wanna keep secrets and shit, fuck all y'all," he spat, with a quick, dismissive wave of his hand.

It was obvious Jorell wasn't going to back down, not even for his own mother. In an attempt to calm him, I turned and grabbed him by the back arm as he tried walking away. But the way his nostrils flared in disgust, and that hateful look in his eyes, when he turned to look at me were enough to make me take a step back from him.

"Just stay the fuck away from me, breh. And I mean that shit," he said, looking me square in the eyes just before stomping away.

I don't know what I had expected, but it damn sure wasn't *that* reaction. Over the past few years, Jorell had held only admiration, lust, and maybe even a hint of love in his eyes for me, so to see him look at me like I was a piece of shit that was stuck to the bottom of his shoe hurt. In that moment, I was no longer his perfect little Nika, the girl he had once thought was too good for him. I had now been reduced to being a bitch . . . just one of his trifling-ass baby mamas, or at least that was what it felt like.

All of a sudden, uncontrollable waterworks sprang from my eyes, and I couldn't breathe. I fanned my face, trying my best to gain control of myself, but everything was now tight, from my heaving chest to the burning muscles in my throat. Jornelle squeezed her tiny arms around my waist and laid her head against my stomach, as if she knew the pain I was going through.

"Calm down. Just breathe," Ms. Annette told me, demonstrating how to inhale through my nose. "I'm gonna go talk to him."

Clarence walked up just then. "What's wrong?" he said, placing a concerned hand on my shoulder.

I was still in the process of trying to regain my breath and my control of my emotions. Taking short inhales, I felt like a person who'd just hyperventilated.

Ms. Annette spoke for me. "She's gonna be all right. Just dealing with my crazy son," she said.

"Did he put his hands on you?" Clarence asked.

Both Ms. Annette and I whipped our heads toward him so fast. "Now, why would you ask me something like that?" I asked, suddenly catching a second wind, as I wiped my eyes.

"Well, with the way he acted out yesterday . . ."

"What happened yesterday?" Ms. Annette asked, tilting her head to the side.

I shook my head. "Nothing. He just—"

"Nothing?" Clarence exclaimed, interrupting me. "That man choked me, then tossed me in the pool like I was *nothing*," he scoffed.

I rolled my eyes at his dramatics. "Jorell just thought that Clarence and I were together."

Ms. Annette's brow wrinkled in confusion. "And what if y'all were? Jorell don't have no claims over you."

Clarence nodded. "Same thing I said."

"That boy's done lost his damn mind. Bad enough we hardly ever see or hear from him these days," Ms. Annette said, taking a quick glance down at Jornelle. "And now I come all the way to LA, to see he's out here showing his ass. I promise you that I didn't raise him that way, to be so dern disrespectful. And I know he's hurting right now because we knew about the baby and he didn't, but still, it's no excuse for the way he's been acting. I'm going in there to talk to him."

"No. I'll go," I said to stop her, shaking my head. "I'm the reason he's so angry right now, not you," I told her.

"Are you sure? I don't want the two of you to get into it."

"I agree. Or at least let me go with you," Clarence said.

Letting out a light snort of laughter, I shook my head, thinking inwardly that if Clarence were to go in there with me, it would only piss Jorell off more. "I'll be all right by myself."

"All right. Just holler if you need me. Come on, baby," Ms. Annette said, taking Jornelle by the hand.

While Clarence just stood there, staring at me blankly, I took the liberty of stepping out of my high-heeled shoes. I leaned down to scooped them up from the grass, hooking my two fingers in the back, then stood up straight right in front of Clarence.

"You know you don't owe him anything, right?" he stated more than asked.

I released a deep sigh. "Clarence, I kept his son from him. I think he at least deserves an explanation." I shrugged, then said, "Probably even an apology."

Without giving Clarence a chance to respond, I turned around and trekked barefoot through the grass toward the house. When I was only a few feet away from the back door, I ran into Plus.

"What's wrong?" he asked, grabbing me by the elbow to stop me in my tracks.

"I'm going in there to find Jorell. He's pissed at me," I explained.

He gave me a sympathetic look. "Is it about the baby?"

"Damn, Perri," I muttered. I don't know why I thought she would hold my secret for a full forty-eight hours, especially from Plus. "Yeah, about the baby," I told him.

"I just saw him a few minutes ago, flying up the stairs, looking pissed. Let me go in there with you."

"No. You don't need to be caught up in our mess. Where's your bride?"

"Camille spilled something on her white dress, so she's helping her change. I'll just run you up there real quick. Make sure my boy is all right," he said.

I didn't understand why no one wanted me to go see Jorell by myself, but for whatever reason, I didn't protest this time. I allowed Plus to lead the way inside the house and up the stairs to Jorell's bedroom. The long hallway was dark and quiet, which was to be expected, since everyone was either downstairs or outside. When we got to Jorell's door, Plus gave two hard knocks, which went unanswered.

"Jorell! Open up, yo!" He banged on the door a little harder this time. After giving Jorell a few seconds to come to the door, Plus glanced over his shoulder at me. "Maybe he's not in there."

Since he acted like he was scared, I stepped in front of him and turned the doorknob myself. I opened the door, and my gaze wandered around the room. Jorell's unmade bed was empty, and as far as I could tell, he wasn't in there, but then I heard the muted sound of running water. I stepped crossed the room and knocked on his bathroom door. Still no answer.

"Jorell!" I called out, pounding on the door again.

When I turned this doorknob and pushed, I couldn't get the door all the way open. It was like something was blocking it. Plus stepped up and gave the door a hard shove, revealing Jorell's legs and feet, which were lying on the floor.

"Oh my God!" I gasped.

Both my eyes and my heart were unprepared when I witnessed Jorell's unconscious body sprawled out on the floor. Once I was inside the bathroom, I dropped down on my knees and lifted his head onto my lap. I could feel a faint stream of air seeping from his nostrils, which told me that he was still breathing, although barely.

"Jorell, wake up!" I cried. I tried to shake him, only to see his eyes roll to the back of his head. "What's wrong with him?" My eyes shifted up to find Plus holding a ziplock bag half full of white powder in his hand. Although I had never done drugs or been around them, I'd seen enough on TV and in the movies to know what it was.

"Fuck!" Plus shouted. "I gotta call an ambulance."

"Hurry! His pulse feels weak." I let out a shaky breath. At this point my entire body trembled out of fear, and tears were pouring from my eyes. Seeing my son's father like that, someone whom I clearly loved and cared for, just did something to me.

Not even ten minutes after Plus made the call, paramedics filed into Jorell's bathroom and tried to get him to respond. When he didn't open up his eyes, I watched them lift his lethargic limbs from the floor, place him on a stretcher, and administer to him. Then they carried him down the stairs, with an oxygen mask covering the lower half of his face.

Unfortunately, Jornelle was down there when they rolled her father out the front door, and I swear, the sound of her crying out for him literally broke my heart in two. Ms. Annette jumped in the back of the ambulance to ride with him, while I stayed back and got Jornelle settled down. Once she had calmed down, I left her with Myesha and the rest of the family. Then Plus, Perri, and I jumped in the car and headed over to the hospital.

Chapter 23

Jorell

I slowly peeled my eyes open one at time, taking in the sounds of machines beeping and people talking around me. Through blurred vision, I struggled like hell to focus my eyes. The lights were dim, and Nika's face was, surprisingly, the first to come into view. I tried to speak, but my mouth was extremely dry, and as I tried to sit upright, I felt tubes tugging at the veins in my arm.

"Here," Nika said, guiding a cup and straw closer to my face.

I took a few sips of water, then cleared my throat. "What happened?" I asked groggily.

"Why don't you tell us?" My eyes shifted to the other side of the room, where I saw Plus still dressed in his tux. He held that same disappointed gaze in his eyes that he had the day I showed up late for practice. Perri, who was no longer in her white gown, sat there beside him, looking just as discontent.

When I didn't say anything, Nika chimed in. "You overdosed, Jorell."

It took a minute for my mind to register what she had just said; then I sucked my teeth. "Mane, ain't nobody overdose."

"Yeah, *you did*, yo, and the shit is all over the fucking news," Plus said.

That bit of information gave me enough strength to sit up in the bed. "In the news?"

Plus and Perri both nodded their heads. "Yes. The media's been crawling all around Holmby Estates ever since they heard about our wedding," Perri explained.

"How long has this been going on? When did you start using?" Nika asked.

"That's what I wanna know." I looked up at my mother, who had just entered the room, with a cup of coffee in her hand.

"I . . . I'm not—"

"Don't even fix your lips to tell that lie," my mother said, cutting me off. "The doctor already told us you ingested a large quantity of cocaine. That, mixed with the alcohol, had your heart beating three times its normal speed, and then it knocked your ass unconscious." When my mother let out a tearful sigh before closing her eyes, I knew that this had hurt her. "You almost died, Jorell," she said in a stern whisper.

"I only do it sometimes. Just for fun or when I'm stressed."

My mother shook her head in disbelief. "You're lying."

"You need to get some help, yo," Plus added, pressing the issue.

I looked around the room and saw that expressions of sadness had washed over everyone's faces. "Why are y'all treating me like I'm some sort of junkie? Like I'm some kinda fucking addict!" I said, raising my voice.

Nika reached behind me to rub her hand up and down my back. "You scared us, Jorell. We all just want you to get better," she said softly.

The tranquility in her voice was almost enough to silence me and to make me understand, but then a quick reminder popped into my head as to why I'd snorted those last few lines in the first place. "Get your fucking hands off me, breh!" I shrugged her away.

The hurt in her eyes was evident as she slowly took a step back from the bed.

"Don't act like that toward her, Jorell. She's the one that found you. She's the one that comforted your daughter after she witnessed you being rolled out on a stretcher. She's the mother of your child, for Christ's sake!" my mother yelled.

I snorted at that assertion. "Mother of *my* child? What child?" At this point, I was beyond agitated, and nothing or no one could calm me down. It was bad enough that the whole world was going to know my business, but now my own mother was sitting here, defending Nika's lying ass. "That bastard-ass baby ain't mine," I said, glaring at Nika, whose mouth had suddenly dropped open from shock. "Mane, I don't know who she's been fucking," I said in disgust as I looked her directly in the eye.

"Jorell," Perri said, dragged out my name, begging me to stop.

Nika put her hand up to quiet her. "No, Perri. Don't say nothing," she said before turning her eyes to me. "You know what? Fuck you, Jorell! I should've left your crackhead ass right there on the bathroom floor to flatline. Don't call me! Don't text me! And don't try to come see about my *bastard-ass* baby, none of that!" She snatched her purse up from the chair and stormed out of the room so fast that she was gone within the blink of an eye.

Feeling slightly weak and even more frustrated, I groaned and allowed my forehead to fall into the palms of my hands.

"Now, why would you do that? That girl loves you," my mother said.

I looked up and off to the side and saw Perri nod her head in agreement.

"I'm not tryin'a hear that shit, Ma. If she loved me, then her ass wouldn't have lied. I can't fuck wit' shawty like that no mo','" I told her. "I mean, who the fuck keeps a baby a secret?"

Sinking her fingers into her temples and giving herself a brief massage, my mother looked at me with glossy eyes, then pushed out a deep breath. "What's this all about, Jorell? And since when did you start using drugs? Is this about your father?" she asked.

Plus turned to me with a questioning look on his face. "I thought you didn't know your father."

Before I got a chance to respond, my mother cut in and said, "He doesn't. Sorry-ass bastard just showed up at his doorstep last month. Wanting money, of course." She rolled her eyes up toward the ceiling.

"Damn," Plus muttered under his breath.

"Yeah, well . . . fuck him too," I snarled. At this point, I was giving the entire world my ass to kiss.

Suddenly a knock sounded at the door. I was expecting a doctor or a nurse, maybe even Nika, but instead it was Coach Jackson, who was followed by a bunch of suits. There was the Lakers general manager, Mr. Mitch; my agent, Frank Barnett; and Diane Lange, the VP of league operations. I swallowed back the lump in my throat before sitting up a little straighter in the bed.

"How you feeling, champ?" Coach Jackson asked.

"Better," was all I said. In that moment, I was actually feeling sick to my damn stomach, and let's not even talk about how embarrassed a nigga was.

"We need to talk to you, son. Important business stuff." Coach tapped the foot of the bed before his eyes floated around to everyone else in the room.

I looked over at my mother, then Plus, silently asking them to give us some privacy. Once they had all left the room, Coach and the rest of his crew took a seat.

Although I already felt like I had an inkling as to why they were here, I asked, "So what's up?"

"Well," Coach sighed, "what's up is that you've broken the league's antidrug agreement," he said, widening his eyes.

"Y'all kicking a nigga off the team?" I asked flat out.

He shook his head. "No, but you're being suspended for the remainder of the season, and you'll be required to complete ninety days in an inpatient rehab facility. And then an additional ninety as an outpatient."

I did the quick math and added it up in my head. "Six months?" I questioned in disbelief.

Mr. Mitch stood up, with a no-nonsense expression on his face. "You don't have to go. The decision is solely up to you, Jorell. But just so you know, if you *don't* go, your days of playing in the league are over. Your professional basketball career will be *finished*," he said evenly, like it was no skin off his back.

I cupped the lower half of my face with my hand, suddenly wondering how all of this would impact me financially. "But how . . . ? I have a family to feed. I can't take off for six months."

"It's not an option, son," Coach said lowly. Pressing his lips together, he gave me a compassion-filled look. "You're just gonna have to figure it out."

For some reason, my mind quickly drifted back to Brenda. "Can I at least try to get some personal things sorted out before I leave?"

Diane Lange finally spoke up. "One week from Monday, you're expected to be in rehab," she said. She stood up from her chair, with a packet of documents in her hands. "I need you to sign here, here, and here." She pointed to the earmarked pages. "This is to acknowledge your suspension from the league. Upon successful completion of an accredited rehab program, you'll be fully reinstated, but until then . . ."

I nodded, understanding the terms, before I took the papers from her hands and signed where she'd instructed.

Once they had all left the room, I was expecting my mother to come back in, but only Plus returned. He had completely abandoned the jacket of his suit, while his tie was draped loosely around his neck.

"What'd they say?" he asked, slipping his hands into the pockets of his pants.

I threw my head back on the pillow and stared up at the ceiling. "Suspended, and I gotta go to rehab."

"Well, at least you're not out. How long are you gonna be in rehab?"

I tightened my jaw, not wanting to release the words that were about to come out of my mouth. "Six months," I groaned.

"Man, it'll fly by. You'll see. The most important thing is getting you better."

"Mane, y'all act like I'm out here strung out on this shit. I can quit anytime I want."

Plus hiked his shoulders, then opened his mouth like he was at a loss for words. "I don't know what you can or can't do. All I know is when I seen yo' ass laid out on the floor like that . . . unresponsive, I thought I had lost my brother."

"I'm fine, breh," I told him. "Really."

Plus didn't look the slightest bit convinced. "You need to get your shit together and *fast*, yo. Stop focusing on the shit you don't have, and focus on what you *do* have. I mean, shit, we play for the fucking LA Lakers," he said, shaking his head. "My whole life I dreamed of playing in the NBA, and now that it's a reality, every day for me is like a dream come true. You have a beautiful daughter, Jorell, and she really needs you, man. Probably more than you even know. And regardless of the shit you have going on with Nika, you gotta whole son out there that's gonna need someone to look up to. You got a lot to live for. You just gotta remember that," he schooled.

After letting his words sink in, I ran my hand down my face before nodding my head in agreement. He was right. I needed to do better, if not for me, for my children. Over the next few days, I would head up to DC to get a DNA test done for Brenda's baby, and then I'd settle up with Nard's lawyer before spending some quality time with Jornelle. Everything else would just have to wait until I was out of rehab.

"I got it under control, breh. I promise," I said.

He cocked his head to the side, a skeptical look crossing his face. "Yeah, you always say that."

"Well, I mean it this time. I've already done fucked up yo' wedding, so after y'all win that game tomorrow, take shawty on her honeymoon, a'ight?"

He reached over and dapped me up before pulling me in for a brotherly hug. "A'ight, yo. I'ma leave you to it. Your mama said she'll be back in an hour or so," he said, then started for the door.

Just when his hand reached out to open it, I said, "Aye, Plus?"

He craned his neck to look back at me.

"Thanks for having my back, man."

Plus quickly tipped his chin up and said, "No doubt."

Chapter 24

Nika

"And you're sure that this is what you want to do?" Grandma asked through the phone.

Balancing my cell phone between my ear and shoulder, I stuck the key into the lock on Jorell's apartment door. "Yes Grandma. Don't worry. I'll still come back to visit you," I told her, thinking that we'd already had this talk about a hundred times.

"You better bring that baby back to see me. I don't want to have to put you over my lap, little girl," she warned playfully.

I smiled and shook my head before pushing the door open. Funk immediately smacked me in the face as I stumbled over a wad of unopened mail on the floor. "Grandma, let me call you back."

"All right, and don't you forget," she said, then ended the call.

I reached down and picked up the mail before letting the door close behind me. A quick glance let me know that most of the mail was bills that were past due, which was partly the reason I was there in the first place. Ms. Annette had called me a few weeks after the wedding, asking if I'd help her with some of Jorell's affairs. At first, I'd been like, hell no. I hadn't wanted anything to do with him or whatever bullshit he was wrapped up in. But after several more attempts, and her telling me that Jorell had actually been making progress in rehab, my position had softened a bit.

Jorell had still yet to lay his eyes on Nicholas, and even after all the ugly, hurtful things he'd said to me that day in the hospital, it still bothered me. Not only did I want my son to know his father, but I wanted him to know the man I had fallen for too. The one I'd, at one point, openly given my heart and body to. So after a lot of prayer, careful consideration, and persuasion by Perri, who just wanted me nearby, I had moved out to LA. For the time being, Nicholas and I were living out of Plus and Perri's guest bedroom, but we all knew that it was only a temporary situation. I'd already found a job as a radiology tech at one of the local hospitals, and because Perri was still out of work, she'd agreed to keep Nicholas for me during the day.

"Yuck," I muttered when I found a month-old slice of moldy pizza sitting on the leather chaise in the living room. On the end table was a half-empty bottle of beer and an open bag of Doritos, which I knew were beyond stale. My eyes darted all around the foreign space, and I quickly noticed the lack of furniture and the minimal decor.

I walked farther into the apartment and eventually landed in the kitchen, with the expectation of seeing dirty dishes piled up high in the sink. However, to my surprise, the kitchen looked fairly clean, but still there was a bad odor. As soon as I pulled open the refrigerator door, I had to cover my nose and mouth from the horrid smell. I had discovered spoiled food, which had been sitting in there for God only knows how long. I shut the refrigerator door, then glanced over at the stainless-steel trash can. Reluctantly, I stepped over to the trash can, pushed my foot down on the lever, and raised the top, to reveal a heap of trash covered in maggots. I instantly gagged.

"Lord, have mercy," I grumbled under my breath like an old person. Jorell had taken this whole bachelor-pad thing to a whole other level.

After sitting my purse and the mail down on the counter, I sent Perri a quick text message. Since she was keeping baby Nicholas for me, I had to let her know that I was going to be longer than I had originally expected.

About an hour after repressing several urges to vomit, I'd cleaned out Jorell's entire fridge. I had also tidied up around his living room and had even taken out the trash. Once that was all complete, I found my way back to his bedroom. Of course, his bed was unmade, and he had what I perceived to be drug paraphernalia lying right there on the dresser. The white powdery residue and the mirror were what gave it away. I quickly cleaned that up, along with his entire bedroom and en suite bath. Along the way, I found things that I wished I hadn't: lace thongs, panties, and condom wrappers, just to name a few.

Now that everything was tidy and odor free, I made my way down to the small dining room area. Prepared to focus at last on what I'd actually come for, I sat down at the small round table. "Where do I start?" I muttered to myself. Tapping my fingers on the wooden surface, I stared at the laptop screen in front me.

Sitting on the table was a stack of bills, which I had promised Ms. Annette I would go through to help sort out some of Jorell's financial affairs. Apparently, before he left for rehab, Jorell had paid Nard's lawyer for a year of services; however, his own rent was past due. His Lamborghini was on the brink of being repossessed, and sad to say, he was also behind on his child support. I didn't know how much Jorell's contract with the Lakers was for, but apparently, it wasn't enough to cover his astronomical spending habits. I was completely shocked to learn that he didn't even have an accountant to help manage his money.

No, I wasn't Jorell's wife, but Ms. Annette, as his power of attorney, had told me what needed to be done and had assured me that she would handle the rest. My trust in her was what had ultimately led me to his apartment. She had given me not only his key but also his bank account information, along with several other log-ins and passwords, which I knew I shouldn't have had access to.

After logging in to Jorell's online bank account, I learned that he had a little under nine hundred grand sitting in his account. Most people would've been impressed by that number, but after looking at page after page of his bank statements, I learned that less than a year ago he had five million dollars in his account. The rent on this mediocre apartment was five thousand a month, and the monthly payment on his Lamborghini was . . . *Christ* . . . even more than that.

When I saw that he was paying Meechie a little more than five thousand a month in child support, I vomited a little inside my mouth. "You know what . . . . ?" I rambled to myself, with an attitude. "It does not take that much money to help provide for a child."

Then there were these six-hundred-dollar transfers that he made routinely every single month, with the description "Brenda" beside them. My mind instantly drifted back to when the name Brenda flashed across his cell-phone screen that night after Plus's birthday party last year. As I kept going, I also discovered that he had paid off his mother's mortgage last year, which, even under the circumstances, impressed me.

Overwhelmed would be an understatement as to how I felt upon seeing all Jorell's debt, but after two and a half long hours of going through his mail and then paying all his bills online, I let out a deep sigh of relief. I looked down at the table and saw that there was one last envelope that hadn't been opened yet. It was from a DDC DNA Diagnostic Center.

Hmm?

It had been ten weeks since Jorell had left for rehab. It saddened me to say that at four and half months old, my son had yet to meet his father. Unfortunately, I was partially to blame for that. I drew in a deep breath and momentarily closed my eyes before knocking on the door to his room at the rehab facility. My heart galloped inside my chest from anticipation, and although they were mere seconds, it felt like hours before he finally opened the door.

Leaning against the doorframe, shirtless, with his locks freely falling past his shoulders, Jorell stood before me. He wore gray sweatpants on his lower half, with white socks and Nike slides covering his feet. My mouth went completely dry, and shamefully, my eyes meandered down his chocolate corded frame. His chest had thickened over the months, and his previously lanky arms even seemed a bit more swollen with muscle. As my eyes traveled down to the familiar bulge in his pants, I had to swallow back my unexpected arousal.

"H-hey," I stammered, feeling my face suddenly growing hot.

Jorell chucked up his chin and peered down at me with his dark set of hooded eyes. Although he wasn't frowning, there was no hint of a smile on his lips. "What you doing out here, shawty?" he asked.

I knew I wasn't his favorite person in the world these days, but for some reason, I was expecting him to be a little bit surprised to see me. And I had expected a warmer greeting than the one I'd received. I reached down into my satchel purse and pulled out a yellow envelope. "This is for you."

As he silently read the words on the front of the envelope, I could see his mind starting to turn. Then his eyes suddenly widened a bit from recognition. "A'ight. Thanks," he said.

My heart dropped when he grabbed the edge of the door, like he was going to shut it in my face. "Is that all you have to say to me?" I asked, placing my hand on my hip.

He let out a snort, then scratched his eyebrow with his thumb. "I mean . . . shawty, what you want me to say?" He shrugged. "Did you bring my son?"

"You mean my *bastard-ass* baby," I said, regurgitating his words. Like the true Scorpio I was, I eventually forgave Jorell for saying that, but it was highly unlikely that I would ever forget it.

Jorell swiped his hand down his face. "See, breh, this is why I didn't invite you in. I been doing good, and I don't need the fucking stress."

I stepped up close to him, practically on the verge of pushing my way inside. "Well, we have a lot more to discuss, so let me in."

Releasing a low groan, he did a half roll of his eyes, then took a step back, allowing me inside.

When I walked in, my eyes did a quick circle around the room, and I realized this was a small studio apartment. It housed not only a queen-size bed but a small sofa and a kitchenette area, as well. Unlike his apartment during my last visit, everything here appeared clean and tidy. Before taking a seat, I looked out his window, which overlooked the community's pool and grounds that featured lots of palm trees.

"It's real nice here," I admitted.

"It's a'ight." He let the words roll nonchalantly off his tongue.

I turned around to see that he had already taken a seat on the small sofa. Legs gaped open wide, he looked like he was more than ready for me to leave.

"So how's it going for you in here?" I asked, trying to keep the conversation light.

He shrugged. "Straight, I guess. Been going to therapy and whatnot. Just doing my time, ya feel me?"

I nodded. "You've been keeping in shape?" Of course, I already knew the answer to that with just one look at him.

"Ever' day," he answered coolly, scratching at his temple. "So how long you in town?"

After dropping my purse down on the edge of the cushion, I took a seat in the single chair directly across from him. "I live here now. Well . . . in LA," I explained. The rehab facility he was attending was actually in Pasadena.

Jorell squinted his eyes. "Since when? And how'd you get this?" he asked, holding up the envelope.

"Well, that's why I'm here. A couple of months ago, your mother asked me to come help out with some of your affairs that weren't in order."

His head suddenly cocked to the side. "My affairs?"

"Your bills weren't being paid, Jorell," I told him bluntly. "And your mother couldn't come all the way out here, because she's been keeping Jornelle during the week," I explained.

Jorell started shaking his head in a way I knew wasn't good. "So basically, you telling me she put you all in my fucking business," he said, aiming his finger at me.

"It wasn't like that—"

"Nah," he muttered, shaking his head again. "Where the fuck did you get this from?" He raised the envelope again.

I released a long, exasperated sigh. "From your apartment, Jorell."

He let out another one of those sarcastic snorts of laughter before reaching for his cell phone, which was sitting on the end table.

"Your mother gave me the key to your apartment, and she also gave me your bank information," I said.

His rapid typing on the cell-phone screen came to an abrupt halt before he looked up at me. "My bank information?"

"Your rent was past due, your car was going to be repossessed, and . . ." I cleared my throat. "And you were behind on paying Meechie," I said. I flexed my jaw just to hide my irritation with that.

Jorell tossed his phone on the cushion next to him, then sat back on the sofa. "Fuck," he muttered, wiping both hands down his face.

"Look, I handled it, so it's fine."

His eyebrow shot up as he glared at me. "What you mean, you handled it?"

I took a deep swallow. "Your rent is current. Meechie's getting her child support," I said, rolling my eyes. "And . . ." I bit down on my bottom lip, wondering if I should even mention the next part. Hell, I didn't want him to relapse. "I returned the Lamborghini."

With his eyes ballooning, Jorell shot up from his seat. "You what!" he roared.

Naturally, I flinched and cowered a little. "I had to. You couldn't afford it," I said, softening my tone.

"Nah, stop playing wit' me and go get my shit, shawty!"

I shook my head. "I'm sorry, but it's already gone."

"It's gone?" he repeated, narrowing his eyes in disbelief. "How did that even happen? You know I should sue the fuck outta you for identity theft and fraud, right?"

"As your power of attorney, your mother has signed off on everything. Look . . ." I finally stood up, stepped right up to him, and placed my hands against his chest. I swear my only intention was to calm him down, but feeling those muscles suddenly flex beneath my palms—my first real physical connection with the opposite sex in well over a year—just did something to me. Now concentrating only on the unexpected pulsing between my thighs, I had completely forgotten what I was about to say.

Jorell circled his hands around my waist and pulled me into him. "Look, what?" he asked.

Between the fresh, soapy smell of his skin and the sudden warmth radiating between us, I had completely lost my train of thought. My mouth had gone desert dry again, and I was finding it difficult to even speak. "I—I," I stammered.

Jorell leaned down and buried his face in the crook of my neck. "You what?" he whispered, lips gently teasing at my skin.

Although my eyes were closed, I shook my head in protest. "I can't," I breathed.

"You know I miss the fuck outta you," he said, sliding his hands down to my ass.

He knew exactly what he was doing to me.

Despite everything Jorell had put me through, my body still longed for him. I still responded to his touch, and there was even a part of me that still felt like I was his. *But* Jorell had charmed me out of my panties one too many times. Until he made things right with my son, I had decided that he would never be able to reach that part of me again.

"This is not why I'm here," I told him, quickly wiggling out of his hold. I went over to my chair and reached inside my purse. "Here." I pulled out a folded piece of paper and handed it over to him, along with a pen.

He opened up the paper and thumbed his nose as he read. "What's this?"

"You need an accountant to handle the rest of your money, Jorell. Plus gave me some information on the person that manages his money, and he seems to be pretty good. You just need to sign there for him to get started. Also, your lease is coming to an end, and my suggestion is that you find an apartment that you can actually afford."

He let out a snort. "Shawty, you really think you running shit, huh?"

Instead of answering him, I simply gave him a one-shoulder shrug.

"So when you gon' bring my son?" he asked. After placing the paper down on the end table, he leaned down to sign it.

"Once I know for sure that you're better." My response was quick, because I had asked myself that same question over a million times.

"I *am* better. I ain't on that shit no more," he said, obviously referring to his former drug use.

I let out a deep sigh and nodded my head. "I know you're better. I can clearly see that," I said, with my eyes lustfully traveling over his physique. "But I need to know that Nicholas will be a priority to you, just like he is to me. For the past few years, I've been trying my best to figure you out, but you're a hard one." I shook my head. "I don't want that kind of uncertainty for him. He needs to know that you love him and that you're always there for him, no matter what."

With a hint of amusement in his eyes, he tilted his head to the side. "You talking about our son or yourself?" he asked, licking his lips.

Shamefaced, I tucked my curly hair behind my ear and took a deep swallow. "We don't need to be together for you to be a father to your son, Jorell," I said curtly, looking him in the eyes. "I promise I won't keep him from you."

"You've already *been* keeping him from me, or did you forget?"

Shit. He was right. "You're right. I'll make sure you meet him soon." I removed another envelope from my purse and passed it over to him. "Here," I said.

After he pulled the pictures out of the envelope, I watched Jorell's dark eyes immediately light up. He took his time, silently examining each photo of baby Nicholas. "Damn, la' baby," he muttered, with a half smile on his face. I moved closer to him so that I could see the pictures for myself, although I had seen them several times before. "He looks like me. Jornelle too," he admitted.

"What? You mean to tell me you don't want a DNA test?" I asked sarcastically, pursing my lips to the side.

He released a light snort of laughter. "Nah, I trust you," he said, keeping his eyes cast down at the pictures in his hands.

"Speaking of a DNA test . . . who else did you get pregnant, Jorell?"

Chapter 25

Jorell

After looking at each of the photos of baby Nicholas, carefully studying each of his familiar features, I put them back inside the envelope. I knew Nika wanted an answer about who else I had gotten pregnant, but I just ignored her. We had actually been getting along for the past ten minutes, and I didn't want to ruin it. If I had it my way, we'd be spending the rest of her time here in the bed, but I knew she wasn't having it. And I guess I really couldn't blame her; I had shit on her time and time again.

"So . . . are you just gonna ignore me?" she asked.

I ran my hand down my jaw and let out a deep sigh. "Why you being nosy, shawty?" I asked, turning around to take a seat back on the sofa.

Nika planted her right hand on her hip and shifted her weight to one side. "Well, I guess I want to know if Nicholas has another brother or sister out there somewhere."

My eyes traveled up the new curves of her body until they met her pretty face. "Come here," I said, licking my lips and gesturing with an upward tilt of my chin.

She must have recognized the lust in my eyes, because she immediately shook her head. "Uh-uh. No," she said.

"Come sit with me for a minute," I told her, patting my thigh. "I need to talk to you."

Although she still had a reluctant expression on her face, she slowly ambled over to me and stood in between my legs. I reached up and grabbed her by the arm, then pulled her down into my lap.

"What do you want, Jorell?" she asked, looking across the room. Her back was upright, and her body felt completely unrelaxed against me.

I hooked my finger under her chin and forced her to look at me. "Aye, I need to tell you something."

"What?" she asked defensively, folding her arms across her chest.

With my hand cupping her chin, I ran my thumb across her cheek. "I'm sorry for hurting you."

Her eyes softened at first; then she let out a snort like she didn't believe me. "Hmm. I've heard that before."

"I know I hurt you last year, when I didn't follow through on my word—"

"You *never* follow through on your word, Jorell. Never!"

I nodded. "Yeah, you right. I don't," I agreed. "Not when it comes to you."

She rolled her eyes and let out a snort like she was at her wit's end. "And why is that? What did I do to you for you to treat me like this?" I could hear the tears slowly building in her voice.

"You scare me—"

She put her hand up and twisted her body a little so that she wouldn't have to face me. "Save it, Jorell!"

"Nah, mane, let me finish," I said, grabbing her legs to turn her back around. "When I told you I loved you, shawty, I meant that shit. I'm just scared of loving you, only to lose you in the end."

She cocked her head to the side and narrowed her eyes at me. "That's bullshit! You're scared to commit because that means you can't go around fucking every female dog with a pussy between her legs!" she yelled, hopping up from my lap. "Let's face it. You don't love me. You love only yourself, Jorell."

I stood up in front of her and grabbed her by the arms. When she tried to jerk away, I tightened my grip a little. "I *do* love you, Nika," I said, then watched as she turned her face away in anger. "Let me show you."

She shook her head, still unable to look me in the eye. "No! Show your children! They you need you . . . I don't."

I moved in close, so that my lips were grazing her ear. "So you don't need me no mo'?" I asked through a whisper.

Closing her eyes, she shook her head again. I knew shawty was lying out her ass, but I understood that she was doing what she thought she had to. Even though the shit hurt, I knew she was only saying that to protect herself from me. I leaned down and gently kissed the side of her face before wrapping my arms tightly around her for a hug. Although I knew she wanted to resist, her body immediately melted into mine.

"I'm gon' show you," I told her.

We stayed like that for a few minutes, with me embracing her and just kissing the top of her head every so often. Once I let her go, I took a seat back down on the sofa and reached over to the end table for the yellow envelope, the one that she had given me when she first walked in the apartment.

She sat down beside me. "Brenda, right?"

I widened my eyes a little before cutting them over at her, and then I slowly nodded my head. I didn't need to act surprised that she knew about Brenda, given the fact that my mama had her all up in my business. I exhaled a deep breath, then created a cross over my chest before kissing my two fingers and lifting them up to the sky. Then I tore the envelope open and pulled out a folded sheet of white paper. My eyes scanned the random data on the page before I finally saw it.

"Probability of paternity is point-zero-zero percent," I read out loud. "Yes," I uttered, briefly closing my eyes to thank God. Although I'd knew the chances of my being the father were slim to none, because we'd never fucked without a condom, a weight was still lifted off my shoulders in that moment.

"Well, that's one less thing you have to worry about," Nika said, standing up from the sofa to stretch. "I'm getting ready to go, but—"

"Wait. Don't go," I told her, sounding damn desperate. I was lonely as fuck from being cooped up in this place around the clock.

"I have to. Myesha is keeping Nicholas for me, and I told her I wouldn't be long," she explained.

"Myesha? What? Her and Tez back in town?"

She shook her head. "Nah. They moved out here a couple of weeks after the wedding. Remember he opened up another security firm out here?"

"Damn," I mumbled to myself, thinking about how I was being kept out of the loop on everything these days.

She reached for her purse, then put it over her head in order to hang it across her body. "Just do me one favor?" She looked at me with pleading eyes.

"What's that?"

"Call Jornelle. She asks about you all the time."

Damn. Hearing her say that made me feel like such a deadbeat father. Sure, I sent a child support check every month, but the fact of the matter was, I wasn't there for my baby girl, just like my father had never been there for me. I wasn't contributing to who she was becoming in this world, and that shit fucked me up inside.

"I know," I sighed, wiping my hand over my face. "I'ma call her."

"Good. And one other thing. She asked me if she could come out here for fall break. She wants to spend time with her brother."

Jornelle wanting to spend time with baby Nicholas, coupled with the fact that she had taken a liking to Nika, made me smile a little bit. "Yeah, shawty, gon' 'head and set that shit up. That sounds good."

It had been seven whole days since I'd last seen or heard from Nika, and the truth was, I was missing her feisty little ass like crazy. Even though I had called my mama and fussed at her for putting Nika all in my business, I was grateful. If I didn't already know it before, I was quickly starting to realize that shawty was a real one. Having her in my corner was like a breath of fresh air, and the moment she walked out my door a week ago, I had made myself a promise that I was going to do whatever it took to get back in shawty's good graces.

To keep my mind on track, I continued working out three times a day, and I even made sure to call Jornelle every single night. Of course, every other word out of her mouth was "Nika this" and "baby Nicky that." It was crazy how just a few years ago, I wouldn't even mention Jornelle's name in front of Nika, because I didn't think she would fuck with a nigga that had kids, but now it seemed as though those two were tighter than a vise grip.

As I buttoned up my collar shirt, I glanced at myself in the mirror. Today was the last day of my inpatient rehab program, and they were having a little ceremony to celebrate our ninetieth day of sobriety. Because I didn't want the reminder of knowing just how badly I'd fucked my life up, I hadn't bothered inviting anyone. Plus was coming to pick me up afterward, and that was all I really needed.

After throwing my chain around my neck, I sprayed on a little bit of cologne before heading toward the door. Just as I reached for the doorknob, I glanced over my shoulder and saw my packed bags sitting on the bed. I couldn't wait until I got out of this place. I mean, yes, I would still have to go to rehab on an outpatient basis, but at least I wouldn't be cut off from the outside world. Plus, I had promised my baby girl that I would fly back home to Alabama just to see her, and I was looking forward to that.

Once I stepped out of my living quarters and locked everything up, I headed down the hall behind a few other recovering addicts in the program. When I got downstairs and entered the ceremony room, I noticed a lot of people were already there. The room was decorated with banners and balloons, and off to the side was a long table laden with cookies, cakes, and cups of red punch. To me, it was a bit juvenile, but it really didn't matter to me either way. I was just here to get my paper, in hopes of being able to play ball again.

As I made my way over to the separate seating area that was designated for those of us in the program, the sound of a baby crying immediately caught my attention. I turned around and was surprised to see Nika sitting there, bouncing my son in her lap. Although I had said I didn't want anyone to come to this ceremony, an instant smile formed on my lips. I thought it would be odd to see her with a baby . . . *my* baby, but it wasn't. In fact, she was somehow sexier to me in that moment. Her curly brown hair was pulled up loosely on the top of her head, allowing me to see all the silly faces she was making specifically for our son.

Her eyes were still cast down and focused on him when I walked over to her. "Shawty, you just a glutton for punishment, huh?" I asked jokingly.

When her eyes flew up to meet mine, we greeted each other with a matching smile. "Hey," she said coyly, standing up from her chair. "Congratulations."

Although I heard her loud and clear, I didn't respond, because my focus was on the chubby brown baby in her arms. He was wearing a Lakers jersey that snapped between his legs like a onesie.

Nika must have noticed, and she cleared her throat. "Um, Jorell," she said, gaining my attention. "This is your son . . . Nicholas."

"Damn. I thought it was just the pictures, but li'l nigga really ain't got no hair, huh?"

Nika smacked me on the arm and rolled her eyes.

"Nah, I'm just playing," I said with a chuckle. "He's handsome, just like his daddy." I took him from her and cradled him in my arms.

"Say hey to your daddy, Nicholas," she cooed.

When I leaned down and kissed the top of his soft little head, it reminded me so much of when Jornelle was this age, what with that baby smell and the extra softness of his skin. I was quickly realizing that I had a lot to live for, and I knew that if I didn't do better, I was going to lose it all. "Thank you," I told her.

Her eyebrows knit in confusion. "For what?"

"For coming today and bringing my son. Shit . . . ," I uttered, with a shrug. "For everything."

I knew that Nika wanted to respond, but there was this look in her eye that told me she couldn't find the right words.

All of a sudden, our moment was interrupted by the program director, who spoke into the microphone. "May I please have all the residents come up to the front?"

"Well, I guess I gotta get up there," I told her, placing baby Nicholas back into her arms.

She nodded her head. "Yeah. We'll be right here when it's over."

Taking the edges of her fingers into my hand, I leaned down and placed a quick kiss on her cheek. Then I kissed the top of my son's head once more. "I'll see y'all when this is over."

Chapter 26

Perri

With my face resting against Plus's shoulder, we both rode in the backseat of the car in complete silence. After a solid battle over the years, cancer had finally won the war against Ms. Rita. Although Plus and TK were no longer friends, we felt it was only right that we fly back home for his mother's funeral. Ms. Rita was one of the many women in the Millwood projects who had looked after us when we were young. While we were growing up, there'd been many nights when both Plus and I had eaten right from her kitchen table. And it had been nothing for Plus, Jamal, and me to camp out on her living-room floor after playing Madden until the wee hours of the morning.

When we first pulled up in front of Riverdale Baptist, I glanced out the tinted window. The church still looked the same, with the same large white pillars in front of the red double doors. There were so many people standing outside, on the church steps, waiting to get in, that I knew Plus's new security team wasn't going to let us out of the vehicle. They were with us around the clock these days.

After we waited another ten minutes or so, I felt Plus's hand slide down to my exposed knee. "Aye, look." He nodded forward with his head.

I scooted up to the edge of my seat and peered out the window. Stepping out of a black limousine, and dressed in an all-black suit, with shades blocking his eyes, was TK. I then noticed a little person getting out behind him. "Is that his son?" I asked, looking over at Plus.

With his eyes still looking out the window, he nodded his head. "Yeah, I think so."

I didn't know if Plus was expecting to see Tasha among the crowd or not, but from what I could tell, she wasn't here now. However, we did see Jamal and Shivon out there, along with a few other people from around the way. I watched as TK led his son by the hand up the stairs of the church. Behind them was a long line of people whom I assumed were other family members. That was the cue for our security team.

"Mrs. P," our security guy, Big John, said as he opened the car door. He was just as tall as Plus, only he had about a hundred pounds more of muscle on him. For the past couple of months, Big John and I had pretty much been inseparable. Every trip to the grocery store, the pediatrician's office, he had been there, and he'd even taken me to my job interview last week. Thank God I actually liked the guy.

I eased out of the car and stepped onto the curb before taking in the gray sky. It seemed like the weather had somehow captured the solemn mood of the day's events. When Plus got out after me, my eyes shifted to his tall frame. He was dressed in a navy blue Tom Ford suit. My husband had *always* been fine in my eyes, but these days Plus looked like money. Gently, he pulled at the lapels of his jacket before grabbing my hand to link his fingers with mine. Side by side, we walked up the brick stairs of the church. We could already hear the organ playing inside.

"Damn, yo. I can't believe Ms. Rita's gone," he said lowly.

"I know."

Both Big John and another security guard on the team opened the church doors and led us the rest of the way inside. The sounds of people in mourning echoed all throughout the church nave. It was sad, to say the least, and even though I hadn't spoken directly to TK, my heart went out to him. I had lost my mother to cancer when I was just six years old, and even though I was now a grown woman, the shit still hurt, so I could only imagine what he was going through.

When Plus and I quietly slid into a row behind Jamal and Shivon, I could suddenly feel people's eyes on us, accompanied by the sound of their hushed whispers. Plus was now a celebrity, and whether he was back home or not, he still got stares. Before sitting down in the pew, Plus placed his hand on Jamal's shoulder, letting him know that we were there. Jamal gave a quick pat to the top of his hand in acknowledgment.

After all the programs and Kleenex had been passed out, Reverend McDonaugh walked out and took the podium. Midway through his sermon, during which he spoke of Ms. Rita finally resting in heaven, I caught someone strolling past my peripheral. It seemed to me that my and Plus's head both turned at the exact same time, and our eyes were met with the sight of Tasha traipsing down the aisle. She wore a black minidress, with black pumps. On her head was a floppy black church hat, and she, too, had her eyes hidden behind a pair of oversize black shades.

Plus pushed out a little snort of laughter through his nose before shaking his head. "That's Tasha for you," he mumbled.

"Shh," I told him, following her with my eyes. I thought she was going to sit up front with TK and the rest of the family, but she surprised me by finding a seat on the opposite side of the church.

When it was time for us to say our final goodbyes to Ms. Rita and walk up to the casket, Plus held on to me real tight. Other than getting a little teary eyed, he hadn't cried this entire time, and he didn't now. But another grown man's crying finally broke me. TK's sobs were so loud, I was sure he could be heard all the way outside.

As we got closer to Ms. Rita, my heart beat faster and faster inside my chest. When we finally approached the casket, my legs grew weak. I wept over her lifeless body, and Plus held me up by the waist and did his best to comfort me. Before we walked back to our seats, we stopped in front of TK to give our condolences.

"I'm so sorry, TK," I said. Sniffing back tears, I leaned down to hug his neck.

He embraced me back and nodded his head to acknowledge my words of comfort. Although he still had those shades covering his eyes, I knew tears were flowing underneath from just how flushed his face was.

"I'm sorry for your loss, man," Plus offered.

"Thanks, man. Y'all coming back to the house? For the repast?" TK said, sounding hopeful.

With a reluctant expression on his face, Plus scratched the top of his head. We had decided to come to the funeral only out of respect for Ms. Rita, but going back to TK's home wasn't a part of the plan. However, the despair in TK's voice made me realize just how much he really needed Plus to be there.

"Yeah, TK, we'll be there," I told him.

Once the service was over, security escorted us to our car and drove us back to Millwood. Big John strongly advised against it, because of the "rough" area, but Plus and I assured him that everything would be okay. *Hell*, we were back at home.

As soon we turned in, I half expected to see dopeboys on the corners and kids running up and down the littered streets, but today the neighborhood was actually quiet. When we pulled up in front of TK's home, Big John got out and jogged around the car to let us out. For some reason, that seemed to catch the attention of everyone standing outside.

Stepping out, I could hear people shouting out Plus's name.

"Taylor!" they said.

"That's my nigga Plus!"

"It's big homie!"

They were snapping pictures and recording videos on their phones, all a part of showing him some love. After this past year I had finally gotten used to Plus's celebrity, but he still didn't care for it, especially not at times like this. Humbly, Plus chucked up his chin and threw his two fingers in the air to salute as we made our way inside.

As we inched into the small home, which was damn near crowded from wall to wall, we searched left and right for TK. With our two bodyguards squeezing in behind us, we finally found him. He was at the back of the house, in the kitchen, with Jamal and a few of his family members. When we walked in, I quickly recognized his aunt Jackie, who was uncovering aluminum trays of food on the counter. TK sat at the table with Jamal and two other guys, and they were playing a game of dominos. His suit jacket was off, and a few top buttons of his shirt were undone, giving him a more relaxed look. He, along with everyone else in the house, didn't appear as sad as he had in the church.

Feeling our presence in the tiny room, he lifted his eyes up from the table. "Y'all made it," TK said, eyes lighting up with surprise.

Plus slipped his hands into the pockets of his pants before he rocked back on his heels. "Yeah, yo, we told you we was gon' fall through."

Upon hearing his voice, TK's aunt Jackie whipped her head around to face us. "Oh my God! Little Plus," she said, shaking her head. She came over and immediately gave him a hug. "Every time someone talks about Ahmad Taylor from the Lakers, I tell 'em I knew him since he was a little boy. That's Plus," she said, beaming.

Wearing a bashful smirk, Plus tilted his head.

"And how you been, baby?" She cut her eyes over at me.

"I've been doing all right," I said.

"I tell everybody I know his wife too. I seen y'all's beautiful wedding pictures in one of the magazines at the grocery store. You looked absolutely breathtaking," she said. Her eyes instantly dropped down to my Prada-covered feet, then slowly roamed back up to my face. "You sure have grown into one gorgeous young woman." She turned back to TK and the group sitting at the table. "Ain't she, y'all? Remember when she used to run behind y'all like she was one of the guys?"

I shook my head. "Nah, they used to run behind me," I said quickly, correcting her.

Everybody in the room fell out laughing at that.

Suddenly I could feel someone running up behind us. When I turned around, Big John already had his hand up to block a couple of guys I'd never seen before. "Aye, we just wanted an autograph, yo," one of them said, holding a small white piece of paper in his hand, along with an ink pen.

"Back up," Big John warned.

"It's all right, Big John," Plus said. He grabbed the pen and paper from the young guy's hand and signed a fast autograph for him. Just as he was passing it back over, a few more people rushed into the kitchen, wanting the exact same thing.

With a scowl etched on his face, TK slid his chair back and stood up from the table. "Nah, he ain't come here for all 'at, yo. Go back into the other room!" he told them.

"Aw, man," I could hear a few of them moan.

"My bad," TK said. Then he pulled up an empty chair. "Come have a seat, yo."

I glanced over at Plus, and because we were so in tune with one another, I already knew what he was thinking. He'd come only to pay his respect; he didn't want to be too friendly with TK, not even given the situation. Placing a soothing hand on his muscular back, I nodded my head toward the chair. Hesitantly, he walked over and sat down before patting his thigh. I knew that was for me, because all the other seats were taken.

When I sat down in his lap, TK let out a snort of laughter and shook his head.

"What?" I asked, giving him a curious look.

"Girl, you don' changed," he said, then let out a light laugh.

I shrugged. "I'm not a girl anymore. I'm a—"

"She's a married woman," his aunt Jackie said, cutting in. She placed a plate down on the table in front of me. "Y'all eat up."

I glanced back at Plus, who discreetly shook his head. I, on the other hand, was completely hungry, and the fried chicken, collard greens, and macaroni and cheese in front of me were calling my name. I quickly grabbed a fork and dug in.

"Yeah, Jamal was telling me all about the wedding and shit," TK said, placing a domino down in the center of the table.

"And I guess he told you about our disastrous reception too?" I asked, then took a swallow from the memory.

Jamal chuckled, then placed his domino next to TK's.

"Nah, but he ain't have to. Shit was all over the news." He paused. "How's your boy doing, anyway?" TK asked, looking over at Plus for a response.

Plus scratched behind his ear and let out a deep sigh. "Jorell's doing good. Getting his shit together."

Although TK nodded his head, I could only imagine the sense of jealousy coursing through him. I mean, let's face it. Jorell had, it seemed, taken TK's place when it came to Plus. Jorell was now Plus's right-hand man and had even been a part of our wedding.

"Where's your daddy?" I suddenly heard behind me.

I turned around in Plus's lap to see Tasha standing in the entryway of the kitchen. My eyes then shifted down to her son, who was planted by her side. He was a cute little boy, with skin a shade darker than TK's pale complexion, and he had a head full of soft brown curls. Those same bright blue eyes that I'd familiarized myself with during elementary school flickered back at me, and I couldn't help but to smile.

Tasha looked at Big John, who was positioned in the corner, before smacking her teeth. "Do I need to leave him here or take him with me?" she asked, with an attitude.

"Just leave him here," TK said, sounding annoyed.

"Well, who's gonna watch him?"

"Man, all this family around here, he'll be all right. Besides, who else watches him while he's here?" It was obvious that, that was a rhetorical question.

Tasha rolled her eyes before nudging the little boy farther into the kitchen. Without uttering another word, she spun around on her heels and took off. It was all of five seconds after she left when everyone erupted in laughter.

"Damn," TK muttered, then gave a light chuckle. "The biggest mistake of my fucking life, yo." He shook his head and placed another domino down on the table.

"Nah, don't say that," Plus said, cutting his eyes over at the little boy. "What's your name, li'l man?"

In my head I said a quick silent prayer that it wasn't still Ahmad, Jr., after all this time.

"Terrance," the boy whispered, with his eyes cast down to the floor. He was shy.

"Well, my name is Plus."

With his head and eyes still hung low, the little boy twiddled his hands and whispered, "I know who you are."

I glanced back at Plus, saw that his eyebrows had hiked up out of curiosity. "You do?"

"Yeah, you're my uncle. The one that plays ball for the Lakers." Little Terrance sounded so sure.

My eyes shifted over to TK, who wore a less than embarrassed expression on his face.

But I think Plus surprised us all when he said, "Yeah, man. Now come give Unc a five," and held out his hand.

Terrance ambled over and slapped his palm against Plus's before running over to grab ahold of his aunt Jackie's legs.

"This boy is so shy," she said, looking down at him as she stood by the kitchen counter. "I told his mama he needs to be around kids more."

"Well, he can play with Camille this week, while we're here," I offered.

TK nodded his head. "Yeah, that sounds good." Then he paused. "I thought y'all were heading back today."

"Nah, man. We'll be here all week, before camp starts next Tuesday," Plus said.

"Yeah, I guess it is that time again. Y'all did good in the playoffs, though. Sorry y'all ain't make it to the finals," TK told him.

Plus shrugged his shoulders, then licked his lips. "It's all goodie, yo. We definitely gon' be there this year."

I nodded my head, silently agreeing. We had lost to Golden State, which had resulted in them playing against the Cavaliers in the finals.

For another two hours, we sat around the table, talking, and at one point, we even joined the game of bones. When I gazed out the window, I saw that nightfall had hit. More than half of TK's guests had left, and his aunt Jackie had cleaned the entire kitchen. I grabbed the back of my neck for a brief squeeze before letting out a little yawn.

"Aye, man, we getting ready to get outta here. The missus is tired," Plus said. He lifted me from his lap, then leaned over to slap hands with Jamal.

"Y'all be safe, man," Jamal said.

TK rose from the table. "Let me walk y'all out," he offered.

After giving TK's aunt Jackie and little Terrance a hug, we followed Big John to the front door. When we got out to the porch, we heard the crickets chirping in the night.

TK placed his hand on Plus's shoulder. "Aye, I know I didn't say anything before now, but I just want to thank you for the money you sent for the funeral," he said.

I had completely forgot that when we found out Ms. Rita had passed, Plus sent a check for ten thousand dollars to help out with the funeral.

Plus shook his head, unwilling to accept TK's gratitude. "Nah, Ms. Rita was like another mother to me."

TK put his hand out for Plus and brought him in for a brotherly hug. "Don't forget about getting the kids together this week."

"I won't forget," I told him.

With that, we walked to the car and got in, and Big John closed the door behind us. As we rode back over to Tez's old place, which was now occupied by Ms. Tonya, I laid my head on Plus's lap. He softly grazed my scalp with his fingers, making my heavy eyelids flutter.

"That was good," he said lowly.

"What?"

"Not the reason why we were there, but . . ."

"You and TK?"

"Yeah. I think I'm finally over that shit. I mean, don't get me wrong. I'll never trust that nigga again, but as far as him and Tasha goes . . . I'm over it."

I patted the top of his knee with my hand. "Good, *honey*." I yawned before closing my eyes.

After a few seconds of silence had passed, with Plus still massaging my scalp, he said, "Bae?"

"Hmm?"

"You asleep?"

When I didn't answer, I felt him shift back in his seat to relax. I hated that Ms. Rita had had to pass in order for Plus and TK to finally speak, but I was truly thankful. It was one less negative thing that Plus had to carry with him from day to day. We had too many positive things going on in our lives these days to let something from our past be a burden. TK was family, even after all the wrong he'd done. I was just glad Plus was finally coming around and recognizing that.

Chapter 27

Nika

"You need any help in there?" Grandma asked from the living room.

I snapped the lid shut on a bowl of potato salad, then looked at the pots cooking on the stove. "No, Grandma. I got it. The turkey's almost done," I told her.

It was two days before Thanksgiving, and we were celebrating early since the Lakers had a game. After I cut the fire down on the gravy, I went to join Grandma on the sofa, where she was holding Nicholas on her lap. At nine months old, he was as fat as could be, with rolls under his chin and even on his arms. He still didn't have much hair on his head, but what he did have, I made sure to brush down smooth against his scalp. His skin was dark chocolate, and I was often told that he looked like a Cabbage Patch doll.

"You have spoiled this baby rotten, chile," Grandma said, looking down at Nicholas, who was trying to squirm his way over to me.

"Aw, he's not spoiled," I cooed, holding my arms out for him to come to me. "He just loves his mama."

Just as soon as I had him in my arms, a knock sounded on the door.

I stood up and, with Nicholas on my hip, went over to look out the peephole. It was Jorell.

"Well, hello there," I said after opening the door. I felt Nicholas bounce excitedly in my arms at the mere sight of his father. If Grandma thought that I was the sole culprit when it came to Nicholas being spoiled, she would soon learn otherwise.

Jornelle stepped into the apartment first. "Hey, Ms. Nika," she said, greeting me with a hug around the waist. Meechie and Jorell had finally come to a shared custody agreement, and according to it, he would get Jornelle every other Thanksgiving and Christmas, every spring break, and for the entire summer. So far she had kept her word and had even agreed to back off on raising his child support.

Before Jorell could even make it in the house, Nicholas reached out for him, with a soft cry.

"There goes my li'l man," Jorell said, taking him from me.

Holding Nicholas in one of his arms, Jorell reached out to hug me with other. I leaned in and wrapped my arms around him, took in the earthy scent of his cologne as I closed my eyes. Although Jorell would often talk of us getting back together, I had tried my best to keep our relationship strictly on a co-parenting level. Jorell had hurt me too many times for me to even be open to that idea, and as long as he was a good father to Nicholas, that was all that mattered.

While I removed Jornelle's coat, Jorell walked over to greet Grandma. "Hey, Grandma," he said, bending toward the sofa to kiss her cheek.

"So it's you that's been spoiling that baby, huh?" she asked, peering at him over the top rim of her glasses.

"See? I told you it wasn't me," I tossed over my shoulder as I made my way back to the kitchen.

While I bent down and checked the turkey in the oven, I felt Jorell come up behind me. I stood up straight and jumped a little before turning around. "Boy," I squealed, smacking him across his swollen chest with the kitchen towel that was in my hand.

He licked his lips and cracked a sexy grin, exposing the gold in his mouth. "Shawty, what you burning up in here?"

"I can cook, thank you," I sassed, closing the oven door. I peeled back the aluminum foil on the candied sweet potatoes that were on the counter and dipped into them with a spoon. "Here. Taste this," I said before blowing off the heat.

Jorell stood with his legs wide apart and placed his hands on each side of my hips as he opened up his mouth. His eyes closed in a sensual-like manner when I placed the spoon in his mouth. "Mmm," he groaned. "Yeah, you put yo' foot in that, shawty," he complimented, nodding his head.

"See, I told you." I spun back around to face the stove and cut off my pot of greens.

"What else can I try?" he asked, placing his chin on my shoulder. Whenever we were around each other, Jorell was always flirty and touchy feely, so I was used to it.

"Nothing. You're gonna have to wait till it's time for dinner."

He sucked his teeth, then moved beside me and rested his lower back against the counter. "I like what you've done to your new place," he said, glancing back into the living room.

I'd been in my new apartment for only about a week, but it was already fully furnished and decorated. My job at the hospital had afforded me three bedrooms and two baths in Moorpark. I really liked the area, and I already had plans in my head to purchase my own home around here in about another two years.

"Yeah, you need to let me do something to yours," I told him, taking a clean spoon to stir the pot of gravy. Jorell had also moved recently into a less expensive apartment out in Burbank.

"For what? I'm gon' barely be there," he reminded me. After completing his outpatient rehab program, Jorell had been fully reinstated with the Lakers and had been on the road a lot.

"Well, I'm sure you want Jornelle to feel at home when she comes to visit, and Nicholas too."

"But we can just all stay here with you," he said matter-of-factly.

I cocked my head to the side and looked at him like he was crazy. "Your children need their own space in your home, Jorell."

He reached over and pinched the side of my waist. "When you gon' stop playing with a nigga, anyway?"

I sighed. "What are you talking about?" I asked, knowing *exactly* what he was referring to. There hadn't been a single time since I saw Jorell at the inpatient rehab ceremony that he didn't mention us getting back together.

"I'm talking about us being a family. Let me move in here—"

I cut him off with a shake of my head. "Uh-uh, Jorell. That's the problem. You and I always move way too fast." I was always opening my heart and legs for this man without making him work for it. Without thinking of the repercussions.

"Well, look," he said with a stroke of his chin. "Why don't you let me take you out?"

My left eyebrow rose. "Like a date?"

"Yeah. Like a date."

Mulling it over in my head, I released a deep breath. "If you set it up, I'll find a sitter." When he started grinning, I held my finger up. "*But*, there will be no fucking," I

whispered, to make sure Grandma or Jornelle wouldn't
hear me in the other room.

Jorell sucked his teeth again and gave a slight roll of his
eyes. "Shawty, you know you miss this," he said, reaching
down to the front of his gray sweatpants to grab himself.

Lord knows I did.

With my heart rate picking up speed, I didn't confirm
or deny it. I just kept my eyes preoccupied with the stove
in front of me.

He let out a light snort from his nose. "It's all good, la'
baby," he said, making me turn to look over at his handsome face. "I'ma work for it. You deserve that much." He
licked his dark brown lips, then circled around and exited
the kitchen.

Blowing out a deep breath, one I hadn't even realized
I was holding, I leaned forward and grabbed the edges
of the stove. After I cut off the remaining burners, along
with the turkey in the oven, I yelled out into the other
room, "Jornelle! Come help me set the table, baby."

Today was Jorell's first free day after being on the road
for two weeks, and he'd followed through by asking to
take me out. Since Perri was busy with her new job as the
assistant coach of the women's basketball team at Loyola
Marymount University, I had asked Myesha to babysit. It
seemed that ever since I'd dropped Nicholas off with her
earlier this morning, my nerves had grown by the hour. It
was completely unexplainable, because this wasn't some
first date with a man I didn't know. I was around Jorell
all the time. This wasn't our first time going out, nor did I
believe it would be our last.

Because I knew it would be chilly later on, I decided on
a long-sleeved cream-colored sweater that crisscrossed
in the back. High-waisted light blue jeans hugged the

curves of my lower half, and I wore a pair of rust leather riding boots on my feet. Natural brown curls framed my bare face, and I coated my lips with a nude gloss I had just gotten from Sephora. After misting my wrists with Versace Bright Crystal perfume, I gave myself the once-over in the long mirror on the back of my bedroom door.

Just then a hard series of taps sounded at my front door, and I glanced over at the digital clock on my nightstand.

Five twenty-eight. He's early.

Tugging down my sweater a tad bit more, I ambled to the front of the apartment. Although I knew it was Jorell on the other side of the door, I still glanced out the peephole. I smiled when I saw his face, partly hidden by what appeared to be a dozen red roses. I quickly unlocked the door and yanked it open.

"Well, hello there," I said, greeting him with unforeseen excitement in my voice.

Without uttering a word, he leaned in and placed a gentle kiss on my cheek before passing me the bouquet of flowers.

"Aw, thank you. They're beautiful," I told him, realizing that this was the very first time he'd ever bought me flowers.

"Beautiful flowers for a beautiful woman," he said, with a wink of his eye, obviously putting on the charm.

My eyes slowly consumed him, taking in his freshly twisted locks, which were pulled back from his dark, handsome face. He was easy on the eyes in dark blue Balmain jeans and a white fitted T-shirt that clung to his chest. On his feet were black leather Balmain boots, which paired nicely with the leather motorcycle jacket he wore. Then there was what I liked to call his "sparkle" or wow factor. It was the diamond-encrusted watch on his wrist, the platinum chain around his neck, and the sparkly earring in his ear.

"You look nice," he said, obviously noticing that my eyes were observing him.

I cleared my throat. "Um . . . so do you," I said before bringing the flowers to my nose for a quick sniff to mask my slight embarrassment.

After putting my flowers in a vase of water, I grabbed my leather jacket, and we headed out the door. As we took the stairs, I could feel Jorell's hand guiding me at the small of my back. It was a simple gesture, but just enough to send tingles down my spine. Once we were outside, with the evening breeze hitting our faces, I saw a black Jaguar S-Type stretch limousine parked out front. I didn't want to assume that it was for us, so my eyes immediately started roaming, in search of Jorell's cherry-red Impala. But then I caught the limo driver opening the back door.

Taken aback, I cut my eyes instantly over at Jorell. "For us?" I asked.

He gave a slow nod of his head. "Of course," he said, directing me to the limo with his hand.

Once we were inside the limo and were cruising down Highway 405, Jorell reached over and grabbed me by the hand. After interlacing his fingers with mine, he pulled my hand up to his mouth for an easy kiss.

"Come sit with me," he said, referring to the scant inches of space between us.

I let out a small laugh before scooting my frame closer to him. "Where are we going?" I asked.

"You'll see," he said, looking out the window. Then he shifted his gaze back to me. "You trust me?"

I gave him what I was sure was a skeptical look.

"Too soon?" He smirked.

"Too soon," I agreed.

After another fifteen minutes, we reached Marina del Rey. I stared out the window in awe, taking in the bright Christmas lights that floated across the water.

"You ever been to the Christmas boat parade?" Jorell asked.

With my eyes still on the pier, I shook my head no.

After we exited the car, Jorell strapped two folding chairs to his back, along with a backpack. As we trekked among the crowd of parade goers, he stopped to buy me a funnel cake, something he knew I'd been craving for the longest time. I quickly dug into it as we walked, listening to the Christmas carols that poured from the outdoor speakers. Then we arrived at this perfect spot on the pier, where we could see the lights on every boat out in the water. After we sat down in the chairs he had set up for us, Jorell draped my shoulders with a warm blanket he must've had hidden in his backpack.

As I peered out at the boats, I heard Jorell chuckling beside me. "What?" I turned to look at him.

He shook his head. "Nothing," he said, and then he softly grazed his thumb across my cheek. "You just got white powder on your face." Our eyes locked, and a surge of butterflies fluttered in the pit of my stomach. "Shawty, you pretty as hell, you know that?"

Even in the cool night's breeze, I could feel my cheeks heating up. "Thank you," I mouthed.

Jorell reached down into his backpack again and pulled out a thermos. From it, he poured us two cups of hot chocolate. As we drank and nibbled the remains of the cold funnel cake in my lap, loud, bright bursts of color scattered across the darkened sky. I swear, the scene before us was a sight to behold, with the boats beautifully decorated in colorful Christmas lights and the sparkling fireworks soaring high above us in the air. I felt like a wonder-struck child as I watched all the magic unfold.

When the fireworks show was over, I turned in my seat to face him. "Thank you for this," I told him, grabbing him by the hand.

He shrugged his shoulders, as if it were no big deal. "What? It was a cheap date."

My head flew back from my laughter as I smacked him lightly on the arm. "Well, you could always feed me, you know," I suggested.

He stood from the chair and reached for my hand. "Come on," he said, tipping his head in the other direction.

"What about the chairs . . . and your blanket?" I asked.

"Leave them."

Again, his fingers locked with mine, and he led me down the pier until we were facing a row of small white yachts.

"What's this?" I could feel my eyebrows gather.

A smirk played at his lips before he gave me a wink. "You'll see."

He led me up the small stairs of a yacht named the *Betty Lou 6*, and at the top we were greeted by two women wearing black vests and dress pants.

"Welcome to the *Betty Lou 6*. Are you ready to take a ride?" one of them asked.

I glanced over my shoulder at Jorell, who seemed to be amused by my staggered expression.

"You ready to take a ride, la' baby?" he asked, making his eyebrows jump.

Unsure of what to say, I gave him a closed-lip smile.

We were then led to a small area of the boat where a small table covered in a white linen cloth had been set up. Fire flickered from the two pillar candles that had been placed on top of the table, and a red rose was nestled in between them. Off to the side was a cart, and on it were meals arranged on silver trays.

When I realized what he had done, I planted my palms on my cheeks. My mouth was practically on the deck. "Wow! You did all this for me?" I asked.

Jorell brought my hand up to his lips again. "Why not? You deserve this and much more."

I shook my head, unsure of exactly what else to say. I had never been on a romantic date like this, where everything had been so well thought out. *So perfect.*

Just as we sat down at the table, the yacht pulled off into the bay. We were served filet mignon, garlic mashed potatoes, and asparagus tips, along with a glass of Dom Pérignon. While Jorell seemed to devour his food, I chewed and sipped rather slowly.

"What's wrong? You don't like it?" he asked.

I shook my head. "No, it's delicious. I just want to take my time and enjoy it," I told him honestly.

Tilting his head, he narrowed his eyes, in doubt. "Shawty, you sure? 'Cause they got shrimp too."

"No, everything is perfect. Really," I assured him before forking a dollop of mashed potatoes into my mouth.

"So how's the job coming?" he asked casually, slowing down his intake to match mine.

"It's going really good. I think they want to pay for me to go back to school."

"Back to school?" He cocked his head to the side. "For what?"

"To get my MRI certification."

The corners of his lips curled as he gave a slow nod of his head. "That's what's up. I'm proud of you."

"Thank you."

Things got quiet for a second, so I took that opportunity to cut off another piece of steak. But that was when I heard him push a large breath of air from his lungs.

"So, look," he said, causing my eyes to lift from my plate. "I know I've said this to you a time or two before, but I really just want to say thanks for holding me down when I really needed you."

Hearing this same speech of gratitude for what felt like the hundredth time, I slowly nodded my head. I knew Jorell wanted me to know how appreciative he was for all that I'd done, but what he didn't seem to realize was that I'd do it all over again without so much as a second thought. Not only was he my son's father, but he was also my friend.

He went on. "I know I cussed your black ass out for being all in my finances and shit." He licked his lips and placed his hand over his heart. "But I'm forever grateful. After all the stuff I pulled with you, it's just a blessing that yo' ass is even still talking to me."

I let out a laugh and shook my head. "It wouldn't benefit me not to talk to you. You're the father of my son," I said.

He lowered his chin and peered into my eyes. "That's all I am to you?" he asked evenly.

"And . . . a good friend," I said, hiking my left shoulder in a semi-shrug.

His tongue glided sexily to the back of his mouth before his lips curved into a smirk. Then, slowly, he nodded his head, as if to say touché. I knew he wanted me to say that we were more, perhaps that I even loved him, but tonight was all about me for once. On the inside, I fought against my natural urge to further boost his ego. Silence fell over the table, and I got lost in contemplation.

Our quiet thoughts were suddenly interrupted by the sound of his cell phone buzzing on the table. He glanced down at it and quickly silenced it with a tap of his fingers.

"Answer it," I told him, surprising myself. Although it wasn't my exact intention, I thought he and I both knew it was some kind of test.

"Nah. We on a date. I ain't doing that."

My shoulders hiked in a nonchalant manner. "Just answer it. It's fine," I urged.

He looked down at the screen again before letting out a deep sigh. "Yuh," he answered lowly, agitation playing all over his face.

Then, nervously, he scratched the top of his head. "Nah, I'm out with my girl right now," he said, shifting his gaze to me. There was a brief pause before he shook his head and said, "I doubt it." Then, slowly, he wiped his hand down over his lower jaw before letting out another deep breath. It was obvious that he was uncomfortable. "Shawty, I'm done with that shit, fa real. I'm not 'bout dat life no mo'," he declared, allowing his deep Southern accent to finally cut through. He nodded his head a few more times, then said, "A'ight. Check you later. Fo' sho'." And then he ended the call.

He looked at me. "You wanna know who that was?" he asked.

I shook my head almost too quickly unsure if I really did or didn't want to know.

"Well, I'ma tell you, anyway. That was this stripper chick that I used to fuck with."

My nose scrunched up at that.

"She was the one that put me onto that white girl, ya feel me?" He looked at me with a raised brow to make sure I fully understood.

"So what'd she want?" I asked out of curiosity.

He shrugged his shoulders. "For us to kick it, I guess. But fuck that. I ain't finna go back to the shit I was into with her."

A moment of silence passed between us before I finally said, "Can I ask you something?"

"Yeah, shawty. What's up?"

"What made you turn to drugs? I mean, you're an athlete, so I can't even imagine what . . ." My voice trailed off, as my inner thoughts took over and I tried to understand.

With a reluctant expression on his face, Jorell scratched the side of his nose. I could tell he was mulling over exactly what to say and how to say it. "To be honest, it was a lot of shit. I just felt like I was being smothered. Smothered by debt, smothered by drama wit' my baby's mom. I wasn't getting no play time, when I felt like I was one of the better players on the fucking team. Then, when Nard got locked up, that shit really fucked with me. We grew up more like brothers than cousins, ya feel me?"

I nodded my head, understanding. "I know how close you two are."

"Then, out of the blue, some nigga pops up at my door, talkin' 'bout he's my father." He let out a snort and shook his head. "I got a whole sister and brother out here that I ain't even met before." I could hear the pain in his voice. Then suddenly his eyes shifted over to me.

"What?" I asked.

"Then there was you."

"Me?" I was confused. I knew I had withheld Nicholas from him, but his habit had started well before he even knew about the baby.

He nodded his head. "Yuh, you. I knew a while ago that you was where I wanted to be, but I kept telling myself, 'I'm not good enough for her right now. But I'm gon' get my shit together, and then I'ma go scoop my girl.' Ya feel me? But it was always something, one thing after the fucking other, that seemed to make that shit impossible for me and . . ." He shook his head. "I just couldn't breathe no mo'. I needed something, *anything*, to take all the bullshit away. To make me stop thinking of it all. And that coke . . ." His eyebrow lifted at the mere mention of that drug. "That shit seemed to work, up until I saw you at the wedding."

I reached across the table and gently gripped his hand. "Jorell, you've always been good enough for me. I've never asked you to be anybody else but who you already are."

He nodded his head. "I'm finally getting that now," he said.

"What I need is for you to be there for Nicholas."

"And what if I wanna be there for you too?" he asked lowly.

"Then we need trust and complete honesty."

When we were done eating our entrées and the crème brûlée for dessert, we took a seat over by the window. I immediately got comfortable and removed the boots from my feet. Peering out, I took in the moonlight that hit the soft ripples of the bay. As we traveled along, the Christmas lights grew smaller in the distance. Then suddenly, out of nowhere, I released a full-bodied yawn.

"You sleepy?" he asked.

I quickly covered my mouth in shame.

"Damn. It's like that? I'm boring you?" he said with a chuckle.

I shook my head. "No. It's just that being on the water is so relaxing, and you know Nicholas doesn't really let me get much sleep."

Jorell pulled at my feet, which were tucked under my thighs. "Here," he said, taking my feet in his hands. "Just lie back and close your eyes."

I pursed my lips to the side. "I'm not going to sleep on our date, Jorell."

"Why not? You're a working mother, and you need your rest too."

I thought about it for a few seconds before lying back against one of the decorative pillows on the bench. My eyes immediately closed when Jorell began kneading my feet with his hands.

An involuntary moan slipped from my lips. "Mmm."

"Look, I'm tryin'a be good, shawty, but don't start that moaning shit, a'ight?"

I howled in laughter before sitting up on my elbows and locking my gaze with his. Jorell must have caught on that the heaviness in my eyes wasn't just from fatigue. Without warning, he leaned over and crashed his soft lips against mine. I didn't hesitate to push my tongue into his mouth and kiss him back with complete fervor and intensity.

When he finally pulled back, he brushed the backs of his fingers across my cheek. "I love you, Nika," he whispered, causing my lips to part slightly from shock.

He shook his head and put a single finger over my lips. "Don't worry about saying it back. I know I still got some proving to do, too, and I'm still committed to doing that. I just wanted you to know how I feel."

In that moment, I could literally feel my heart as it skipped a beat inside my chest.

Chapter 28

Plus

Summer 2012 . . .

Carrying the ball down the court between my legs, I pitched a quick glance up at the play clock. We had one minute and twelve seconds left till the buzzer. It was us versus the Celtics in the championship , and through every quarter, we'd been shot for shot. We were now down by five, and the entire arena seemed to be on their feet, erupting in a chanted roar. Out of forty-five minutes total, I'd played thirty-six in the game. I was beyond exhausted but knew I still had to fight.

"Aye, yo. Get open," I called to Jorell. He was low post, trying to get free, but Cook was on his ass. After being back seven months in the league, Jorell had proven himself threefold and was now getting almost as much play time as me. Both the fans and the media loved his comeback story.

As I approached the top of the key, my eyes shot down to Bynum, who was battling Durant under the rim. *Fuck.* He wasn't open, either. Making a split-second decision, I faked to the right on Harden, then pulled up for a three.

Swoosh!

The crowd went wild again, as it was now a two-point game. After we charged back to the other side of the court, I kept close to Harden, making him pass the rock over to number fourteen. He tried for a three, but the ball bounced back hard off the rim. Bynum recovered the rebound and did a chest pass down the court to me. As soon as I felt the ball in my hands, my eyes went up to the play clock. We were down to twenty-two seconds.

My heart was pounding so loudly, it seemed to drown out the sound of the crowd. I slowed the ball in an effort to eat time off the clock. My eyes cut down to Bynum, then over to Jorell, who was surprisingly open. I dribbled past Harden toward the goal, then faked a finger roll before shooting the ball over to Jorell, who was posted low for three. He didn't hesitate to pull the trigger. My breath stalled as I watched the ball float in midair, in what seemed to be slow motion. *Three, two, one.* At the exact same time the buzzer sounded in the arena, the ball fell through the net of the hoop. Cheers went up from the crowd.

We are champions.

As purple and gold confetti fell on us from the ceiling, fans rushed onto the court. Everyone was so excited, I couldn't hear a thing, and although I could barely see through the crowd, I searched all over for my brother. Jorell had been lifted on the shoulders of a few team-mates, but when I approached, they let him down. Even though it wasn't the manliest of moments, tears were in our eyes. We dapped each other up and held each other in a one-arm embrace, which only he and I understood. That was until Coach brought the championship trophy over to us. Together, we lifted it high in the air and held it up, allowing the various photographers to take their shots.

Then suddenly I felt a pair of familiar hands going around my waist. I looked back to see Perri standing behind me. She was all smiles and had nothing but pride in her bright-colored eyes. I released my hold on the trophy, then spun around and lifted her up in the air.

"Oh my God, Plus! You did it," she squealed loudly against my ear.

Not caring about the sweat covering my face or my dampened clothes, she wrapped her arms around me and suffocated me with a kiss. I knew the media caught the moment, based on the bright flashing lights in our faces, but I didn't care. I sucked on her tongue and enjoyed the sweetness of her mouth, as if we were the only ones in the arena.

Just when I put her down and her feet touched the court, the sportscaster Erin Andrews appeared, with a microphone in her hand.

"Ahmad Taylor, how does it feel to be this year's NBA champion?" she asked.

I was smiling so damn hard, my face hurt. "It feels amazing. I've worked so hard to get here, and I'm just thankful for such an amazing team."

"You had a total of thirty-four points in tonight's game, playing thirty-eight minutes total. What kept you going?"

"Where I come from, you don't stop. No matter how tired you are, you don't give up. And it's always this little lady right here that keeps me going." I pulled Perri around from where she was hiding behind my back. "She and my daughter are all the motivation I need."

Erin grinned. "So, MVP?" she asked.

"That's what they're saying." I shrugged. "But it's however it shakes out. I'm just happy for the win."

She nodded her head in understanding. "And now that you've won, what's your next move?"

I glanced down at Perri, who was tucked under my arm, and let out a light laugh. "We're going to Disneyland!"

Even though the saying had been coined at the Super Bowl, ever since Michael Jordan won in ninety-one, I'd wanted to say that shit. Perri knew the inside joke, too, so she and I quickly locked eyes before we burst out laughing in unison.

Perri was in our bedroom closet, gathering up a few more things for us to take on our trip to Disney World. Two days after we'd won the championship game, we'd gone to Disneyland with the team, but now we needed a *real* family vacation. Somewhere we could get away and take Camille along with us. Not only were we going, but Jorell and Nika wanted to tag along too. That had led to Tez and Myesha coming as well. My mother, Mr. Phillip, and Aria were also flying down to Orlando. It was going to be a true family affair.

I walked into the closet and showed Perri the screen of my tablet. "Bae, you see this?"

She glanced down at the photo on the screen, then quickly scrunched up her nose. Numerous pictures of her and me had been posted on E! News. There were some of us on our wedding day and others of us on our honeymoon last spring in Saint-Tropez. There was this one photo in particular that stood out: it was of Perri standing in a white, two-piece string bikini. She exuded sex appeal, with droplets of water dripping from her hair and down her body. Even on her athletic frame, she had these full, melon-sized breasts and a nice fat ass, something she always kept hidden beneath oversize T-shirts and basketball shorts.

According to E! News, we were now #couplegoals, a hashtag that was also trending on Twitter, which had even more pictures of our faces. Just last year the media had cast Perri as the ugly duckling by my side. The woman I'd chosen to be with only because she was my baby's mother and had been with me since day one.

But ever since the photos of our wedding had got out, with Perri looking better than Beyoncé herself, she was getting more positive press than she could stand. And the fact that she coached at Loyola Marymount seemed only to add to her appeal. After the pictures had surfaced of me tonguing her down on the court at the NBA finals, we were wanted on the covers of *Essence*, *Ebony*, and even *Sports Illustrated*.

"What?" She shook her head and frowned.

"Well, you was crying when they were calling you ugly. Now that they're saying you're beautiful, you still crying, yo," I half joked.

She slapped me across the chest with the shirt in her arms. "Ain't nobody crying," she said, rolling her eyes. "I just don't like people all in our business."

I let out a little snort of laughter. "I'm this year's MVP, baby. Just got three more endorsement deals. What'chu want them to do?"

"You so damn cocky, I swear," she muttered, then went back over to remove something else off a hanger.

I went up behind her and pressed my hard dick up against her ass. Her body immediately tensed, letting me know I had her attention. "But nah, for real, though. You gonna do the covers with me?" I whispered in her ear in what was almost a whine.

When she nodded her head, I started kissing on the nape of her neck, allowing the tip of my tongue to glide to the side. Her long brown hair was thrown up in a sloppy ball on top of her head, allowing me full access of her flesh.

"And Tez told you about the court date with Brianna, right?" I asked between kisses.

"Yeah, unfortunately," she mumbled, slowly nodding her head. After partnering with a detective firm, Tez had found out that it was Brianna who had been sending all that crazy shit to Perri. As a result, she had been charged with stalking and harassment, and a court date had been set for next month. Back at Georgetown Brianna had seemed so sweet to me, but apparently, she was obsessed with the kid, and my NBA stardom had only seemed to make matters worse.

As I kissed and sucked on Perri's neck some more, pulling her closer to me by the waist, she moaned. Her head collapsed back against my shoulder from pleasure, and I could hear the sound of her breathing gradually picking up speed.

"Mmm, you think we have time for a quickie?" I mumbled against her skin. Although we had four hours until our flight, I knew the traffic getting to LAX would be brutal.

"I don't know," she whispered, slowly shaking her head from left to right.

I took that as a green light and slipped my fingers into the waistband of her Lakers cheerleading shorts. I had bought them for her in hopes that she would at least wear them around the house, and fortunately, she did so without me even asking. Every time she had them on, I caught myself staring at her ass. Her cheeks would just spill out from the bottom of the shorts, and, I swear, that shit would make my dick so hard. Although she didn't know it, tomboy or not, Perri was one sexy *muthafucka*.

Once I got her shorts all the way down, exposing the bareness of her lower half, I tugged down my own basketball shorts just enough to free my dick. Bae eagerly reached back and took my hard muscle in the palm of her soft hand. I loved it when she got all aggressive like that, but at this particular moment, I wanted to be in control. I wanted to fuck my wife like she was a *gahdamn* ho. With my knee, I forcefully spread apart her thighs and pushed her torso against the wall. Her back automatically dipped, forming a natural arch.

"*Honey*," she moaned and let out an anxious pant.

Sliding the head of my erection up and down her slick folds, I watched her body slowly unravel. "Please," she pleaded beneath her breath, grinding her hips, as she tried to rush me into entering her. I knew it was wrong for me to tease my wife like that, but there was something about the sound of her begging for my dick that excited the inner me.

Without warning, I entered her hard and fast from the back. "Fuck, P," I breathed, biting down on my lower lip as she gasped. "My pussy wet as fuck." Perri's body felt the exact same as it had when we were just eighteen years old. *Fucking incredible.*

I pulled her hair back by the ball on top of her head, making it all come undone. She knew exactly what I wanted. Immediately, she craned her neck around to kiss me. As I penetrated her deeper from behind, I sucked on her lips.

"Oh God," she moaned into my mouth. "It's too deep," she cried.

Those words somehow encouraged my fingers, which intuitively reached down between her thighs and softly strummed at her clit.

"Plus . . ." She let out another breathy moan.

As I drove in and out of her, she gradually began pushing her hips back in a rhythm, matching me stroke for stroke. "That's right, shorty. Take this dick," I murmured, feeling my head start to spin. Although we both knew it was a quickie, she was now trying to put on a show.

"Ooh, Plus."

That was when I started to feel her muscles slowly contract around me. It was happening. "Cum for me, P," I coached, gripping her tighter by the hair.

"Ah, fuck! Wait," she urged, but my thrusts inadvertently picked up speed.

"Uh-uh. Cum on this muthafucka now, P!" I told her, hearing the flesh of her ass slap against me.

All of a sudden, her body quaked, and she gave a sweet, orgasmic moan. "Ahmad!" she wailed.

Unexpectedly, a tingle of my own started to stir in my groin, and after just a few more strokes, I was exploding inside her. As we both tried to catch our breath, I ran my hand across her stomach and placed gentle kisses along the edge of her shoulder. "I love you, shorty," I whispered.

"I love you too."

For a few moments more, we stayed glued together like old photos in a picture book, then finally pulled apart. When I started for the bathroom, Perri was right on my heels.

"And, by the way, if anybody asks why we're late, I'm not lying, yo. I'm straight up telling them that you was at the house, fiending for the dick," I teased, tossing her a wink over my shoulder.

"I swear to Gah, Plus, you better not," she warned, slapping me playfully on the arm.

Chapter 29

Nika

After flying into Orlando this evening, we were finally settling in our hotel rooms. Plus had chosen a private wing of the Hyatt Regency, and everything was beautiful. The hotel sat on a clear-water lake that seemed to stretch for miles, and right by the oversize pool were man-made waterfalls and palm trees. We each had our own personal suite that included two bedrooms, two baths, a small living room, and even a kitchen.

As I laid Nicholas down in his portable crib for the night, I sensed Jorell walking up behind me. I peeked over my shoulder and saw him standing just a mere foot away. After tucking our son beneath the thin blanket, I turned around to face him. After stepping into his personal space, I pushed my breasts up against his abs. I naturally reached up to slink my arms around his neck when he pulled me into him by the waist.

He softly kissed the tip of my nose before pecking me on the lips. "I ordered you spaghetti and shrimp," he said.

Tilting my head to the side, I gave him a mocking expression. "You think you know me, huh?" I asked.

"Shawty, you my la' baby. Of course I know you," he said with a smirk, winking his right eye.

Since that one cool night in December, when Jorell took me to the boat parade out in Marina del Rey, we'd become closer than ever. We were now dating exclusively, and I honestly couldn't have been any happier. Over the months Jorell had proven to be both an amazing father and a terrific friend.

He made sure to spend all his free time with both Nicholas and Jornelle. When he'd got his first endorsement deal a few months ago, he had made sure to cut me a nice chunk of his earnings as back child support. Even when I'd told him it wasn't needed, because he always bought Nicholas the things he needed, he'd refused to hear otherwise. And although I knew there would always be some tension between him and Meechie, they were actually getting along much better than what they had been before.

As far as our romantic relationship, Jorell had courted me for three months straight before I'd finally given him the goods. That was when we had ultimately made things official. Since then, he'd been trying his best to get us all under one roof. On those frequent evenings over at my place, where he'd call himself just "falling asleep" with Nicholas, I would give in and allow him to stay. To be completely honest, I found it to be such an amazing feeling to wake up to him in my bed, but I was still a bit guarded and wanted to take things slow.

"Come on. Let's meet everybody out here for dinner," he said, taking me by the hand.

When we walked out into the open floor plan of the suite, I saw that the long wooden dining-room table was already set for six. Then we heard knocking at our hotel door.

"I got it," Jorell said.

When he opened the door, Myesha was the first to appear. Following behind her were Perri, Plus, and Tez.

"Where the kids at?" Plus asked, looking around.

"They're all in the other room, asleep," I told them. After being fed Happy Meals from McDonald's, MJ, Camille, and Jornelle were all fast asleep in bed.

"Aye, and don't think we gon' be babysitting er' night this week, while y'all over in the next room, fucking. We taking turns, breh," Jorell said, making everyone laugh.

"Godma will be here tomorrow, so I ain't even worried about it," was Tez's response.

While we went to the table and sat down, Tez made his way over to the minibar and poured three glasses of Rémy. Jorell decided to keep me close and pulled me down onto his lap. At the very same time that Tez was bringing over the drinks, another round of light knocks sounded at the door.

"It's probably just the food," Plus said, hopping up to answer the door.

His assumption was right. As everyone got situated at the table, a hotel attendant walked in behind Plus, rolling our dinner in on a cart. I remained on Jorell's lap and watched as the attendant served dinner to everyone around the table. The attendant even poured us each a glass of the hotel's most expensive wine. Once he was finished serving, Plus gave him a generous tip and escorted him back to the door.

When I shifted slightly to get off Jorell's lap, he firmly held my hips in place. One of his large hands then reached under my curls and brought my face in for a kiss. For some reason, he had been big on PDA with me lately. It didn't matter how shy or embarrassed I felt; I couldn't help but to just go right along with it. His touch just felt too good. As he swirled his sweet tongue around in my mouth, kissing me like he hadn't seen me in months, I could feel his dick slowly starting to rise.

"Damn, yo. Is you gon' let shorty eat, or y'all just gon' sit here and fuck at the table?" Tez asked, obviously annoyed.

As I pulled back from Jorell and gave a little laugh, Myesha said, "Well, *I* think it's sweet."

"Yeah, you would," Tez mumbled.

Once I slid into my own seat, I took a swig of wine. After Jorell cut into his steak, he offered me a small piece on his fork. We were that couple who shared just about everything we ate. Opening up my mouth for him to feed me the steak, I gave him a sexy hooded gaze. As I chewed the tender meat, he leaned over and whispered in my ear. "Shawty, I just wanna fuck the shit outta you."

With my eyes still cast down on the spaghetti in front of me, I raised my brow and said, "Oh, trust me, baby, you will. Just gotta be patient." I was trying to talk in code.

"What are y'all over there talking about?" Perri asked from across the table.

"Niggas over there making plans to stretch that pussy later on tonight. I already know what time it is," Tez said.

Myesha promptly nudged him on the side of his arm.

"What? He *is*," he said as he turned to her in all seriousness. "But, shorty, don't worry. I'ma stretch yo' shit out tonight too." When Tez softly sank his teeth down into his bottom lip, Myesha's brown cheeks turned a bright shade of red.

"So . . . what's the plan for tomorrow?" Perri asked, cutting in.

"Well, you already know the kids want to go to the park. So it's going to be an all-day thing," I told her.

"Yeah, Camille wants to go to Blizzard Beach and Animal Kingdom," Perri announced.

"Well, y'all already know MJ don't care, as long as he can run behind them girls," Myesha said.

"I swear, I think I'm more excited than them," Perri said with a laugh.

"Girl, me too, and this resort is so beautiful. You really outdid yourself when picking this place, Plus," I said.

"'Preciate it," was all he said.

After we ate our dinner, the guys all went out on the balcony to smoke a blunt and polish off the bottle of Rémy. Meanwhile, Myesha, Perri, and I decided to hang inside for a little girl talk. Although we all lived in California, we didn't see each other every day, and this was a nice opportunity for us to do some catching up. We each sat lazily across the oversize couches in the living room.

"So how's married life, Mrs. Taylor?" I asked Perri.

A wide smile stretched across her lips before she said, "It's . . . great. Plus is all I've ever dreamed of in a husband. I couldn't ask for a better man."

"That's good. You guys deserve to be happy. Especially after everything you've been through." I paused for a moment, thinking about the miscarriage she'd suffered last year. "Do you guys want more kids?"

"Maybe one day, but definitely not no time soon. I'm working toward a head coach position at Loyola Marymount," Perri revealed.

"I'm so jealous that you two have your own careers," Myesha confessed. "Tez just wants me to stay at home with MJ, and now that I'm . . ." Her voice trailed off as she shook her head.

"What? What's wrong?" I asked.

Myesha put her hand up, hoping to squelch my concern. "I'm fine. Really."

"So when are y'all getting married?" I asked. Tez and Myesha had been engaged for a few years now, but no wedding had ever taken place.

Myesha shrugged her shoulders and let out a slow huffy breath. "Girl, I don't know. I don't even ask anymore."

Perri placed her hand on Myesha's arm in an attempt to comfort her. "You want me to talk to him, sis? 'Cause you know I'll cuss his ass out," Perri said.

Myesha adamantly shook her head at that. "No, he's been so busy trying to get his security firms off the ground. And now that he's gotten so many celebrity clients in LA, he's running himself ragged. He's even talking about opening up one in Atlanta for some celebrity clients out there."

"Damn," I muttered. "With all that going on, is the nigga ever even home?"

"Not much, but enough to get me knocked up again," Myesha replied, letting the news slip out. She immediately covered her mouth with her hands.

My eyes immediately widened after hearing such a huge secret spill from her lips.

Perri shifted in her seat and leaned toward her. "Does my brother know?" she asked. I already knew that Perri was thinking about the last time Tez had found out Myesha was pregnant.

"Not yet, but I'm going to tell him."

"How long have you known?" I asked.

"Well, I went to the doctor a few weeks ago. I believe I'm about ten weeks along," Myesha admitted, pulling her knees up to her chest.

"Do you think he'll ask you to get an abortion?" I asked.

"Fuck no! He better not," Perri snapped. "Matter of fact, let's just call him in here and tell him now. I don't like keeping secrets like this from him."

Myesha shook her head fervently. "No, please! I don't want to ruin our vacation. I'll tell him as soon as we get back home, I promise."

Suddenly, I heard the sliding-glass doors of the balcony being opened. "What y'all in here talking 'bout?" Tez called, as if he already knew that he was the topic of our discussion.

"Nothing. Just making plans for when we get back home," I said, thinking it wasn't a total lie.

As Tez entered the suite, I could see Jorell and Plus coming in right behind him. They all came over to the couches we were sprawled on, and Tez reached down and grabbed Myesha by the hand to help her to her feet. "Come on, shorty. It's getting late, and you got a lot of work to do," he said, softly slapping her on the ass.

She smiled and wrapped her arm around his waist. "Well, good night, y'all," she said. When they reached the door, she turned and gave a little wave.

Once they were gone, Plus stretched his arms out wide and let out a loud yawn.

"You tired, honey?" Perri asked, standing up from the couch.

"Yeah. Just let me check on the kids right quick," he told her.

When he went over to crack the bedroom door, I asked if he could check in on MJ too. He went into both rooms, and when he came out, he gave us a thumbs-up, indicating that all the kids were still asleep. Once he and Perri had left, I got up front the couch, with plans of hitting the hot shower, but Jorell must have had other plans. He caught me by the wrist and brought me back to him, so that I was standing there between his legs. As his hands slowly traveled up my bare thighs beneath the yellow sundress I wore, he looked up with dark, hooded eyes. Although we'd been off and on for years, my breath still stalled, like it was our very first time at physical contact. When his fingers finally met the edges of my panties, skimming lightly across my skin, a quick tremor shot down my spine.

"La' baby, you know I'm finna eat the fuck outta ya pussy, right?" he asked before wetting his dark brown lips with his tongue.

Inside my head, I was screaming out, *Yas*! But for some reason, I only nodded my head. After he slid my panties down over my hips, he gently dipped his index finger inside me.

"Mmm," I moaned. Just that itty-bitty touch from him gave me a small gush of pleasure.

When he pulled his finger out of me, he quickly slipped it inside his mouth. "Mmm, that muthafucka sweeter than candy. Come're, baby," he said, summoning me with a chuck of his chin.

As he lay back on the couch, I moved to straddle his lap. But then he abruptly grabbed my waist and brought me farther up his chest.

"What are you doing?" I asked, bracing myself against his shoulders.

"Tryin'a get you to sit on my face. A nigga finna show you just how much I luh yo' ass."

"Oh," I gasped in surprise, knowing full well that I loved every single time his country ass would talk dirty to me. With his help, I eased myself up the rest of the way, until I was positioned exactly where he wanted me. When I finally felt his wet tongue flickering against my center, my head couldn't help but fall back from delight.

"Mmm, baby," I moaned, little by little circling my hips. "I love you so fucking much."

Chapter 30

Jorell

We had been back home from Disney World for just a little over a week, and it was now the Fourth of July. Tez was throwing a poolside barbecue a little later on at his crib, but before we headed over there, I had a surprise for my girl. As Nika and I cruised along Parkway Calabasas, with the kids asleep in the backseat, I noticed her staring out the window. I knew that she was trying to figure out exactly where we were going.

Reaching over, I placed my hand on her knee. "You all right?" I asked.

"Where are we going, Jorell?" she asked, hating the suspense.

Shrugging my shoulders, I smirked. "I 'on' know, la' baby. I guess you gon' have to wait and see."

Letting out a little huff, she folded her arms across her chest and sat back farther in the seat. Quietly, I chuckled to myself at just how cute shawty looked when she was angry. After about another ten minutes of driving, I slowed down and pulled into a guard-gated community with a fancy sign that read OAKS OF CALABASAS. When we pulled up to the booth, I passed the guard a small slip of paper. Without us exchanging words, he lifted the gate and allowed me to drive in.

Nika turned to me with a puzzled expression on her face. "Who do you know that lives out here?" she asked.

"Shh," I told her. "Shawty, just sit back and ride."

As we drove down the winding street at the neighbor-hood's entrance, I could hear her letting out more huffs and puffs. "Shawty, you doing all right over there? You breathing like a gahdamn dragon," I teased.

She rolled her eyes and said, "Shut up, Jorell."

About another half a mile down road, I pulled into a long cobblestoned driveway. Nestled on two acres of land was a huge white Mediterranean-style mansion with a ceramic-tile roof. The front yard was lush, with the most perfect blades of green grass. There were even a few palm trees along the way.

"Wow. Who lives here?" she asked, in awe.

I pulled my Impala in front of the four-car garage and shifted the gear into park. "I do," I said, dangling a shiny silver set of keys.

As her eyebrows dipped, she twisted her glossy pink lips to the side. "Yeah, right."

I let out a snort of laughter before giving her a sideways nod of my head. "Shawty, just come on here."

After we unstrapped the kids from the backseat, wak-ing Jornelle up in the process, the four of us headed up the walkway. After I unlocked the wrought-iron double doors of the house and we stepped inside, our eyes were met with the sight of a grand foyer and a spiral staircase. It was truly something out of a magazine. We walked across the travertine tile and caught the view to the pool out back.

"Wow! This place is so beautiful," Nika said lowly as she looked up to observe the high ceilings and pendant chandelier.

"Where we at, Daddy?" Jornelle asked, rubbing the sleep from her eyes.

Feeling Nicholas's fat butt squirm against my chest as he slept, I looked down at my daughter and said, "This is our new house, baby girl."

She quickly stretched her eyes and looked around the place again.

"You're serious?" Nika asked, cutting her gaze over at me.

"Shawty, I'm dead ass. Now come on, so I can show you the rest of it."

"All right. Well, pass me my baby before you show us around."

The house had six bedrooms and five baths and was just under ten thousand square feet. Carrera marble poured over the kitchen counters, and the kitchen even featured a stainless-steel gas stove and a double oven. As we went from room to room, I watched Nika run the tips of her fingers over the walls, in awe. She was definitely impressed. And when we stepped through the double doors of the master suite, which looked more like three or four bedrooms combined, she gasped.

"Wow! This is huge, Jorell, and it has a fireplace. What are you gonna do with all this space?" she said, taking it all in.

"Whatever you wanna do to it."

"Aw. You're actually gonna let me decorate your home?" She beamed.

Shawty just wasn't getting it.

"Nah, I'ma let you decorate *our* home," I told her.

Her lips parted, but I could tell she was finding it hard to even speak.

"You can move in and then get Grandma out here to help with the kids," I told her.

"You know Grandma's not coming all the way out here," she said, finally finding her voice.

The sound of Grandma's voice suddenly resonated behind her. "Chile, don't speak for me. I got a whole guesthouse out back."

Recognition dawned immediately, and Nika spun around fast on her heels. "Grandma! What are you doing here?" She ran over and gave her grandmother a tight hug.

They embraced for a bit before Grandma said, "And give me that baby." She took Nicholas from Nika's arms.

Confused by it all, Nika asked, "Grandma, really, what are you doing here?" Then she turned back to look at me, more than likely for answers. Her eyes instantly dropped, and she gazed right in front of her, having found me down on bended knee.

"Jorell," she whispered, placing her hand up to her mouth, as tears glossed over her dark brown eyes.

Feeling my airway suddenly constrict, I sucked in a huge breath of air to get my nerves under control. "Shawty, I know that you wanted to take things slow, and after all the bullshit I put you through, I really can't blame you. But . . ." I placed my hand over my chest. "I can assure you that I've seen the error of my ways. From the very first time I laid eyes on you in that hospital waiting room, I knew you were something special. And, baby, where I come from, niggas like me don't get girls like you. You're some shit we see on the TV screen or in the movies. Someone that niggas like me can only dream about. And now that I actually have you and realize that you've always just loved me for me, I can't lose you. Shawty, I can't live without you . . . I *don't* want to live without you."

Reaching down into a pocket of my cargo shorts, I blew out a short, quick breath. I pulled out a white leather ring box and popped it open in her direction. "Nika Aleese Turner, will you marry me?"

She damn near covered her entire face with her hands and nodded her head vehemently.

"Nika, is that a yes or a no?" I asked above the sound of her murmured cries.

When she removed her hands, her face was completely red and wet from her tears. "Yes," she breathed. "I'll marry you."

I reached up for her hand and placed the sparkling four-carat diamond ring on her finger. That was when Jornelle and Grandma started clapping.

"Praise God. Ain't got to hear about this child crying over you no more," Grandma said jokingly.

"Grandma." Nika sniffed back a laugh.

I stood up and grabbed Nika by the face, then brought her in for a passionate kiss. *Breh,* I was so in love with this girl that these days I could only picture my future with her in it. Somehow, she made the air I breathed fresher, my rainy days brighter, and bad news sound *okay.* Shawty was my everything. Everything I'd ever wanted in a wife and even more, as the mother of my kids. As long as I had her by my side, I felt like there wasn't nothing on this earth I that couldn't achieve.

Nika held out her hand and marveled at her ring. "Baby, can we afford all of this?" she whispered.

"Yuh." I chuckled. "I just signed a new contract, and because of the championship win, I got two more endorsement deals. We gon' be straight, Mama," I told her.

She stepped in close and wrapped her arms around my neck. "I love you," she said softly, looking up into my eyes.

"La' baby, you know I'm gon' always love you more."

When we pulled up to Tez's place, it was just about four o'clock. As we walked up to the front door, I could hear people splashing out back in the pool. After we rang the doorbell twice, Myesha opened up the door, wearing a white one-piece bathing suit and a sheer white sarong.

"Hey, y'all," she sang, then leaned in for an individual hug from each of us before she let us in.

As we trekked along the mahogany floors behind her, my eyes scanned the various rooms. Much like the home I'd just purchased, their place was a sight to behold. Tez had always joked around about Plus and me having all the money because we now played for the league, but truth be told, he was the one who had been getting money hand over fist. Tez had turned into a successful businessman and was now a multimillionaire in his own right.

When I opened the French double doors to the back, I saw Plus playing with Camille in the pool. She had bright yellow floaties on her arms, and she was kicking around in the water like she knew how to swim. Perri and Ms. Tonya were seated off to the side, playing with MJ, and I noticed Tez over by the grill. I stepped outside and rubbed my hands together at the scent of barbecue that was floating past my nose.

"What Tez got burning on that grill?" I asked, moving my hand to rest above my eyes to shade them from the sun.

"Ribs and chicken. I think he got some hamburgers up there too," Myesha replied as she led Nika and Jornelle through the double doors and out back.

Since Jornelle had already changed into her swimsuit back at the house, she didn't hesitate to get in the pool. This summer, she and Camille had quickly become the best of friends, and whenever they spent time with one another, they'd be stuck together like glue.

"Jornelle, come put your floaties on, girl. You know you can't swim," Nika said. Squatting by the shallow end of the pool, she placed the floaties around Jornelle's little arms. "There you go, baby," she said.

I glanced down at Plus in the pool and gave him a quick chuck of my chin before Nika and I walked over to greet Perri and Ms. Tonya.

"Where y'all been at?" was the first thing Perri asked.

"Well, hey to you too," Nika said, waving her hand in a manner that allowed the sun to reflect off the new diamond on her finger.

"Yo, I know that's not what I think it is," Perri said, hopping up from the lounge chair.

Myesha caught on quickly and joined the two women in their semi-huddle so she could see Nika's ring for herself.

"Oh my God, it's beautiful. Congratulations!" Perri said, giving Nika a big hug. As they embraced, rocking from side to side, it looked as though the two hadn't seen each other in years.

"Damn, Baby Mama, a nigga can't get no love?" I asked Perri, holding my arms out wide.

Perri tossed a knowing smirk, then ambled her way over to me. "You did so good, yo. I'm proud of you," she said, giving me a one-arm squeeze.

"Now come're and let me see that rock," I heard Ms. Tonya say.

As Nika held out her hand, flossing, for Ms. Tonya to see, I noticed that Myesha hadn't said much. She had this pensive look on her face, like she was deep in thought.

Tez suddenly approached the group. "What's all the commotion over here?" he said.

"We're engaged," Nika boasted, again holding out her hand.

After grabbing Nika by the wrist, Tez thoroughly examined the ring. "Just making sure that nigga ain't get you no shit out the bubble-gum machine," he said seriously.

Nika, Perri, and Ms. Tonya all snickered.

"Aye, breh, why you try'na play me? What happened to 'Congratulations. I'm happy for y'all'? You know . . . the shit normal people say," I joked.

Tez shook his head. "Nah, you right, considering how your crackhead ass was living just last year. I'm proud of you," he said, putting his arm around my shoulder.

I let out a light chuckle and pushed him off me. "Nigga, fuck you. Wasn't nobody no crackhead."

"That's right, baby, 'cause crack is whack," Nika chimed in, trying to help.

Cocking his head to the side, Tez narrowed his eyes at Nika. "Aye, shorty, you on that shit too?" he quizzed. "'Cause yo' ass sounded just like Whitney Houston when she did that interview with Bobby's crackhead ass."

Nika scoffed before her mouth fell open in shock. "You know what?" she said coldly, obviously offended.

"Nah, I'm playing. I'm playing, yo." Tez chuckled, holding both of his hands up in surrender. "But fa real, though, congrats. That's a good look." He turned to me. "You got your shit together this past year, and now you try'na lock shorty down and make her your wife. That's what's up. I'm proud of you," he said, extending his hand.

As I slapped hands with Tez and brought him in for a brotherly hug, the sound of Myesha's loud crying brought everything to a halt. When I glanced over at her, she had her hand covering her mouth, in an attempt to trap her emotions.

Tez craned his neck back and asked, "What's wrong, My'?"

Although Myesha shook her head, I could tell she was unable speak.

Tez walked over to her and pulled her hand down from her face. "Baby, what wrong?" he asked again.

"Nothing," she finally told him.

"Have you told him?" Perri asked, holding MJ on her hip.

Confused, Tez looked back and forth between the two of them. "Told me what?"

"No, Perri, I haven't told him!" Myesha snapped. "For what? He's not tryin'a *lock me* down. All he wants to do is keep pumping babies inside me. That's all I'm good for to him." With tears spilling from her eyes, Myesha ran full speed back into the house.

"Man, the fuck wrong with her?" Tez asked. He was completely bewildered and had no clue as to what was going on.

Perri held her hand up to her forehead out of frustration before she said, "She's pregnant, Tez. Again."

Tez's neck jutted forward. "She's what?"

"Pregnant. About three months, and it's bothering her because of how you acted when she got pregnant the first time with MJ. And aside from that, you still haven't even married her yet, although you proposed," Perri explained.

Unable to take any more, Ms. Tonya stepped directly in front of Tez. "Look, take your ass in that house and make things right with that girl. 'Cause if I gotta take you both down to the courthouse tomorrow morning myself, I will," she fussed.

Tez ran his hand over his face, trying to quickly get himself together. "I don't know why shorty tripping. She know I'ma marry her," he said.

Against her better judgment, Nika chimed in. "She said that whenever she mentions having a wedding, you always toss out your work schedule and business commitments. She said that all you care about is money."

"Nika," Perri gasped, not believing that she had just divulged the things that Myesha had clearly told them in confidence.

Nika looked at Perri and said, "What? He needs to know." Then she turned her attention back to Tez. "Look, Myesha loves you and the funky drawers on your ass, but if you haven't noticed, she's a beautiful woman with a big heart and a good head on her shoulders. If you don't step up, all you're doing is leaving the door wide open for the next man to step in," she schooled.

For a moment there, I could tell that Tez was pondering Nika's words. "If she wanted to get married that bad, all she had to do was say so. She know I love her ass," he muttered.

"Well, go in there and make things right," Perri said, encouraging him. She stepped closer and placed her hand on his back. "Tell her that you guys can get married whenever she's ready and that you're excited about the new baby."

I could tell that the last part was a stretch, because Tez scratched the top of his head, with a hesitant expression on his face. We all knew that Tez didn't want any more children, but after everything he and Myesha had been through, there wasn't a chance in hell he'd admit that shit out loud. "Yeah, I'ma go in there and holler at her. Make things right," he said, nodding his head.

"You better," Ms. Tonya warned.

As he went inside the house to find Myesha, I went to turn his meat on the grill. When I came back over, I joined Nika and Perri on the edge of the pool and dangled my feet in the cool water. Plus swam over and stood in between Perri's thighs.

"Did I show you this one?" Nika said as she showed Perri pictures of our new house on her phone.

"Wow. It's beautiful. When are you guys moving in?" Perri said.

"Next week," Nika said, with a proud smile. "And Grandma said she's gonna move out here too."

"Oh yeah. Why didn't she come over here today? And where's Nicholas?"

"Girl, Grandma said she was tired from her flight. And since Nicholas was fussy, we dropped both of them back off at the house," Perri replied.

"Aye," Plus said, interrupting the girl talk. "Y'all ever think we'd be living out here in LA like this? Living out our dreams?"

"Mane, hell nah," I said, shaking my head. "Even though I could ball, I never thought I'd amount to shit."

"Well, now that I got the job I've always wanted, the family," he said, shooting a quick glance at Camille over his shoulder. "And the girl of my dreams, what's next?"

Looking over at Nika and me, Perri shrugged her shoulders. "Yo, anything our young hearts desire. You already know the sky's the limit when it comes to matters of love and game."

When she winked at Plus, he responded by pulling her into the water. With her legs wrapped around his waist, the two of them shared a passionate kiss and floated off to the deep end of the pool. Throwing my arm across Nika's shoulders, I glanced over at Camille and Jornelle, who were splashing around in the shallow end. Although I knew this was only a small snapshot in time, I smiled. Everything just seemed perfect. Not only had I gotten my job back, but I had a great family and loyal friends too. Those were now the things that motivated me to be a better man.

Epilogue

Perri

Summer 2018 . . .

As we walked through the doors of the Alexandria Ballroom, I gave Plus's hand a gentle squeeze. The lighting in the room was dim, spilling only from scattered crystal chandeliers. If it hadn't been for Trey Songz playing on the track, I would have thought this was an overly ritzy affair. As we waltzed our way inside, my eyes roamed the ballroom, in search of Tez.

"There." I pointed. He was standing next to a very pregnant Myesha, who was now in her second trimester with baby number three.

His fingers interlaced with mine, Plus led the way across the marble floor. When we approached my brother, he was standing there in a full black tuxedo, talking with Kendrick Lamar. The well-known rapper had just signed on to Tez's security firm a few months ago. I went right over to Myesha, whose eyes were solely on her husband. Five years ago today, she and my brother had got married on Guana Island, a private island in the British Virgin Islands. Since Myesha didn't have any family from her side, it had been only us, but it had been perfect.

I gently touched her on the arm to gain her attention. "Hey, sis. Happy anniversary," I sang.

Her eyes lit up when she turned and saw the two of us. "Thank you," she gushed. "You guys made it." When she pulled back from giving me a hug, her eyes made a full sweep down my frame. "I absolutely love this dress, girl. You look beautiful," she said, complimenting me for the white Oscar de la Renta gown I had chosen for the night. "And you look sharp too, Plus."

With one of his hands casually tucked in a pocket of his pants, he gave a one-shoulder shrug. "Thank you, but I think you and my wife are the ones stealing the show tonight," he said.

As Myesha blushed, I looked her over, thinking that he was absolutely right. Myesha looked beautiful tonight. I didn't know which glowed more, her beautiful pregnant face or the long silver gown that sparkled against her chocolate skin. Her black curls were pinned high on the top of her head, showcasing her dark, slanted eyes, and her lips were painted a soft hue of pink. Large diamond drops dangled from each of her ears, adding a touch of elegance.

She tapped Tez on the arm. "Baby, Perri and Plus are here."

In the middle of a full, hearty laugh, Tez craned his neck back in our direction. "Oh, shit," he said, amber-colored eyes lighting up at the sight of us. "We got NBA royalty in the house," he joked, slapping hands with Plus.

Instead of gold fronts, my brother now sported his own perfectly straight white teeth. The days of his sandy-brown locks were long gone; they'd been replaced by low-cut waves. Instead of the Tims and gold chains, Tez wore the finest Armani suits and Ferragamo shoes four to five days a week. And although he still talked and walked like my brother, he had grown into a fine businessman. No, my brother had never graced a TV screen or heard his own voice on the radio, but he was somehow considered a part of black Hollywood, someone everyone in the industry should know.

"Yeah, right," Plus muttered humbly, bringing Tez in for a half hug. Although my husband was being modest, NBA royalty was truly what he was. Over the past six years, he had won two more championship rings.

Once Tez's gaze shifted to me, he held his arms out wide and took in the sight of me. "Ma would be so proud. You look beautiful, baby girl," he said.

I wrapped my arms around him and whispered thank you in his ear. "You ready for another one?" I asked, looking down at Myesha's swollen belly.

"Whatever the little lady want, yo. I'm wit' it," was his response. I could attest to that being a truthful answer. Although they'd had their fair share of ups and downs over the years, he had given her everything she had ever asked for.

Squinting his eyes, Tez looked over my shoulder, across the room. "Aye, is that Michael over there?" I turned around to see Michael B. Jordan walking in with Trevor Jackson. As I strained my neck slightly, I could also see Teyana and Iman coming in behind them. "Aye, I'ma be right back," Tez said.

As Tez took off toward the other side of the room, I looped my arm through Myesha's. "Looks like everybody came out to celebrate you two tonight," I told her. This whole extravagant shindig was in honor of her and Tez's five-year wedding anniversary.

Smiling, she inhaled a deep breath. "I see. Everything turned out perfectly," she said.

I looked over at Plus and noticed him staring down at his phone. "Honey, you ready to go sit down?" I asked.

With his eyes still down on the screen, he quickly nodded his head. "Yeah, I could use a drink."

I looked down and saw that he was now texting TK.

TK: Did you guys get the wedding invite?

Plus: Yeah. Perri just put the RSVP in the mail yesterday.

TK: Good looking out.

"Do you really think he's going to marry that girl?" I asked.

Plus casually shrugged his shoulders. "Probably so, but that ain't none of my business. Or yours, either," he said, giving me a stern look.

In the middle of me rolling my eyes, Plus grabbed me gently by the chin and leaned down to plant a soft kiss on my lips. "And you gon' stop rolling them pretty-ass eyes at me too, Mrs. Taylor," he said, with a quick wink of his eye.

In the midst of me blushing and becoming aroused, Myesha came up and pointed her finger at the other side of the room. "I put you guys at our table. Right over there," she said.

As Plus took me by the hand and started leading the way, we saw Nika and Jorell entering the ballroom.

"There goes Nika and Jorell right there," I said.

"I'm surprised they made it. I know Nicholas wasn't feeling so good tonight," Plus said, recalling the conversation that we'd had with them over the phone earlier.

As we made our way over to them, I took in just how perfectly matched they were, Nika in her beautiful

powder-pink, strapless gown and Jorell in his gray suit
and pink silk tie. He, too, had since gotten rid of his locks
and now sported a low-cut fade. Although he was still a
flashy guy, with small diamonds in his ears and an iced-
out watch on his wrist, he no longer wore the gold grills
on his teeth.

Walking over toward them, I saw Nika tap Jorell on
the arm, then nod her head in our direction. They started
in our direction and met us halfway. My lips naturally
pouted from envy when I spotted the champagne flute
already in her hand.

"What's going on, Mr. ESPN?" Plus said, greeting
Jorell with a slap of his hand. After Jorell tore his ACL
last season, he was forced to retire early from the league.
But as luck would have it, ESPN quickly signed him on
as the lead sportscaster of his own show, *In the Paint*.
Of course, the money wasn't nearly as much as he had
made while playing ball, but thanks to Nika, they were
financially set for life.

Jorell flashed a proud smile at the mention of his new
contract. "Ain't shit, breh. Just trying to get Nick over
this cold."

"How is little man?" I asked.

"His fever finally broke, so hopefully, he's on the road
to recovery. Grandma's there with him now," Nika said.

"Aye, our table's over there," Plus let them know, with
a dip of his head in that direction.

Suddenly one of the waiters passed by with a tray of
champagne flutes in his hand. "You want me to grab you
one?" Nika asked, cutting her eyes over at me.

"Nah, not tonight," I told her with a soft smile.

As we began walking to our table, an old-school joint
from Babyface started to play. It was "Every Time I

Close My Eyes," the one song that Daddy had always told me reminded him of my mother. Glancing up at my husband, I gave him a knowing look while tightening my grip on his hand. Without uttering a word to anyone, he led me out onto the dance floor.

As he pulled my body in close, I naturally folded my arms around his neck and started to sway from side to side. Laying my face against his chest, I sealed my eyes and enjoyed the feeling of his hands sliding across my lower back. Just above my ear, I could hear Plus's deep tenor as he sang the lyrics to the song.

"And you're, you're every bit of a dream come true, yes you are, yes. With you, baby, it never rains and it's no wonder the sun always shines when I'm near you. It's just a blessing that I have found somebody like you."

Between the sound of his voice, the inviting scent of his cologne and, most of all, his touch, I was completely lost in the moment. Forgot all about where we were and who was watching. As my hips began to sway a bit more sensually, I could feel the sudden swell of his pants. But he didn't stop: he just kept me wrapped in his arms, gently rocking me in the dance.

"See, this is why you knocked up now," he whispered.

Opening my eyes, I gave him a sheepish smile. Just two weeks ago I had found out that I was pregnant again. Although it was totally unplanned, we both were genuinely happy about it. But given my miscarriage all those years ago, I wanted to keep this pregnancy a secret at least until my second trimester.

"When are you going to tell your job?" he asked.

I shrugged my shoulders. "I don't know. Barbara's going to flip," I said, thinking about my boss. I had just taken the head coach position at Loyola Marymount last season, so I knew she would feel some type of way about me having to take a leave. Not to mention the fact that Plus wanted me to take a few years off. I was still undecided.

As Plus's finger started to travel down to my ass, I peered up at him and asked, "You wanna cut out early?"

Lowering his dark brown eyes, he bit down on the corner of his lip. "You know we can't leave right now, but . . . maybe Big John can take us for a spin around the block."

Shit. My center started to pulse just from hearing the idea.

After telling Jorell and Nika that we'd be right back, we scurried out, hand in hand, to the limousine. Once Big John had opened the door to let us inside and we had climbed in, Plus immediately raised the partition. With urgency, I started unbuckling his pants. I honestly couldn't blame my behavior on the pregnancy, because Plus and I were always like this—fucking any and everywhere, like some horny teenagers.

As I watched his long erection jut out from his pants, I began to pull my long gown up around my waist. When Plus grabbed ahold of my waist and brought me over to straddle his lap, my heart rate started to pick up speed. He crashed his lips against mine with such force and passion that he nearly took my breath away. Gradually, his hands made their way between us, and I could feel him sliding my panties to the side.

When I slid down on his length, I purposely fought against closing my eyes. I loved the sight of Plus biting down on his bottom lip.

"Fuck, bae," he breathed.

He pushed my hips down, forcing me to take all his length, and a pleasurable pain shot through my spine.

"*Ahmad*," I cried.

As he lifted me to ease himself in and out of me, I could only whimper in delight.

"I love you so much," he whispered against my lips.

Rendered speechless, I slowly nodded my head.

"Always have, P, and I always will."

The End